WILD HEART
of the
MAGIC

WILD HEART
of the
MAGIC

ERICA SEBREE

SQUIRRELED AWAY PUBLISHING

AUSTIN, TEXAS

First Edition: May 2024

Book Cover design by MiblArt

ISBN 979-8-9866118-5-3 (paperback)
ISBN 979-8-9866118-4-6 (ebook)

Squirreled Away Publishing
Austin, Texas

For Bella.
Thank you for choosing me.

Contents

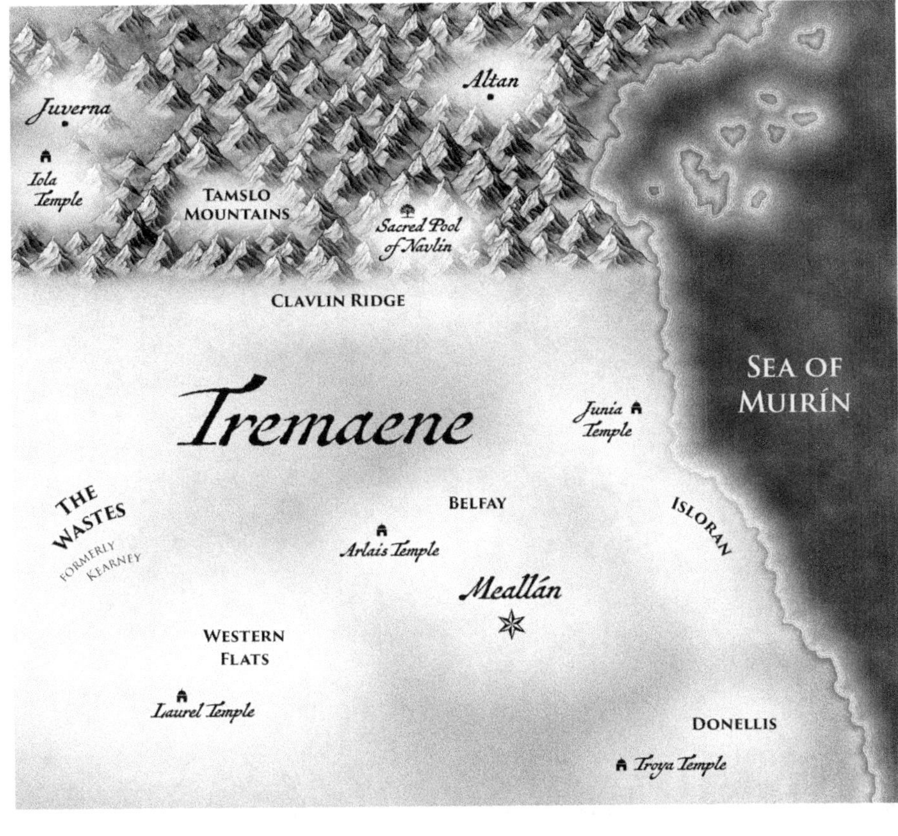

Juverna
Iola Temple
TAMSLO MOUNTAINS
Altan
Sacred Pool of Navlin
CLAVLIN RIDGE
Tremaene
SEA OF MUIRÍN
Junia Temple
THE WASTES
FORMERLY KEARNEY
BELFAY
ISLORAN
Arlais Temple
Meallán
WESTERN FLATS
Laurel Temple
DONELLIS
Troya Temple

PRONUNCIATION GUIDE

People

Abaigeal: ab-ah-gail

Aeveen: aa-vEEn

Aindreas: AHN-dree-ahs

Alastar: AEL-aa-staar

Alpina: al-pee-nuh

Armel: AR-mell

Athdara: aeth-DAAR-AH

Audris: ow-DRIYS

Barram: baa-RaaM

Beglan: BEG-lahn

Brighid: brEEJ-id

Cadwyn: KAD-wayn

Cahir: KAW-heer

Carrick: CEH-ruhk

Catriona: kah-tree-OH-nah

Ceridwen: keh-RI-dwen

Cora: kaw-ruh

Edlyn: EHD-LihN

Eimhir: AE-veer

Ellison: EHL-ihS-SahN

Erena: EHR-ae-nah

Esme: EZ-may

Fergus: FER-gus

Ffion: FEE-on

Firinne: FEER-in-yeh

Fulton: FUL-tn

Genvieve: jhehn-VIY-V

Gorman: GUR-mawn

Griselda: gruh-ZEL-duh

Gwen: gwehn

Harlow: HARR-low

Hazel: HAY-zl

Jaime: JAY-mee

Jarlath: JHAAR-lah-th

Keelin: KIY-lihn

Kenrich: KEHN-RihK

Keva: KWIY-Vah

Killian: KIL-ee-an

Leenan: lee-NAN

Lennox: LEN-uhks

Luxovious: luhx-o-vee-uhs

Madoc: MAAD-aak

Mairtín: MER-tn

Mallory: MAA-Low-Ree

Marta: MAAR-tuh

Moira: MOY-rah

Molly: MOL-EE

Muirín: MWIR-in

Myles: MYLZ

Neala: NEE-lah

Niall: NEE-ul

Olan: OH-len

Orianna: aw-ree-ON-AH

Pallya: pahl-yah

Pearce: pih-RZ

Quinlan: KWIN-luhn

Regan: REE-gun

Rion: ree-ahn

Roderick: RAHD-rik

Shawndrell: shAWhn-dryl

Sheridan: SHEHR-i-dehn

Sullivan: SUL-uh-vuhn

Sybil: SIHB-ahL

Tahra: TAE-rah

Tearlach: TCHAR-lakh

Torin: TAOR-ahN

Vevila: vey-VIY-LAH

Winifred: WIN-e-frid

Zaira: ZEHR-ah

Places

Altan: AWL-tin

Arlais: aaR-Ley

Belfay: BEHL-faye

Bilberry: BIL-buh-ree

Debarrow: DEH-bah-row

Derval: DUR-vel

Donellis: DOH-nel-lis

Iola: EE-O-lah

Isloran: ees-LOH-rehn

Junia: JOO-nee-uh

Juverna: joo-VUR-nah

Kearney: KAR-nee

Laurel: LAOR-ehL

Meallán: MEL-awn

Navlin: NAH-vlin

Periwen: peh-ri-when

Rhoswen: RAAS-wahn

Tamslo: TAHM-sloh

Tremaene: TReh-meyn

Troya: TROY-uh

Other

Loinnir: LUN-neer

Mios: mhee-os

Neve: NEEV

Triskele: tris-keel

Chapter One

"YOU'RE CERTAIN?" TEARLACH'S voice was deceptively low, but his fury was evident in his advancing strides.

"I am." Esme gave a single nod. "Lord Luxovious used—"

"*Lord Luxovious?*" he growled. "That *thing* wasn't a man, much less a lord."

"All right," she acquiesced, no more willing to relive Lord Luxovious's memories than Tearlach was to hear them.

It had only been a matter of minutes since Esme had stumbled back onto solid ground. The memories she'd witnessed in the Sacred Pool of Navlin had presented one disturbing revelation after another about the former Lord of Kearney.

So far, she'd only conveyed to Tearlach the most unnerving memory she'd accessed down there—that Lord Luxovious had been singularly responsible for provoking the uprising that had led to the Dark War and the slaughter of thousands. She'd yet to reveal everything he'd done before that, nearly a thousand years prior.

Tearlach's chest expanded as he took a slow breath, flexing his hands like it might keep them from curling into fists.

Esme knew that his thoughts had strayed to the war. She'd seen the horrors herself, through Lord Luxovious's eyes. Visions of battlefields bathed in blood and ash...the kingdom overrun by creatures wielding powerful, dark magic...

Tearlach and the others never spoke about the gruesome things they'd witnessed in the battles against Lord Luxovious's underlings. All Esme knew was that out of Tearlach's faction in the north, only four had survived.

"What else?"

Esme shook the nightmarish images from her mind and glanced up, finding Tearlach visibly calmer. It was a trait he'd long ago mastered, one that concealed the turmoil she knew was churning just beneath the surface.

The desire to reach out for him was so strong Esme nearly tripped forward. She could still feel the echoes of the emotions he'd let slip through their connection when she'd first emerged from the cavern.

With a steadying breath, she sifted back through the memories she'd bartered for. Objects of power forged by Alastar's hand...Lord Luxovious imbuing them with dark magic...hundreds of channels sealed off in an instant...false gods and narratives...high-priestesses controlling the world's magic...

"The channels," Esme started. "They weren't destroyed as we thought. Only closed off."

Tearlach's shoulders loosened a bit. "Good. That's good." He nodded.

"It is," she agreed, though that was the only piece of non-distressing information she could offer.

"Let's get some rest."

"Now?" Esme looked through the branches to where the sun hung high in the sky. "Shouldn't we return to camp?"

"We'll wait until nightfall. Wake the others in the morning." He pulled a canteen from his pack.

They'd left her entire royal guard—as well as Myles, who'd guided them into the mountains—in a state of deep sleep the night before. With Tearlach's magic, they wouldn't wake until he released its hold. It was a power Esme was none too comfortable with, having had it wielded against her more than once when she'd refused greatly needed rest. But the situation, unfortunately, called for it.

Much as Esme wanted to trust everyone in her retinue, the information she'd uncovered with Tearlach and Cadwyn regarding the channels—namely that there'd once been hundreds scattered throughout the kingdom—had been somewhat conflicting. Until they were able to verify the truth, and whether or not there was even a possibility that the channels could be restored, it was best not to spread the information.

However, her unintentionally lengthy stay in the cavern beneath the ancient tree would delay the *official* purpose of their journey.

"What about the meeting with the priestesses? They'll be expecting..." Esme trailed off, her mind clouding with confusion. She could remember asking Sully to send word when the unordained priestesses replied to her request. And he'd delivered—

Oh no. He hadn't. She hadn't seen Sully since the morning they'd left Meallán.

If the women of the Triskele hadn't responded to her letter, there'd be no one waiting at the temple when she arrived.

"I'll send someone on ahead, alert them as to our delay." Tearlach tossed his empty canteen into his pack, then ducked under one of the low-hanging branches.

Esme followed, shielding her eyes against the sun. The darkened clearing beneath the canopy would've been more suitable for sleep, but she'd wager that Tearlach hadn't veered more than a few feet away from the wide, twisted trunk the entire time she'd been trapped in the cave beneath the tree.

It wasn't until she settled beside him that she realized just how exhausted she was. Still, she resisted the temptation to close her eyes, fearing Lord Luxovious's memories would return the moment she did.

When Tearlach's breathing evened out, Esme eased back against the branch. After a while, she allowed herself to sink further into the tranquility that surrounded them, finding her mind blissfully blank.

"What was the cost?" Tearlach asked softly.

Esme's breath hitched. She held it for a second, letting it out slowly in hopes that she might fool him into thinking she'd fallen asleep. Though she knew it would never work.

After a moment, she twisted to look up at him. "One of my memories for...one of his."

Tearlach stared down at her, unblinking, his jaw tightening.

"I'm sorry." His voice was unexpectedly rough, and Esme wondered how many of their shared moments she'd given up.

———————

Breathing in a warm, familiar scent, Esme knew immediately that she'd drifted off to sleep curled up next to Tearlach. Slowly, she opened her eyes to the lilac and emerald colors of the Loinnir Lights playing across the smooth lawn of his shirt. Night had fallen and they needed to head back, but she didn't move, mesmerized by the glow of light dancing and swirling, growing brighter, then fading.

The lights were far more brilliant above the ancient tree than anywhere else in Tremaene—yet another reminder that the magic of their world was locked away, their land becoming more and more barren with each passing day.

And finally, she understood how it'd all happened.

She shoved the thought away, refusing to let that monster rob her of another precious memory.

Returning her attention to the hard planes of Tearlach's chest, expanding with each powerful breath, she wished they could stay a little longer. *Just a few more minutes*, she pleaded silently.

"Did you sleep?" Tearlach's voice rumbled through her, making the skin at every point of contact they shared shiver with awareness.

"A little. I think."

"We should get moving."

Reluctantly, Esme pulled away. She straightened her clothes and replaited her braid before turning back to face him. He held up her pack, his hands grazing her arms as she slid them through the straps. Even through her shirt and the protective layer of fine mesh chainmail she wore beneath, she could feel the heat of his touch.

Without speaking, they wended their way through the thick foliage between the ancient tree and the ridge that obscured the small oasis, then climbed the mass of vines that covered the rock face. At the top, Tearlach halted her and offered a pouch of dried fruit.

Her thoughts instantly scattered.

A dull pain radiated at her temples.

It wasn't that she couldn't recall when last she'd eaten; it was the gesture itself that bewildered her.

She stared down at his outstretched hand. There was something eerily familiar about it. He'd handed her food before—countless times during their journeys—but she couldn't stifle the feeling that she'd somehow...*forgotten* something. Lost something.

She glared back at the tree. How many moments had she sacrificed?

"They're not lost," Tearlach said softly. "Whatever it took from you, you'll find again. We'll help you remember. I'll help you."

She worried her lower lip between her teeth, thinking back on her years in Periwen. Even when she'd thought she'd been alone, Tearlach had been there.

She only wished she'd known at the time. Not because it felt like a violation—having someone watch over her without her knowledge—but because, for all those years, she'd thought she was alone. When Tearlach had been right there, so close.

Esme looked up. His dark eyes tangled with hers, and she knew he was thinking the same.

"Are you going to remind me of the time you trapped me on the ladder?" she asked, hoping to ease some of the tension swelling between them. "Because I can assure you, I remember that quite well." She forced a tight smile.

The determination in Tearlach's eyes remained.

"No," he said simply, taking a step toward her. "I'd tell you about the time I watched you build the fence around your garden, how you were intent on weaving every branch yourself instead of hiring help in the village. Then I'd tell you about the ducks who congregated in the pond just past your orchard, and how you'd calm them whenever they grew agitated. Usually after a storm. I'd remind you about the way you'd hum to yourself when you picked apples or when you walked through the forest."

Esme swallowed, her throat suddenly tight.

"I'd tell you about the way your hair would fall loose after you tended to your plants for hours on end in the late summer heat, how it would curl at your temples. How your face could be smudged with dirt, but your eyes were always bright and glittering."

He took another step, and Esme's face grew warm. The intimate recollections should have made her feel exposed, vulnerable, but they only made her feel...*seen*. Cherished, almost.

"I'd remind you of the dresses you'd wear every time you dared to venture into town, nervous of other people's judgments." His eyes trailed down her body as though imagining one such dress. Her skin prickled in response. "I'd tell you how it never mattered what you wore." He paused a moment, then added in a near whisper, "You were always beautiful."

Her breath caught. She pressed her lips together as declarations threatened to tumble forth.

I didn't leave her behind. The words Tearlach had said late one night, back at the palace, echoed in her mind.

He took one more step, then reached up to brush a lock of hair that had fallen across her forehead, tucking it behind her ear. She inhaled a shuddering breath at the feel of his fingertips grazing the tip of her ear before they trailed softly down her neck.

"Always beautiful," he said again with reverence.

Her lips parted on a tiny gasp. Tearlach's gaze dropped to her mouth, his eyes devouring the movement of her tongue as she wet her lower lip. Slowly, he lifted his eyes back to hers. The weight of his potent attention made her blood run hot.

Then something cleared in his vision and he straightened. Only then did Esme realize he'd been leaning toward her.

"We should..." He took in their surroundings, inhaling deeply. "Be on our way," he finished.

"Ah—Of course," Esme stammered, shying away, eyes stinging.

But as they started off across the rocky flats, her eyes kept straying to the broad expanse of Tearlach's shoulders and his long, powerful legs striding ahead of her.

Try as she might, she couldn't stop her mind from turning over every word, every look they'd shared. Tearlach felt something for her, she knew that with certainty. But he'd never acknowledge his *improper* feelings. Much less act on them. Such were things a guard wasn't allowed to feel for his queen. And Tearlach would never compromise his duty.

While she might dislike it greatly, she couldn't help but respect his conviction.

Besides, after all he'd been through—being cast out by his family, fighting in the Dark War, leaving behind the people he loved in order to protect her—Tearlach deserved a far less complicated life than the one she offered.

He deserved someone—

Like Sheridan, Esme suddenly recalled, her heart sinking. How had she forgotten about the woman she'd seen Tearlach with on more than one occasion?

"What was it like? Down in the cavern?" Tearlach halted her tormenting thoughts.

He slowed his pace to match hers as Esme thought about the sacred pool, welcoming the feel of comfort and warmth the otherworldly place had offered. Before Lord Luxovious's memories had wrenched her mind into horrifying atrocities.

Swallowing past the bile that rose in her throat, she described it as peacefully as she could, telling Tearlach about the water that swirled around the central rock, the memories drifting through the cavern as if on a gentle wind, even the scent of magic that saturated the air.

"Didn't know magic had a smell to it." A smile crept into his voice.

She breathed in deeply. "It smells like apple blossoms and misting rain and dewy grass. Like springtime."

Tearlach fell silent for a moment. "Springtime," he repeated longingly, as if it were a place only they knew. And something about that helped her settle back into the easiness they'd long since established.

It's better this way, she decided. Tearlach was her guard. She, his queen.

"Tell me everything." He rolled his shoulders. "From the beginning. Every memory you saw."

Esme stretched her neck from side to side and adjusted the straps of her pack, knowing that reliving each memory would be challenging. But it felt like if she spoke the heinous truths into the night air, they'd infect the entire mountain range. Instead, she allowed the foreign memories to rise in her mind, then opened herself up to the connection that bound her life to Tearlach's, letting him see everything Lord Luxovious had done.

Each moment flickered behind her eyes: the dark magic and the orbs, the light from each of the channels going dark, the creation of the gods and their fictitious origins.

Tearlach could infer the rest. She wasn't about to flood his mind with visions of a war he'd barely survived.

By the time the last of the memories faded from her mind, Esme's heart was thudding violently against her ribs, her hands clenched in rage. She pulled in lungfuls of air as she awaited Tearlach's response.

Several moments passed as they hiked along quietly.

Nothing? He had nothing to say?

Not so much as a comment about the Order? Everything their people had believed as truth for a thousand years had been nothing more than an elaborate tangle of lies...

And Tearlach had no reaction?

Esme resisted pressing him on it. Knowing that the burden of Lord Luxovious's betrayal was no longer hers alone to bear was enough.

Her gaze lifted to the sky. She watched as the Loinnir Lights faded slowly, leaving only the bright moons in their wake. Both Mios and Neve were mere slivers, though not close enough to cross paths. That wouldn't happen again for many months.

Her thoughts turned to the celebrations the darkest night heralded, when the kingdom would honor Aeveen, goddess of fire.

Only there was no goddess of fire.

There were no gods at all. No one orchestrating her life or anyone else's. No grand plan.

In a single night, everything had changed.

As they neared camp, Esme stole glances at Tearlach. As expected, his jaw was set, his eyes dark. But there was an alertness in them that sent a chill down her spine.

When they crested the ridge, she saw why.

The camp was empty.

Her horse and Tearlach's stood beside the remnants of a fire, alone.

"Where are they?" Esme breathed.

"Out looking for you," Killian called from the far side of the valley.

Esme's eyes went wide. Tearlach stiffened beside her.

Neither said a word as Killian rode over—the sharp angle of his brows and firm set of his mouth quickly coming into view. He was furious. And likely, so were the rest of her guards.

But as Killian swung down from his horse, Esme saw the clear relief in his sapphire eyes, softening his stern expression, if only a little.

He looked her over, then turned to glare at Tearlach.

"Where the fuck have you been?"

Chapter Two

ESME FLINCHED AT the words. But she could see it wasn't anger. Killian's words, his posture, even the way his eyes blazed at Tearlach— they all masked the worry beneath. He'd been terrified that something had happened to her. To both of them.

"Not going to tell me, are you?" Killian huffed. "Fine. Keep your secrets." He turned back to his mount and led her down into the valley.

Tearlach and Esme followed silently. They hadn't discussed whether or not they'd tell the others about the memories, and she wasn't particularly eager to relive everything she'd seen in the cavern. Again.

"Am I to assume we weren't meant to wake until you returned?" Killian called over his shoulder.

"That's right," Tearlach replied. His voice didn't invite further commentary.

Killian scoffed as he pulled his horse to a stop. He reached into one of the saddlebags and pulled out a hunk of parchment-wrapped bread. He bit into it, studying each of them as he chewed. "Suppose this means you're not the only one with sleep magic." His eyebrow twitched with satisfaction.

"Who?" Tearlach demanded.

"Wouldn't tell you if I knew." Killian cocked his head to the side, provocation flaring in his eyes.

"Where are the others?" Esme stepped between them.

Killian looked down at her, eyes softening. "Everyone was set to return by sunrise if you weren't found."

Esme glanced toward the western horizon just as Roderick, Harlow, and Armel appeared atop the ridge, silhouetted against the pinkening sky.

"What happened?" Armel asked as he drew near.

"They won't say."

"I see." Armel lowered his head and narrowed his eyes at Tearlach.

Seeing the betrayal on each of their faces, Esme's stomach turned with guilt. They deserved an explanation.

You owe them nothing, Tearlach asserted as Madoc and Quinlan joined from the south.

I have to tell them.

You don't have to do anything. Tearlach didn't spare her a glance, continuing his silent standoff with her guards as if he were the one to blame. *You are their queen, Esme. They answer to you. They do not question you.*

But her discomfort only worsened when Hazel crested the ridge with Cahir and Myles. How could she have asked Hazel to be her lady-in-waiting if she couldn't trust her with the truth?

Armel strode over to Hazel as she dismounted. They shared a few brief words before Hazel's eyes slid from Tearlach over to Esme.

"We'd better get moving," Killian grumbled, securing his horse's pack. "As it is, we won't reach Juverna for another two days."

Esme bit her lip. There'd be no one waiting for them in Juverna. Another of her deceptions.

"Harlow, ride on ahead and wait for the priestesses at the temple. Inform them we've been delayed."

Harlow nodded at Tearlach's command, but Myles stepped forward before she could turn her horse. "I can get us there in time," he promised. "If we travel through the night."

Myles didn't seem to be harboring any anger at Esme's betrayal. Then again, he'd likely sensed the falsity of their mission before they'd even left Meallán. Surely he'd anticipated that something would go awry.

"Not like anyone'll be sleeping tonight anyway," Cahir muttered.

"Good." Tearlach nodded to Myles, ignoring the comment.

"Wait," Esme said a little too loudly, causing everyone to stop what they were doing and turn to face her.

If I can't trust them, I don't deserve their loyalty, she told Tearlach.

"I'm sorry I left without telling any of you. Or rather…I'm sorry I left *without* all of you." Esme dropped her gaze. "There's this place where memories are kept. I wasn't sure if it would yield the information I sought, or whether it even existed…"

"Navlin? The Sacred Pool?" Madoc questioned.

"How do you know about it?" Tearlach asked in a near growl.

"My mother used to tell me stories. 'Bout a lot of things. Never really believed them to be true, though. She told a lot of stories, my ma." He shrugged his shoulders. "So it's real, then?" When Esme nodded, Madoc gave a low whistle.

"Should have taken us with." Hazel lifted her brow at Esme before glaring at Tearlach.

"It was my decision. And again, I apologize. I'll admit it was foolish to keep it from all of you."

"Sure was," Hazel agreed.

Esme closed her eyes for a second as she exhaled a shaky breath. "I was worried I wouldn't be able to find the location, or that it would end up being nothing more than the stories your mother told you." She gave Madoc an imploring look. "So, I kept my plans a secret. I simply couldn't bear the thought of leading everyone off course." She paused, before adding quietly, "Or letting you all down."

With that, something shifted, and Esme felt a brief moment of reprieve as postures became less tense and expressions softened.

But she could sense their forthcoming inquiries, so she summoned Lord Luxovious's memories once again and relayed to the group each vision that led up to the start of the Dark War.

Armel moved closer to Hazel, while sharing a speaking glance with Killian. Myles reached for Cahir, whose eyes looked haunted.

Esme spared them the horrid visuals she'd seen through the eyes of the enemy. And when the sight of her mother appeared in her mind— standing before Lord Luxovious, weary and determined, chest heaving with each strained breath, clothing and armor stained with dirt and blood, a battered sword raised with a trembling arm—Esme gave only the barest details.

No one said a word when she finished. Not even a stomp of a hoof broke the silence—as if the horses were just as appalled by the revelations.

Finally, Quinlan asked, "If the Order isn't what we thought it was, how do we know we can trust the unordained priestesses?"

Esme stared at her. Of all the questions her guard could have asked, of all the rage and disillusion she should've felt after hearing such shocking truths, Quinlan was only concerned about what was to come, and what needed to be done.

"From what I've seen," Esme replied, "I believe the initiates were misled, just as we were. Likely, they trust that the ritual itself summons the elements. Paired with their intrinsic abilities. I've no reason to think that the women who formed the Triskele know the truth."

"I'd wager they know even less about the origins of the Order than their predecessors," Tearlach appended.

"I'm inclined to agree," Killian offered. "But if they were, in fact, ignorant of the true power hidden within their ritualistic garb, couldn't anyone use the objects to summon raw magic?" He paused as the implications settled around them. "Why those women? Why were they chosen?"

"I'm...not sure," Esme admitted. "Though I intend to find out. And until then, I think it's best if we presume no malice on their part."

"Let me get this straight." Cahir stepped forward. "Our mission, as I understand it, is to now locate these...crystals or *orbs*—which are actually keys that will unlock obstructed *channels*. But they've been broken to pieces and cast into silver decorations and jewelry, so...what we actually need to find are rings and necklaces and such." Esme nodded weakly. "And we have no idea where they are or where to look for them."

"That's...correct."

"But without them, we'll have no way of restoring magic to the land. Do I have that right, so far?"

"You do." Esme swallowed.

"And on top of all that"—Cahir spread his arms wide—"this... *Luxovious*—the man who stole magic from our kingdom and created this complicated subterfuge as a way to have ultimate power—is the same man who led those savage creatures across Tremaene, to wipe out every soldier, man, woman, and child—not just on the battlefields, but in every village and town that stood between him and the power he sought?" He dropped his hands as a defeated look crossed his features. Esme's breath caught in her throat as Myles gripped one of his shoulders. When the memories seemed to clear from Cahir's mind, he refocused on Esme and, with a deep breath, continued. "And now you tell us that he wasn't even killed at the end of the war, as we were led to believe. That he's still alive. Is that about right?"

"He may not have been killed, but he is of no threat to our kingdom or our queen." Tearlach inclined his head toward Esme. "Erena herself bound him in eternal sleep, locked him in an iron box, and buried him on a remote island across the sea, far beyond the shores of the mortal realm. And that's exactly where he'll remain."

Cahir seemed to accept Tearlach's assurances, even as Esme's pulse quickened at his mention of the mortal realm. Until raw magic once again flowed freely in Tremaene, the small, thriving continent across the sea was in danger of plunder. It was only because Sully had assured her that only a few of them knew the fog that separated their worlds could be crossed that Esme was able to tuck that particular worry away.

"Our focus," Tearlach redirected, "is to locate the fragments of the orbs and remove the obstructions from the channels." He was met with nods of agreement by each member of the guard.

"Now." He turned to Myles. "You said you could get us to Juverna by—"

"What was the toll? For his memories?" Armel's tone revealed more than his words. He knew Esme hadn't divulged everything. "That kind of knowledge isn't free." He canted his head slightly, his eyes already offering solace.

"It was an even trade," she said carefully, feeling the weight of everyone's gazes. "My memories, for his."

Killian took a step toward her, then stopped. That he was no longer the person to comfort her made her chest tighten. But before the hollowness of the loss could take root, he clasped his hands together firmly. "Well, then," he declared with a falsely bright smile. "Let's go save the kingdom, shall we?"

Chapter Three

"WHERE DO YOU think they are, the orbs?" Cahir asked Roderick as if the man known for his silence might respond.

"They could be scattered anywhere. Or hidden," Quinlan joined in.

Esme listened with half of her attention as the group of guards ahead of her tossed ideas back and forth. She'd already considered more possibilities than her mind seemed to have room for, but hearing them ponder various options reminded her that she no longer carried the fate of the entire kingdom on her shoulders alone. And because no one had questioned how she came to learn of the sacred pool's location, her own visions and the visit with Athdara would remain between her, Tearlach, and Cadwyn. For a time, at least.

"What d'you think happened to them when the Order fell?"

"It could be...I mean, what if pieces were set into every piece of jewelry the priestesses wore?"

"Could be."

"Or maybe one specific item—something that would stand the test of time, something required for their ritual."

Esme's ears perked up at that. She drew forth Lord Luxovious's memory of the summoning ritual. In it, the high-priestesses had worn silver circlets, amulets, rings, cuffs at their wrists...Any one of the items could've held fragments of the orbs.

"We'll search the temples. See what remains." Tearlach's tone was assuring and absolute.

"You think Orianna would've left anything of value to scavengers?" Quinlan asked.

"Payment?" Myles suggested. "For whoever assisted with destroying the Order?"

"That's the *only* way she'd give anything up," Hazel grumbled.

Esme hadn't given much consideration to Orianna's role. She was quite certain the woman had been manipulated at a young age by Lord Luxovious. Jaime's recounting of the strange encounters Orianna had partaken in during their youth—conversing with things that couldn't be seen—only solidified what Esme already suspected. Yet, how much or little Orianna knew about the true source of a priestess's power would likely remain a mystery.

The Loinnir Lights were brighter as they approached Juverna. Wisps of deep green and lavender threaded through the milky swirls. Esme breathed in the pine-scented forest, savoring the sweet smell of growth and flowing water after traveling across the sparse mountain terrain.

A creek widened as the trees thinned, and eventually it was the lights of the small town that lit the night sky. Esme pulled her cloak from Edlyn's saddlebag and covered her head as they rode quietly down the main road.

Behind the sole inn, they stabled their horses. Myles went to find something for them to eat, while Cahir and Roderick secured the rooms that occupied the entire second floor.

Esme was brushing down Edlyn when she noticed Tearlach leave with Armel, Madoc, and Harlow. She'd expected him to stay near, especially in a place they'd never been. Was it distance from her he sought or the need to see to their security personally?

Before she could further analyze his retreat, Killian found her. He'd been assigned to the back of their company most of the journey, and it wasn't until he smiled down at her that Esme realized how much she'd missed being in the presence of his happiness and optimism.

"I'll tell you everything. *Every* detail of every moment since we met. All of it. It's all yours." He glanced down at her again, surely seeing the moisture gathering along her eyelashes. "I'll never let you forget," he vowed.

Then, with a heartfelt grin that coaxed a smile of her own, he strode off.

Esme stared after him until his silhouette disappeared around the side of the main building, then returned the brush to the empty hook and sat down heavily on a wooden chest, struggling to keep her eyes open. She pulled the brim of her hood low to keep her appearance hidden, though she suspected it was too early even for stablehands.

Little air moved through the open doors, and soon her cloak became stifling. She opened the front and felt something crinkle. Reaching inside the pocket, her fingers closed around a tightly folded letter.

She pulled it out, frowning in confusion. Try as she might, she couldn't recall having put anything in her pocket. Especially not a letter she didn't recognize.

Then she noticed the triskele symbol stamped in wax on the outermost flap.

She sucked in a breath and tore it open, quickly scanning its contents.

"They've agreed," Esme whispered.

Turning the page over in her hands, she stared down at it, wondering where it'd come from. Ultimately, she decided that she didn't much care. The only thing that mattered was that the priestesses would be at the temple in the morning. Instead of searching the abandoned structure for silver adornments Esme knew wouldn't be there, she'd actually be able to speak with them, hear their stories, glean a bit more insight into the Order.

Then another thought occurred.

She hurried over to where Hazel was standing guard at the entrance to the stables. But Esme's excitement at finding the letter drained the second she remembered the look Hazel had given her that morning. The betrayal. The anger.

"I'm sorry about..." Esme rushed to apologize, but Hazel waved her off.

"No need. I understand," she replied simply, yet didn't spare her a glance.

"Nevertheless..." Esme cleared her throat. "I should've confided in you. You've selflessly protected me since the day I returned, and I...I've come to think of you as a—"

Hazel shot her a look.

"I owe you more than I've allowed, that's all I mean to say," Esme finished lamely. When Hazel didn't respond, she shifted her tone, infusing it with a touch of command she hoped Hazel would appreciate. "I'll need your help when we meet with the priestesses."

Hazel lifted her chin a fraction—the request clearly acceptable.

"Do you think you could sense objects that contain magic the same way you sense our signatures?"

"It's possible," Hazel allowed, staring straight ahead. "Though I may not be able to distinguish it from its wearer."

Esme considered that. If the priestesses had any of the items, surely they'd keep them close.

"And dark magic?" she dared ask. "Can you sense that kind of presence as well?"

Hazel turned and aimed her full attention at Esme. "When I'm not overwhelmed by hordes of pestilent creatures annihilating every soldier around me with their abominable, flesh-melting sorcery...I might."

Esme clamped her mouth shut. Thankfully, Myles chose that moment to return, or she might have issued another groveling apology. Or worse, tried to offer Hazel physical affection in the form of an embrace.

When everyone was gathered in the largest suite abovestairs, her guards descended on the trays of slightly stale bread, cold roasted root vegetables, and steaming bowls of lentil stew, then took turns with the shared washroom down the hall. Exhausted as they were from riding hard through the day and most of the night, even a cold wash would've been welcome, but Armel ensured that they had hot water for proper—albeit quick—bathing.

Esme had just finished a large helping of vegetables and a second bowl of stew when Quinlan returned to the room, toweling off her hair. Killian nodded for Esme to go next, but she insisted the guards take their turns first. It didn't take much to convince him.

Pushing herself back on the bed, she leaned against the thin pillows that lined the headboard, and let her eyes fall closed, listening to the sounds of dishes being stacked and creaking floorboards.

When next she opened her eyes, the room was dark. The lamps had been extinguished, and the lights from the night sky cast the room in a cool green glow. Esme pointed and flexed her feet against the smooth linen sheets.

Her *bare* feet.

She was tucked in, she realized. Almost too tightly to move.

She felt along her hip, finding her belt and dagger gone. Shifting her shoulders, she managed to turn onto her side.

Then froze, her breath trapped in her lungs.

Beside the bed stood a figure.

Black flames licked up its sides, encircling the billowing garment that looked more like smoke than a heavy traveling cloak. Deep purple cores flickered in the depths of the dark, wraithlike flames.

With a shuddering breath, Esme dared to take in the face of the person she feared dwelled beneath the cloak.

The hood was pulled low, shrouding the head of the figure in shadow. But Esme knew who'd come for her.

Lord Luxovious.

Had he sensed her sifting through his memories? Did he know her true identity as his captor's daughter, that Erena's blood ran through her veins? Or was it simply that she'd seen something she wasn't meant to?

Esme stiffened as a gray, clawlike finger curled around the edge of the fabric.

A ripple shivered through the figure, and for a split second Esme could see through to the wall beyond.

It wasn't fully formed.

He's not really here. He can't touch me, she told herself. Not believing the words even a little bit.

He drifted closer, his gnarled hand reaching for her.

Esme fought against the bedclothes and scrambled to the far edge just as a sliver of light pierced the apparition.

The door across the room creaked open, and Lord Luxovious vanished.

Chapter Four

WHEN MORNING LIGHT filtered through the window's age-warped glass, Esme was still gripping the hem of the sheet and staring up at the beams that stretched the length of the ceiling. Her fear hadn't waned in the slightest.

She'd remained unmoving, feigning sleep during the guard change that had scared off her unwelcome visitor. Though she doubted anything could scare such a man as Lord Luxovious.

After watching the spot where he'd appeared until she was mostly certain he wouldn't return, she'd listened for several long minutes to the heavy breathing of her sleeping guards. His presence hadn't alerted them. None of the three guards sleeping on the floor had woken, nor had any of the seven outside the room, belowstairs, or patrolling outside the inn detected the intrusion.

Because Lord Luxovious had come for her, and her alone.

What if they hadn't been disturbed? If he'd been able to reach out and touch her?

What if he returned? Became stronger? More...corporeal?

How would she defend herself if he attempted to worm his way into her mind as he had with her mother and Orianna? According to her mother's journal, that particular ploy hadn't worked on Erena. But Orianna had easily submitted to his manipulations, his promises. Perhaps because she'd been so young, her magic newly awakened?

Much like Esme.

Her heart quickened at the thought, fresh panic flooding her veins.

Killian and Cahir burst into the room, calling out unsavory names in an effort to rouse the others, each balancing a stack of covered dishes and baskets of bread. Myles followed, gripping the handles of several empty copper mugs.

As the rest of the guards funneled into the room, Esme pushed back the bedding she'd yanked up to her chin like a layer of armor. She was still wearing the clothes that were covered in two days' worth of travel, having not made it to the washroom before falling asleep.

Her gaze sought Tearlach as she remembered that someone had tucked her in at some point during the night, but she couldn't find him.

The more she thought on it, Tearlach wouldn't have shown such intimate attention to her in front of the others. It'd probably been one of the female guards who'd pulled the covers up and tucked them around her so tightly.

It was only when they were alone, when Tearlach didn't need to be a stoic, impenetrable wall of a man, that he expressed any sort of attention that diverged from his official duties. Like the nights when Esme couldn't escape the nightmares that haunted her dreams and he'd stay by her bedside until dawn.

If he'd been there the night before, standing guard over her vulnerable sleeping body, would he have seen Lord Luxovious too?

Esme shook her head. It had been an apparition. A trick of light, nothing more.

Armel filled mug after mug with piping hot water. Only a few were lucky enough to have slept in the scant hours since they'd arrived, leaving everyone eager for strong tea.

Esme used the distraction to slip from the room and make her way down the narrow corridor. When she returned, wearing a shirt that smelled slightly better than the one she'd slept in, she halted at the foot of the bed, her sword belt dangling from her fingertips.

There, on the worn wooden slats, where the figure of Lord Luxovious had stood, was a scorch mark.

Esme swallowed, stealing a glance over her shoulder at the cold hearth, wishing she could place the blame there. But the mark on the floor was in the shape of a ring.

She averted her eyes, fumbling with the ties of her belt, then tucked her dagger in at her hip with a shaky hand. She thought she heard her name. Then came what sounded like her title. But the buzzing in her ears muffled the sound.

"Your Majesty," she heard again, turning to find Killian at her elbow. He looked into her eyes for a protracted moment, then scanned the rest of her body. "Everything all right?" he asked in a low, concerned voice.

Esme nodded, noticing that they were alone in the room. How long had she been standing there staring at the floor?

Killian gave her something warm wrapped in a linen cloth, then handed her a mug. She wordlessly thanked him, downing the bitter contents in only a few swallows. Killian kept his eyes on her as he gently took the mug from her hands. He set it beside the other empty dishes, then guided her out as if she were unable to perform even the most basic of tasks.

Roderick fell in behind them as they stepped out onto the rickety stairs that clung to the side of the inn. Harlow pushed off the wall when they reached the ground, and Madoc moved away from the adjacent building to join them. Esme pulled up her hood after searching once more for Tearlach.

Quinlan brought Edlyn forward and offered Esme a boost. It wasn't until she was in her saddle that Tearlach strode purposefully into the yard. Without sparing her a glance, he tossed sacks of fresh supplies at

Armel and Hazel, then stuffed a smaller pouch into his shirt pocket before mounting his horse.

Esme thought to call him over, anxious to tell him about what she'd seen, but decided it would be best to do so when they were alone. Whenever that might happen.

———————

It was midday when they neared the Iola Temple. The rocky terrain and redwoods had long since given way to a lush and thriving landscape that Esme hadn't seen since fleeing the mortal realm. Moss and ferns clung to lichen-covered trees. Vines dipped down over the seldom-used path.

She stretched in her saddle, straining to see the twisting spires that broke through the canopy. She hadn't expected something quite so opulent. The only temple she'd visited in her youth had been the Arlais Temple in the Belfay territory, near the capital city. And it was nothing like the resplendent structure that rose to greet them as they emerged from the thick stand of trees.

The Iola Temple sat atop a steep incline, its pillars and winding steps hewn from the stone peak. Sunlight glinted off thousands of diamond-shaped panes of colored glass that made up the arches of the dome and the soaring windows that wrapped around every curve of the impressive edifice.

But even as a hallowed place to commune with the gods, it seemed... out of place. Not only among the neighboring villages that dotted the mountain range, but in all of Tremaene. Esme wondered if it had been the first temple Lord Luxovious had commissioned.

Or perhaps the final one—a grand statement to the subterfuge he'd successfully executed.

It certainly looked like a place the gods might occupy. That was what he'd wanted, wasn't it? For everyone to see it as a place where gods would deign to dwell within their world.

Water trickled down from an unknown source, glittering as it fed the shallow creek that circled the jagged mountain peak. Woodland creatures darted from the trees to drink at the white-pebbled banks. Birds with long tail feathers and iridescent black plumage flitted out from behind the many waterfalls to dance through the mist.

Tearlach ordered Cahir and Harlow to investigate the perimeter, motioning for Esme to stay mounted.

When they returned, reporting that there were no horses or signs that anyone had recently arrived, Tearlach considered the rugged ascent and the imposing temple.

"Quinlan." He nodded, then eyed the rest of the guards. "Killian, Armel, inspect the temple. Hazel, I want you on the east side, where that ledge—"

"No," Esme interrupted. "They can't go up there. And we certainly can't have anyone sneaking around, looking for other ways inside."

Tearlach's eyes darkened, and Esme could hear the resounding growl in her head.

"It has to be me." She held his unyielding stare. "Only me."

She swung her leg over, knowing if she didn't act quickly Tearlach would send every guard up before her. Or worse, physically stop her from going up there at all. She shimmied ungracefully off Edlyn's saddle and dropped to the ground, wishing she had the long limbs every other Fae seemed to be blessed with, or even half the agility of her guards.

Tearlach watched as she pulled a sheathed charcoal pencil and a small notebook from her pack. The rest of her retinue remained understandably silent.

"It's not going to happen this way," Tearlach informed her calmly.

"This is the only way; and you know that." She wedged the notebook into her belt before meeting his gaze. His eyes bored into her and Esme added, "I'll bring Hazel." She was already planning to, but if it seemed like a compromise, she might convince Tearlach to stay behind.

When he still didn't yield, Esme made a final, deliberate concession. "Myles too." His ability to sense deceit was also a necessary part of her plan.

"You'll take me," Tearlach corrected succinctly. "Or you'll not go up there at all." He took a step closer. The horses nearest them shifted nervously.

I sincerely hope you're kidding, Esme rebuked. *They'll take one look at you and—*

And what? Tearlach snapped, his gaze hardening. *They'll see that you're well protected?*

Esme stared up at him, feeling the barest hint of aggression echoing with his words.

Did you really think, for even a moment, that I'd let you go up there alone, without—

"Fine," she conceded quickly aloud, unable to bear another word. He'd go wherever she went, she knew that in her bones. But when those declarations—so fierce and dutiful—piled up, it brought a sudden, sharp awareness to the nature of their relationship. What it would always be, and what it could never be.

Tearlach regarded her a moment longer, then shared a look with Hazel, who started up the stone steps without a word. Myles followed after darting a worried glance between Tearlach and Esme.

An eerie silence hovered around them as they climbed, the sounds of running water and trills of birds fading into the air that seemed to grow heavier with their ascent. The steps widened, curving around the foot of the temple as two massive doors came into view. They stood open, though it wasn't a welcome sight as the opening revealed only an empty rotunda. There was no indication that they were in the company of the Triskele, of anyone. Yet the prickle at the back of Esme's neck made her suspect they weren't alone.

As they ascended the final step, Hazel slipped away to scout the narrow circumference around the building. She was gone before Esme could protest.

Tearlach strode into the massive inner chamber, but Esme only approached the threshold, stopping short of entering. Myles came to stand beside her.

The structure was in remarkably good condition. There were no signs of damage or disrepair. It looked as though it had been well cared for, the walls and floors polished. She'd expected the interior to be the same ethereal white of the facade, with soft pastel light filtering in through the glass. But inside, the temple was dark, swallowing the light and reflecting it back as a dense, opaque haze.

"Come on." Myles gently nudged her with his elbow. She blinked up at him. Myles nodded to where Tearlach stood inside the main chamber, hands loose at his side as he continued to sweep his focus around the room.

Esme slid her foot forward, hesitant to make a sound, to leave a mark. Her unease heightened as she moved toward the center of the space, her eyes falling on the massive, nine-pointed star adorning the floor. It was multifaceted, each slice made up of a different dark stone: black obsidian, coppery pyrite, a blue so deep it looked like the depthless waters of the Sea of Muirín. A few opalescent white tiles contrasted the design, but it still felt fathomless, endless. Like its purpose was to shroud the secrets of the Order.

Summoning the memories she'd bartered for, Esme tried to picture the ritual the high-priestesses had performed. There'd been a circle of blue flames, and words that sounded like the Old Language, chanted over and over.

She glanced around. Where were they?

Pulling the letter from where it was pressed between the pages of her notebook, she moved farther into the chamber, rereading their instructions, their demands.

"*This* was not our agreement, Your Majesty," a voice said, halting her.

Esme whirled toward the speaker.

A woman with a dark auburn braid twisting down the front of her gray cloak stepped out from behind Myles. The dim light inside the temple caught the edge of the dagger she had pressed against his throat.

42 WILD HEART OF THE MAGIC

A woman with a dark auburn braid twisting down the front of her gray cloak stepped out from behind Myles. The dim light inside the temple caught the edge of the dagger she had pressed against his throat.

Chapter Five

ESME RAISED HER hands slowly, careful not to take her eyes off the woman holding the blade. Myles was tall by any measure, yet the woman nearly matched him in height. Even if Myles decided to do something foolish, she wouldn't be easily overpowered.

Hazel had returned. She and Tearlach stood on opposite sides of the rotunda. They shifted closer subtly, their movements nearly indetectable. Neither had weapons drawn, or things might have come to a swift and tragic end. And Esme needed information only the woman who was currently threatening Myles could give.

"Leave now, and I'll let him go." Myles grunted as the woman pressed the blade against his flesh.

"I'm sure we can—"

"Was it not you, Your Majesty, who wrote the letter asking—*pleading*—for our assistance? Was it not you who claimed she'd agree tacitly to all of our conditions?" Esme opened her mouth to respond, but the woman hastened on. "This was not the agreement. Your guards"—she jerked her head toward Tearlach, then to Hazel—"should not be here. You were to come alone. Or not at all."

"I've left my guards outside." Esme dared a step forward, halting when the woman flicked her other wrist for her to stay where she was. "Hazel is my attendant." The words were out before she could think better of them. Hazel looked nothing of the sort, and judging by the woman's scrutinizing appraisal of Hazel's attire and the bow strung over her shoulder, she didn't believe the falsehood for a second.

"What does a queen's attendant need with so many weapons, I wonder?" The woman cocked her head to the side, her eyes sharpening.

"You know the answer to that." Esme gave a pointed look to the dagger in the woman's hand.

"And him?"

"My personal guard, Tearlach," Esme admitted. The woman sneered at the title. "He doesn't let me out of his sight. Believe me, I've tried." She attempted a hint of levity. "I assured him there would be no harm in meeting with you and your Sisters alone. And once you lower that blade, I'll gladly command him to wait outside with the others."

The woman considered her for a moment before her eyes slid over to Tearlach. Esme was infinitely grateful he'd assumed what appeared to be a relaxed stance.

"And this one?" The woman nudged Myles again. Esme could see the strain in his throat as he swallowed past the edge of the blade.

"Myles is our guide" was all Esme revealed. The woman aimed a scowl at Myles's profile, though she said nothing.

The silence in the temple tightened around them before the woman finally ordered, "The weapons go. And that one"—she shoved Myles away and pointed her blade accusingly at Tearlach—"stays where I tell him."

Esme remained in the center of the room as Tearlach and Hazel—and to her surprise, Myles—removed their many weapons. Tearlach approached Esme slowly, then carefully pulled the dagger from her belt, his eyes meeting hers for only a second before he stepped away. Her focus quickly returned to the woman across from her while listening to Tearlach's unhurried strides as he carried their cache of weapons out of the temple.

When he returned to her side, though not too close, he clasped his hands loosely behind his back, awaiting further instructions.

The woman looked each of them over again, then, deciding something, ordered Tearlach to stand against the wall to her left. Once she seemed satisfied with his position, she turned and swiftly strode toward the back of the rotunda, where she pulled open a previously unseen door.

Five additional women stepped into view. The woman—their leader, Esme could only assume—took her place in front of the others.

"My name is Moira. And I was charged with starting a new Order."

Chapter Six

QUESTIONS UNFURLED IN Esme's mind at Moira's declaration. She pressed her lips together and mastered her expression as each of the others introduced themselves.

"Zaira," the one on the left began, nodding with far more respect than Moira had offered, her dark curls dancing slightly with the motion.

Ceridwen spoke next. She was more petite than the others, and with her blond hair reminded Esme of Sheridan. Banishing the comparison from her mind, she focused on Keva, who offered her name with a slight tilt of her head as she looked down at Esme. Vevila followed, pronouncing her name with a voice sweet and lilting—welcoming, almost.

"Catriona." The tall, almost wispy woman at the end presented herself last. The single word was flat, delivered without a hint of emotion. And yet, there was something about the woman that caught Esme's attention. The thin, rose gold braids at each of her temples almost disappeared against her pale, shimmery complexion. But her eyes—a blue as light as the tone of her skin—seemed to hold hidden truths and powers unknown.

"Please." Moira gestured for them to take a seat. Esme lowered to the floor and crossed her legs over one another. She glanced over at Tearlach, where he was leaning against the wall.

No closer, he told her. *Keep some distance. She still has that blade.*

Hazel and Myles hesitated a moment before taking their places on either side of her.

"You wished to implore our assistance, Your Majesty. Is that right?" Moira addressed her.

But Esme wasn't ready to negotiate. First she needed to determine what they knew.

"Tell me about your sect, the Triskele. You said you were charged with starting a new Order?"

When Moira regarded her, Esme intertwined her fingers on her lap, making it clear she would hear everything before offering them anything.

Finally, Moira conceded. "Nearly ten years ago, a woman claiming to be Sister Firinne sent me a letter. She inquired as to my abilities—if my magic had begun to manifest—and asked if I would meet with her. It didn't seem like a formal invitation to join the Order—not that I'd ever received one myself. Stranger still, she didn't want me coming here, to the temple. Instead, she wished to meet in private at a tavern in Juverna. A strange request, wouldn't you agree?" Esme nodded. "It made me question whether the sender was truly who she claimed to be. I even thought about informing the city guards that someone was posing as a high-priestess— for what ends, I wasn't sure. But there was an urgency to her words that I couldn't discount. When I requested to know what her interest in me was, I received another letter along with a parcel." The other women bowed their heads as Moira met Esme's gaze. "That was the last I heard from Sister Firinne."

Esme's lips parted as she considered her response carefully. To them, the Order was sacred, each priestess chosen and blessed by the gods. She felt Myles shift beside her. "I'm so sorry. Sincerely." She knew what Orianna had done; it was no secret. Though she wondered if Sister Firinne had suspected something was amiss. "The letter, the parcel, did they give any indication as to..." She trailed off.

Vevila spoke softly. "It was poison, she said. In the letter, Sister Firinne conveyed her suspicions regarding a mysterious illness that had swept through the other temples. She beseeched Moira to begin a new Order—one in secret so the women would be safe, so the power bestowed upon the high-priestesses could not be manipulated or misused." Vevila looked to Moira. The woman gave a slight nod for her to continue. "There was a list of eleven names, potential initiates. She begged Moira to find each of them. Not only to band together and keep each other safe, but to carry on the sacred rites. For, as you know, Your Majesty, without the priestesses, Tremaene would surely perish."

A list? Who could've known which women would possess powerful enough magic? Athdara? She'd given Alastar's name to Lord Luxovious in the beginning, might she have provided the others? Esme ground her teeth at the thought. Until another possibility rose in her mind—that Lord Luxovious had visited each of them, *called* each of them to join the Order. Her stomach soured.

"The women on the list"—she glanced between the six of them—"must have been rather young."

"No younger than you, queen," Keva replied in a challenging tone.

"I meant no disrespect, I simply…" Esme glanced at Hazel, whose steady gaze gave her a small amount of encouragement. "What I mean to say is that your magics must have only recently manifested when Moira found you, and I…Well, I wonder if any of you felt…*compelled* to join the Order before that time." Her neck and chest heated and a drop of cold sweat slid down her spine. It was more difficult than expected to extract information without offending them.

"I don't follow, Your Majesty," Zaira answered when the others only looked at her skeptically.

"It's always been a curiosity of mine, I suppose. The high-priestesses have a connection to the gods that the rest of us could never even fathom, and I've always wondered if any of the *chosen* women experienced an early communion with the gods before joining the Order. A divine calling, if you will."

"I'm afraid not, Your Majesty," Zaira replied. Then her eyes darted to Moira as if suddenly realizing she might have revealed too much.

"You mentioned eleven women," Esme redirected. "What happened..." *Ah*, she realized too late.

"The others had already been killed or taken to the capital city. We never learned what...*became* of them," Vevila explained.

Esme bowed her head. "I'm sorry," she murmured. "Again, I'm so sorry for the losses you've endured."

"It's not you who needs to apologize," Moira cut in. "But I'll ask that you remember from where our concerns stem."

"Absolutely. I do." Esme met the eyes of each woman sitting before her, then said, "I'm glad the six of you were able to find one another, and have managed to remain safely hidden all these years."

"It seems we were not the only ones," Keva commented.

"No, you weren't." Esme looked away and cleared her throat. She was there for the Triskele's secrets, not to divulge her own. "Sister Firinne sent a parcel, you said?"

"It contained a sacred book about the Order, and Sister Firinne's vestments," Moira explained.

Esme's heartbeat picked up at the mention, and that Moira had given the information so freely.

They had the pieces of the orbs. Some of them, at least.

"And with the vestments, you—With the sacred book, that is, you and your Sisters..." Esme inclined her head toward the other women. "You taught yourselves how to summon the elements?"

"Water," Vevila corrected. "Only water."

"Yes." Esme nodded. "You mentioned that in your correspondence." She'd already guessed that the reason they could only summon one element was because Sister Firinne's vestments only held fragments from the water orb. But how had they reconciled that anomaly? "Has that always been so? Have you ever managed to summon the other elements?"

"Water is the least complicated," Moira stated. Esme bit her lip. She wasn't sure Armel, or any other water wielder, would agree with that statement. "We're...*limited* in our power, as you pointed out." She arched a dark auburn brow. "And because our suffering land is best restored with flowing water, it was decided that our gods-blessed gifts be used to draw water from the source."

Myles tapped his finger twice on his knee, but Esme didn't need his detection to know that Moira wasn't telling the truth. Water was all they *could* summon. It wasn't a decision they'd made.

Her attention strayed to the woman at the end. Catriona. She held Esme's eyes for a moment before averting them. Did she know?

"As we become stronger, as our power becomes more precise— though it will require decades of practice and devotion—we will be able to summon the other elements as well," Moira promised.

"Be that as it may, I must offer my sincerest thanks for the work you've already done here in the mountains. It truly is commendable."

Moira accepted the praise gracefully.

"Might I ask, have you been successful performing the ritual anywhere outside the temple?" Esme knew there were only five open channels, each located beneath the five sacred edifices, but wanted to be certain that the dark magic in the orbs couldn't simply unlock the hundreds of others Lord Luxovious had obstructed.

Moira sat a little taller. "The ritual is sacred and must be performed within the walls of the temple. We wouldn't dare anger or disgrace the gods by straying from their ordained edicts."

Myles tapped his finger again. So they *had* attempted the summoning ritual elsewhere. Without success.

"Of course," Esme appeased them, sharing a look with Hazel. When the time came to tell them that everything they'd spent their lives believing had been nothing but lies, it would need to be done delicately.

"Can you tell us anything at all about the ritual or about the sacred book you were given? I'd like to understand as much as I can."

"No," Moira told her bluntly. "The ritual is for priestesses alone. And as for the book, you wouldn't understand the language. Only those destined for the Order have the gift to discern the meanings of the words."

Likely the Old Language, Esme guessed as Myles tapped his finger again. Or an altogether made-up one. Of course Lord Luxovious would keep the ritual mysterious, indecipherable even by its practitioners. Though she was curious if he'd created something convincing, should someone attempt to translate it.

Esme couldn't fault Moira for her dishonesty. They were trying to appear reputable as a sect and competent in their craft. Esme knew all too well what it felt like to be underestimated.

She summoned the memory of the ritual again—three high-priestesses holding raised hands, chanting in an indecipherable language, a ring of blue flames in the center of the temple. She peered down at the star on the floor. Was that where it was performed? The flames had been contained within a curved saucer. Esme wondered how the Triskele had improvised that.

There was something about seeing the flames in the memory. Alastar had created a fourth orb. If high-priestesses could only summon earth, air, and water, what had become of the fire orb? What had it been used for?

Brushing the distracting notion aside, Esme returned her focus to the ritual. In all honesty, she was surprised the untested, untrained women had managed to summon anything at all. And with only fragments to access water magic from the source. She'd always been told that all three elements needed to be summoned together, to create balance.

Lies too, she reminded herself.

If the Triskele only had Sister Firinne's articles, and they only contained pieces from the water orb—as Esme assumed—could the element only be summoned by water wielders? Or did the dark magic allow for anyone to bring forth raw elements?

She considered the women sitting before her, wondering who among them had a water affinity. Which of them had unknowingly wielded dark magic to summon from the source rather than from herself?

Esme suspected it wasn't Moira. She was far too defensive. Esme had a feeling it was someone who didn't want her ability known. Zaira, Ceridwen, and Keva all had dark eyes ranging from blue to green, and hair that curled. And Vevila's warm skin...Esme closed her eyes. It was useless trying to identify someone's magic based on physical appearance. Hazel could sense their magics, but she couldn't very well pull her aside to ask.

Her eyes locked with Catriona's again, and Esme knew. *She* was the sole reason water continued to flow through the Tamslo Mountains. And she'd let her Sisters believe that only with their combined efforts had they managed to sustain the land in the north. Esme admired her benevolence, though she wondered how much Catriona understood. Did she sense something beyond her abilities, or did she simply believe her magic was stronger than that of the other women?

Esme considered for a moment what might happen if she, herself, held the objects that contained dark magic. She wasn't particularly strong in any one element, but she did have a connection to all of them.

After darting another quick glance at Catriona, Esme addressed Moira again. "As I've already conveyed, the rest of Tremaene needs your help. If I'm able to arrange transport and guarantee your safety—by my own guards—might you consider traveling to the Laurel Temple in Derval? The plains of the Western Flats have been impacted the most by the fall of the Order, and I fear the lands will soon be lost to the Wastes, without hope of revival."

The Wastes were a vast, desolate tract of land that Esme suspected hadn't always been so untenable. It had once been known as Kearney, the westernmost territory of Tremaene. That was, until Lord Luxovious had destroyed his own lands in his endeavor to control the raw magic beneath his feet.

The women shared a look. "It will not last long," Moira told her with genuine regret. "This plan of yours is not sustainable. At most, we can bring water to the flats for a month, perhaps longer. But that's hardly enough to establish new growth. So unless other women with our gifts can be found, and a new Order established, our efforts will not be enough to reverse the drought and barrenness that plagues the lowlands. For now, our place is here, in the mountains."

"I understand your reservations, but right now"—Esme let out a breath—"you're our only hope."

Moira seemed mollified by her response. She canted her head and regarded Esme for a long moment. "We will consider your request." She rose from the floor, then paused to add, "Your Majesty."

Esme watched them stand, wondering how she might convince them. But when Myles reached down a hand for her, she knew there was nothing more to say.

Esme thanked them again, but the women did little more than nod, standing stoically as the three of them turned to leave. Tearlach pushed off the wall to join them.

She plucked her dagger from the pile of weapons and glanced back once more before starting down the steps.

Hazel grabbed her arm. "Why didn't you ask to see the items?"

"They wouldn't have let us."

Hazel huffed out a frustrated breath, though she seemed to agree.

"She's right," Myles confirmed.

"Did you sense anything?" Tearlach asked.

A haunted look crossed Hazel's face. "I did."

Chapter Seven

ESME TOOK THE steps carefully, her mind a whirlwind. Having foolishly forgotten to take notes during the interaction, she recited everything the young priestesses had said. But the feeling of permanence her memories had once held was no longer, so at the bottom of the stone steps, Esme hurried across the bridge and settled atop a large flat rock a few paces down the shore. There, she wrote furiously in her notebook—short, quick words that had been said, her impressions about each of the women, architectural details of the temple itself.

When she lifted her head and stretched her arms—feeling a knot forming between her shoulder blades—she heard the low rumble of Roderick's voice from somewhere nearby.

"Could you sense anything up there?"

"Only a little." Hazel's voice was tight. "The objects were there, but not close."

"What did they..." Roderick seemed to pause. "Did they feel like our magic?" Was Roderick a sensor too?

When Hazel didn't answer at first, Esme turned her head slightly to see if they'd moved back to where the horses and the rest of the guards were waiting. Hazel's face was angled up toward the sky. Roderick stood patiently beside her.

"It was like those things." Hazel exhaled heavily and dropped her gaze. "From the war."

Roderick grunted his discontent, then gave Hazel a nudge—which, coming from Roderick, must have been a consoling gesture.

Esme looked back down at her notes, unseeing, as images from the Dark War flickered in her mind—memories she wished she'd never seen. But there was nothing she could do to vanquish them. They were a part of her.

When at last they faded into the recesses of her mind, she closed her notebook and made her way over to Edlyn.

"Same route back? Or would you prefer something…less strenuous?" Myles asked the last part softly, so only Esme could hear.

She considered assuring him that she was fine, but Myles wouldn't even need to sense the lie to know how untrue it was. He could probably see the strain the trip had put on her in every one of her features, in the rigidity of her steps, the shortness of her breath. Every stretch of the journey had been more demanding than she'd anticipated.

"The same way," she told him, wanting to be quickly home. She needed to make a plan to find the missing—*stolen*—items. Needed to fix what Lord Luxovious had done. Nothing, it seemed, could wait.

She also missed Cadwyn and Sully, and hoped the familiar surroundings and routine of palace life would somehow mend the distance growing between her and Tearlach. He'd been pulling away since they'd left the sacred pool. At least, it felt that way.

Myles offered his interlocked hands to help Esme up. She glanced once more at Tearlach, but he was already circling his horse as the rest of her guards fell in line.

"Thank you," Esme murmured to Myles as he boosted her up.

"Any time." He nodded, holding her gaze for a moment. "Truly."

Esme stared after him as he jogged over to where Cahir was holding the reins of his mount.

As they headed south, stopping once at a small village before traversing the rocky peaks of the mountain range, no one spoke of the meeting at the temple. Tearlach, Hazel, and Myles had given the others detailed accounts of everything the women of the Triskele had said. And while Esme's mind churned with questions and theories the meeting had provoked, she was content to keep them contained to her notebook.

The pages of it, however, were filling up rather quickly—not just with details of the journey, but with every one of her own memories that surfaced in her mind. She cherished them all. Held them tight. Wrote down every sight and sensation she could remember for fear that they too would slip from her grasp.

Sudden recollections woke her from sleep each night and distracted her through the long treks each day. She'd clumsily scratch the echoes of each memory in her notebook, balancing it between her thighs while gripping Edlyn's reins.

Days passed without notice, and soon they reached the lowlands of Belfay.

As they left the sparse cover of a copse, Esme blinked against the harsh midday sun. The path toward the knoll ahead was a straight one, and she was surrounded on all sides by her guards and their horses. For just a moment, she let her eyes fall shut. She was so very tired, having not slept more than a few hours at a time in days. The pounding hooves trampling the brittle grass and the muted light filtering through her eyelids lulled her mind.

Her limbs felt loose, heavy.

She felt herself sway.

Felt her head drop.

Careful, Princess. Tearlach's deep voice curled around her. *If you fall off your horse, I'll have no choice but to pull you onto mine.*

A shiver ran down Esme's spine and her eyes sprang open. Her heart hammered behind her ribs as she thought of riding with him again. His powerful thighs bracketing hers. His arm pulling her body flush with his.

She adjusted herself in the saddle, then risked a glance at Tearlach, who was riding close beside her for once.

He stared down at her, and Esme fought the heat flooding her body. He was looking at her with concern, but there was a touch of something more, something she hadn't seen since the night they'd left the sacred pool—when he'd nearly confessed his feelings for her.

She swallowed, her throat suddenly dry.

Like the last time you forced me to ride with you? When I expressly insisted on my own horse? she retorted, somehow managing to sound unruffled despite her thundering pulse. *As we're not being pursued by assassins at the moment, I'll keep to my own, thank you.*

Tearlach gave her a subtle nod that seemed more pleased than dismissive, and Esme realized he wasn't only keeping her from falling off her horse. He was making sure she remembered the moments they'd shared.

And there were many.

The heat he'd awakened in her transformed into something calmer, soothing her nerves with a feeling of contentment, of belonging. No matter what happened between them, they would always belong together. Even if not in the way she truly wanted.

———————

Esme knew they were nearing the capital city when she spied slivers of pale green shoots piercing the dry brush. She glanced around, looking for packed roads, streams, or familiar woodlands, but they must have been at least a day's ride from Meallán. That, or the barrenness had transformed the landscape so dramatically that she no longer recognized her home.

She swallowed the bile rising in her throat and focused on the plans that had been discussed throughout the day. They'd need to find the items that contained the fragments of the orbs. Unfortunately, there was no way of knowing how many silver pieces they'd been cast into.

Were there only three sets for each of the five temples—one for water, one for air, and one for earth? Did every item a high-priestess wore contain the magic—circlets, amulets, rings, wrist cuffs—or just a single item that was designated for each participant?

She should have pressed to see the articles the Triskele had from Sister Firinne, but she'd feared angering or offending them to the point that they'd no longer offer their assistance without great payment. Or withhold it altogether.

The only choice left was to search the remaining temples. Arlais Temple in Belfay was the closest to Meallán, so they'd start there. Esme didn't want to consider the difficult quest that might befall them if the items had been pillaged and sold off in pieces. She hoped—perhaps naively—that they'd been hidden somewhere safe beneath the temples, locked away in vaults.

But what then? she dreaded silently as discussions continued around her. Even if they found them all, what needed to be done with them? Lord Luxovious's memories had only shown the creation of the orbs. They'd offered no clues as to how they might be destroyed. Could they even *be* destroyed? If they could, would that be enough to break the dark magic's hold on the channels?

The thought of carrying out such a task sent a shudder of fear through her body. It would no doubt affect the person who destroyed them.

Perhaps there was another way to remove the obstructions. If they managed to find others like the women of the Triskele, powerful enough to act as conduits between their own magic and the source, could Tremaene simply carry on as it had before, build a new Order?

She felt a heavy thump in her chest, in the place where her magic had resided before Tearlach siphoned it from her. It felt empty, yet answered nonetheless. There was no other option than to destroy them.

Her thoughts eddied from her mind as she felt a tendril of magic return. She inhaled deeply, relishing the feeling, letting it spread out beneath her skin.

She turned in her saddle, searching for Tearlach, only to find that he and the others had dismounted and were pulling items from their packs. Esme looked ahead, surprised to see the city wall sitting along the horizon.

Edlyn stomped her displeasure and Esme quickly swung her leg around and dropped to the ground, which was soft and green with life. She'd been so consumed by her thoughts that she hadn't noticed the verdant landscape swelling around her. The trees above were full, allowing only dappled light to reach the mossy ground.

A fire was quickly summoned and a kettle of tea set to steeping. They'd make camp until midnight, then return to the palace unseen, so the remaining food stores were passed around. Some of the guards meandered to a nearby stream to wash up as a deck of cards was produced with shouts of agreement.

When Esme sipped her second cup of tea, letting the warmth soothe the nervous energy her returning magic had churned up, Madoc called over to her.

"Would you care to join?" He nodded at the cards he was shuffling between dexterous fingers.

"Oh, I..." Esme began, then noticed Tearlach and Armel conclude whatever quiet conversation they'd been having. Tearlach rose from his spot and strode off in the direction of the stream. She still needed to tell him about the night at the inn, when Lord Luxovious had found her.

"Thank you, but perhaps next time," she told Madoc, attempting to stand. But she slumped back down on the felled log, her vision tilting. Magic thrummed through her veins, pounding loudly in her ears.

"Your Majesty?"

Esme blinked up at Madoc, who was standing over her. Quinlan and Killian were there a second later, kneeling down in front of her. She took a slow breath, trying to quell her sudden dizziness, then glanced between the wall her guards had made only to find everyone else staring just as intently at her.

"I'm fine," she assured them, giving her head a little shake—which ended up being a terrible idea.

"Have you eaten anything?" Killian pressed.

The thought of food made her stomach twist. "Only tea."

A murmur went through the group. Hands were moving, and soon Myles pushed his way through to crouch before her. He placed a piece of stale bread in one of her hands, then curled her other around a cup of soup.

They all waited.

Reluctantly, Esme forced the cup to her lips. Then forced herself to swallow a mouthful of the thick soup, nearly choking on a piece of carrot. When that didn't appease them, she bit off a chunk of bread. She chewed for far too long—knowing from the taste that it had come from the palace kitchens, so it was more than a week old—then barely managed to swallow it.

"I'm fine," she told them again. "Really."

It took several more minutes, and a few shared looks, but they finally left her to finish eating without an audience. The card game commenced, though without its previous enthusiasm. While she didn't look over, Esme could feel their not-so-subtle glances. Her eyes, however, were trained on the spot where Tearlach had slipped away. He'd return soon, and Esme needed to speak with him alone.

After waiting another few minutes, she rose on much steadier legs, even as a renewed rush of magic swirled incessantly inside her, making her ears ring. She drew everyone's notice as she made her way through the makeshift camp.

"Where are you going?" Hazel stepped into her path.

Esme opened her mouth, but it took more than a second to formulate a convincing excuse. "I just need to splash some water on my face." *Not* as convincing as she'd hoped.

Hazel gave her a pointed look. "We've water here." She didn't bother to remind her that they also had one of the best water wielders among them. They both knew it wasn't the stream Esme sought.

"I'll escort you," Hazel insisted when she didn't reply.

"You won't. I'll be all right." Esme stared back.

Hazel narrowed her eyes, then stepped aside, folding her arms across her chest, set to await her return.

When Esme reached the stream, she found the bank vacant. She looked upstream, then down, but she didn't see Tearlach anywhere. Deciding to venture a bit farther upstream, Esme followed the bank until a thick bramble blocked her path. Carefully, she picked her way around it and spotted Tearlach sitting on a flat rock at the edge of the water. Without a shirt.

Esme's lips parted—her goal completely forgotten—as she watched water drip from the dark ends of his hair and travel down the powerful muscles of his back.

She stumbled back a step, knowing he could feel her there. Spying on him.

But when she noticed his attention fixed on something cupped in his hands, she wondered if he was too distracted to sense her.

Esme knelt, peering furtively through the prickly branches as Tearlach lifted an object—small and silver with a faceted magenta stone—into a harsh ray of late afternoon light.

An earring? What was Tearlach doing with—

She inhaled a sharp breath.

A gift, she realized. While they'd been journeying to uncover truths vital to the survival of their kingdom, Tearlach had gone out of his way to procure a thoughtful and, dare she say, intimate gift for...for...

Esme swallowed the name as Tearlach lifted his shirt from his lap.

She sank back on her heels, grateful that he was dressing. But instead, he used the soft lawn of his shirt to polish the small stone with a care she'd never witnessed before. Esme thought of the blades he'd fashioned back in Debarrow, how the hands that had dealt death in battle had created such intricate, delicate designs along the hilts.

She kept staring, knowing she should leave. Or make her presence known at the very least. But she couldn't bring herself to move. Not when he polished the matching earring and returned the pair to a small black pouch. Not when he shook out his shirt and finally pulled it back on. And not when he slipped the pouch into the pocket near his heart, then patted it once to make sure the small treasures were secure.

When he rose from his spot, Esme ducked down and squeezed her eyes shut. There was no escaping.

Tearlach cut through the brush swiftly, his boots crunching the undergrowth not two paces from her. She peeked up from beneath her lashes as he passed, but his eyes were focused on something else, something in his mind, she suspected.

Once he disappeared through the oaks, Esme slowly hiked back the way she'd come. Her mind was a mess, but her legs carried her toward the sounds of the camp.

Even if Tearlach had once felt something for her, it was evident he no longer did. Not if he was buying gifts for another woman.

Sheridan.

Had he been thinking of her the entire trip? Even when he'd told Esme she was beautiful, *always beautiful*, had he been thinking of someone else, someone who was waiting for him back at the palace?

Esme stumbled up the low rise and was confronted by Hazel's all-too-knowing gaze, followed by a sympathetic one from Armel.

Rather than indulge the upsetting direction of her thoughts—as torturously tempting as they were—she decided to unburden herself from another of her many secrets.

Once the card game concluded, Esme told the rest of her guards the truth about the nine years she'd been away.

Chapter Eight

IT WASN'T COMPLETELY dark when they crossed the unguarded eastern gate, but given the late hour, the city should have been well asleep.

The sight of tents and caravans crowding stoops and darkened alleyways sent Esme into a panic. Had word of her secret excursion spread? Were they there to witness her return?

The festival, Tearlach's voice soothed.

It had been days since Esme had slept more than a couple of hours at a time, so it took her a moment to understand the words.

"Of course," she breathed, looking up to find banners and flags strung between awnings and rooftops. The Festival of Tahra would begin in only a matter of days.

And at the end, the ball.

Esme refused to think about what would be expected of her that night, of the *eligible noblemen*—as her councilors had referred to them— she'd be formally introduced to. Instead, she tugged on her hood and thought about how the new arrivals in town weren't simply there for the public festivities, but for the ball as well. She'd opened up attendance to include *everyone* in Tremaene before leaving on her journey into the mountains. Which, she could only assume, had not been received well by many of her councilors.

A smile threatened as they entered the yard that circled the palace stables. When she spotted Sully waiting, her smile broke free and she nearly jumped from Edlyn's back to rush toward him.

Sully wrapped her in his arms, and Esme felt tears prick at the corners of her eyes. She cleared her throat and leaned back so she could peer up at him.

"My dear?" Sully's forehead creased with concern.

"I'm fine. Everything's fine. Just need some sleep, is all."

"And a bite to eat, I'd imagine. There's plenty set up in the dining hall."

"That sounds…" She thought of the stale bread and dregs of soup she'd eaten earlier, when she hadn't been able to stomach much. But she'd acclimated in the hours since, and was suddenly, ravenously hungry. "I can't think of anything better."

"And the trip?" Sully asked quietly before she could hurry off. "I trust everything went as planned." He gave her a meaningful look.

Esme stilled at the words. Had Sully…

She could almost feel the weight of the letter in the pocket of her cloak. *Sully* had delivered it to her?

The empty feeling in the pit of her stomach suddenly felt less like hunger and more like a reminder of all the memories she'd given up.

"Yes." Esme nodded, catching sight of Tearlach striding over. "The meeting was…informative. I believe they'll be open to helping our cause."

"Splendid." Sully took notice of Tearlach's approach as well. "Now, go and eat something." He winked, turned her by her shoulders, then gave Esme a nudge toward the palace. She didn't hesitate to stumble off, all too glad to avoid yet another discussion of everything the visit with the priestesses had entailed.

The kitchen staff didn't disappoint. Esme wasted little time filling her plate with fresh greens, berries, poached eggs, and rounds of toast topped with a creamy sauce and steamed spinach. But after she took the first bite, she barely tasted the food as she descended on it with a ferocity she hadn't felt since her days of training in Altan, when food had been nothing more than sustenance.

She loaded helping after helping onto her plate as dishes were passed down the long table, hearing only the faint buzz of conversation.

When at last she looked up from her plate, popping a small chocolate biscuit in her mouth, Killian was staring at her.

"I'd ask if you were hungry, but…"

The rest of her guards chuckled. Esme scanned the empty plates and platters in front of her, awed by the amount of food she'd put away, then managed a tired smile of her own.

After telling them about her time in Periwen earlier, she'd been worried that they'd feel deceived, but everyone had taken the news surprisingly well. Madoc and Harlow had recounted some of the rumors that had arisen when Esme and Tearlach had first arrived in Altan—many of which were laughable, all of them improbable.

"Had enough?" Killian tossed his napkin aside and stood. Esme nodded, stifling a yawn.

Outside the dining hall, she felt Killian's hand come to rest on her lower back, guiding her toward the grand staircase. She was grateful for the assistance as her eyes struggled to remain open.

As they rounded the smooth wall of the rotunda, she felt Killian's supportive hand fall away, vaguely aware that someone had called his name. But Esme trudged on, certain that if she so much as stilled her momentum, she wouldn't make it to her bed. And her bed was where she needed to be. Tucked under fresh linens, scented with lavender and sage.

She hummed sleepily, watching her tired feet move her closer to the base of the steps.

At the edges of her mind, she registered the crisp sound of tailored boots on the marble floor. It was only when those boots pierced her line of sight that she looked up and found Tearlach standing before her.

Wait. That wasn't right. The man looked like Tearlach—*exactly* like Tearlach—but his eyes—

Blue eyes.

"I...Who..." She stammered as her thoughts tried to reconfigure into something that made sense. Blinking away the luring fog of sleep, Esme focused on...*not* Tearlach. She tilted her head as if that might rectify the illusion standing before her.

Then he smiled.

Her eyes widened, and she canted her head to the opposite side.

The man mirrored the gesture, like he found her amusing.

"Your Majesty." He bowed deeply. "Might I introduce myself?"

"Introduce..." Esme repeated the word slowly, as if she no longer understood its meaning.

His smile widened and his blue eyes twinkled with—

Blue eyes, she noted again, since her mind refused to acknowledge that she was looking at anyone other than Tearlach.

"Jarlath of Isloran."

"Jhaar-laaah-th?" She rolled the foreign name around on her tongue. "You're...Are you..." *Tearlach's brother.*

Though not *just* a brother. His *twin.*

Why hadn't Tearlach told her that his one and only brother was *his twin?*

The man chuckled at her obvious confusion and stepped closer. "Lord Torin's son," he clarified.

"Right. Of course. Lord Torin's son." She nodded one too many times, but it only seemed to make Jarlath's fascination toward her grow.

"That's right." He ducked his head to catch her averted gaze.

Esme tried to avoid those charming, utterly enchanting blue eyes—like the glimmering surface of a lake at night, with flashes of gold ringing the irises. Because when she met his gaze, she couldn't look away. She was enthralled by it. By him.

By Tearlach's brother, she reminded herself with a mental shake.

"I'd heard our queen was quite the beauty, but the word seems vastly inadequate."

Heat bloomed along the tops of her cheeks before spreading quickly down the column of her throat and across her chest. He kept his eyes locked with hers, but she felt as though they swept languidly down her body.

Only then did Esme recall her current bedraggled appearance and dreadfully filthy attire. Her blush chilled instantly, cooling as a cold sweat spread along her skin. *I must smell of horses*, she groaned inwardly.

"Your Majesty, you must forgive my thoroughly untoward opinion, for I simply cannot help myself. You are"—he took a breath, as if bracing himself against something powerful—"absolutely astonishing."

And with that, every thought drained from Esme's mind. She could only stare at the man standing before her.

Until Killian's voice fractured the trance. "I'll see her up. I traded my shift with—"

Esme looked over as Killian's approach slowed, no doubt realizing that the man he'd addressed wasn't Tearlach. He shifted his eyes to Esme, then stepped between her and Tearlach's brother. Esme was quite certain the two of them had never met, but Jarlath's resemblance to Tearlach left little question as to his identity.

Jarlath gracefully retreated. An easy smile pulled at his lips at Killian's clear hostility.

Esme wasn't sure what had incited Killian's reaction, but she quickly remembered herself and introduced the two men.

Killian didn't move, but from where she stood Esme could see the muscles in his jaw clench.

The air became heavier as the moment stretched, until finally Killian forced a bow and muttered something under his breath.

Jarlath didn't match Killian's animosity, he simply chuckled and stepped forward, hand extended. "Expecting someone like my father, were you?"

Killian hesitated a moment, his glare cutting between Jarlath's smile and his proffered hand before he accepted it with a perfunctory shake.

"My father's a lot to take. Believe me, I know." Jarlath shook his head as though the man in question exhausted him. "But I assure you, I'm nothing like him. Though I'll admit"—his gaze returned to Esme, eyes softening—"that being summoned by him seems to have had a rather... *delightful* benefit."

"So that's why you're here?" Tearlach's deep voice rumbled through the space as he rounded the staircase.

Jarlath turned toward Tearlach. "Brother," he greeted brightly, hands outstretched.

Tearlach merely crossed his arms over his chest and cocked his head.

Esme looked between them. They had the same dark hair and towering build, but their stances couldn't have been more different. Tearlach stood strong and commanding, impenetrable, while Jarlath's demeanor was open and friendly, his hands returning to their polite, clasped position behind his back.

"In fact, it is," Jarlath confirmed easily. "I'd written to him about a few matters back home and the quarterly commerce reports, about which Torin insisted I deliver in person. And..." Jarlath hesitated a moment, his self-assurance slipping slightly as he lowered his voice. "Mother told me you were here."

Esme's chest tightened at the words, at the longing they contained. He'd wanted to see his brother, after being apart for so many years.

When Tearlach didn't so much as blink at the clear sentiment, Jarlath dropped his hopeful gaze. "Come now, Tearlach," he tried again. "I haven't seen you in more than a century, certainly you—"

"Not long enough."

Esme's eyes widened at Tearlach's unfeeling tone.

What's going on? She fought the urge to shout the question as the tension between the two men made the cavernous space of the palace feel like a cramped dungeon cell.

"You still haven't explained why you're here in the palace, wandering the halls in the middle of the night."

"With the renovations at the town house, I took an apartment here at the palace."

Tearlach widened his stance and angled his head to stare down at the man who was equal to him in height, looking thoroughly unconvinced.

"I apologize for any inconvenience." Jarlath glanced at Esme. "I arrived only yesterday, and was assured that my stay had been cleared by… What was his name? Mairtín? However, if it will be a problem—"

"It won't be," Esme insisted, ensnared in the gaze he turned on her once again. "You're more than welcome here."

"As for the late hour, I confess I was unable to sleep. Meallán is lovely." Jarlath opened his arms, as if to encompass the entire city in his open palms. "And while the accommodations here at the palace are exceedingly generous, I must admit I'm partial to the sounds of waves crashing against the cliffs and…find I cannot sleep without them."

Esme heard the faint, yet unmistakable, sound of Tearlach grunting his disapproval before Jarlath continued.

"I wandered the library for a bit. What an extraordinary collection you have, by the way." He leaned toward Esme, conspiratorially—as if she were responsible for the acquisitions. "I was thoroughly engrossed in a book about the architectural history of our fine kingdom when I heard the rousing sounds of servants in the hall. I came to investigate, and found myself in the presence of our..." Jarlath trailed off, staring down at Esme like she was something beautiful and precious, and not at all covered in days of trail dust.

Tearlach moved between them, fists firmly on his hips, blocking Jarlath's view.

He spoke to his brother in a growl so deep Esme couldn't discern the words. But just as suddenly, Killian was at her elbow, ushering her away.

Taken off guard, she let him lead her, stumbling to keep up and twisting her neck to look back at the brothers. When they reached the servant stairwell, Esme pulled Killian to a stop.

"What was that about?" She jerked her thumb back to where Tearlach was speaking to Jarlath in low, gravelly tones.

"I'm sure Cadwyn is anxious to see you," Killian deflected.

Esme scowled at his blatant attempt to ferry her away. From what, though, she wasn't sure. She turned to stare at the sight once more, but Armel appeared then, blocking her view.

"Is that..."

"His brother," Killian responded ominously as he took Esme gently by the shoulders and directed her toward the stairwell.

"Shit," Armel muttered as a look passed between him and Killian.

Before Esme could inquire again, the two of them had linked their arms with hers and were all but carrying her up the winding stairs.

Indeed, Cadwyn was waiting in her suite. And finding herself far more awake than she'd felt moments ago—Jarlath's inviting smile seemed to have rejuvenating effects—Esme joined Cadwyn on the sofa and recounted everything about the meeting with the priestesses.

When at last she fell into bed, the morning sun was already creeping across the floor. Esme didn't bother to close the curtains. She simply turned away from the light and nestled deeper into the thick bedding.

The image of Jarlath returned to her mind insistently. She envisioned each of his features—so similar to Tearlach's, like mirrors of one another.

And yet her brief encounter with Jarlath—the way his eyes had held hers, softly, gently, the easy curve of his lips, his words genuine and uncomplicated—only exemplified how different the two were. Jarlath might have had the same look as his brother—his *twin*—but he seemed to express himself openly. In a way a queen's guard would never dare.

No, she amended, thinking of Killian and Armel, even Hazel. Especially Hazel.

Jarlath expressed himself in a way *Tearlach* never would.

Why didn't you tell me you had a twin? she demanded of him, unable to resist a moment longer.

Tearlach's reply was immediate. *I told you I had a brother.*

Esme turned her face into her pillow and growled in frustration.

Chapter Nine

ESME FELT SOMEWHAT restored, and was amazed she'd slept
through the night without disruption. The last time she'd woken had
been the evening prior, when Marta had delivered her dinner tray, which
had been followed by Winifred's arrival. And even though the council
secretary had brought with her armfuls of reports awaiting Her Majesty's
signature, Esme had been relieved that only a few required further
discussion—one of which had been another request from Lord Torin
about procuring lumber from the Tamslo Mountains. Winifred had once
again advised against Esme granting it, as they'd both suspected Lord
Torin wanted the redwoods not for lumber, but for pitch. Though neither
had determined the intended use.

With a groan, Esme pulled the sheet up to her chin, thinking how
she still needed to address the issue. Perhaps she could sleep through
another day, put off the many impending conversations, debates, and
confrontations she knew awaited.

Although, she reconsidered, glancing out at the songbirds that
had gathered on the stone railing, Cadwyn's suggestion that Keelin be
given permission to inform the other members of the council about
the meeting with the priestesses seemed sound. It would delay Esme's

obligation to call an immediate session, and afford her another day or so of peace.

She stretched long. It felt so luxurious to sleep atop a soft mattress. Though it hadn't been the hard-packed dirt beneath her bedroll that had kept her from sleep since the night at the inn.

Before the recollection of Lord Luxovious's visit could fully take shape in her mind, Esme reached over and pulled her mother's journal from the bedside table. She knew well what the words on the page would say—that her mother had been visited by him in her sleep, not during waking hours. Esme reread the entries anyway, finding comfort in her mother's words, though it did little to fend off the fear that he might return.

Suddenly the sunbright sanctuary of her room felt stifling. She crossed to the glass doors and threw them open, scattering the birds that had perched nearby. They glided in a cyclone above, then settled beside her hands as she braced them against the railing and breathed deeply.

———

Madoc and Harlow followed Esme as she marched out the south doors, making sure her pace was quick and determined. Unapproachable.

But upon spotting Lord Lennox speaking with an attendant, Esme changed course. The lord of Belfay had presided over the council in her absence, and she simply couldn't ignore him.

Lord Lennox looked up as she made her way across the veranda that rounded the window-lined wall of the council chamber. His deep blue eyes crinkled at the corners as he smiled.

"Your Majesty," he cried, handing his attendant a folio and a stack of papers. The woman kept her eyes downcast and slipped away, pulling the glass door silently closed behind her.

Esme noticed papers strewn across the large table within, and felt a flush of guilt that she hadn't provided him with a private office, or at least a proper desk.

"Lord Lennox, I can't thank you enough for your assistance." The stocky man bowed his head humbly. "I was just on my way to the lake, and I wonder if you might accompany me."

Lord Lennox's gaze turned unsure. He looked to the jasmine-covered stone wall beside them, as if seeing the stretch of grounds beyond.

"I'm afraid I must advise against that, Your Majesty." His tone rumbled with warning. Esme felt her guards move closer.

"Milord?"

"There are predators lurking beyond these walls." He glanced past Esme, toward the main doors at the south entrance, then stroked his long auburn beard. "Within them as well."

When he looked back at her, there was a glint in his eyes. "Noblemen." He smirked.

Esme released a breath and caught Harlow pursing her lips in an attempt to hide her own smile.

"Noblemen," Esme repeated, closing her eyes for a second at the reminder.

Lord Lennox chuckled, his wide shoulders shaking with delight.

"Apologies, Your Majesty. But it's been rather outlandish, what with all these men prowling about in search of you. Not to mention that you weren't anywhere to be found."

"Did they—"

"No, no. You needn't worry. Keelin took good care to redirect their attentions."

"Should I even ask?" Esme scrunched her brow, though her curiosity was piqued.

Lord Lennox chuckled again. "Your Minister of Communications is no fledgling when it comes to constructing a good narrative. She had a couple of your lady's maids don navy cloaks. Made them look very mysterious. Quite out of sorts for anyone to be wearing a traveling cloak about the palace, you know. Keelin left the men to arrive at their own conclusions. And sure enough, dozens were following after *the woman* in the blue cloak. Night and day your maids lured the suitors this way and that. Out of the palace and toward the stables, the gardens, the training yard. Then back into the palace. Around and around, they had them following after like yipping pups."

"And none figured it out?" Madoc questioned, disbelief ringing clear in his voice.

"As I've been told, the women were quick to remove their cloaks should any pursuers get too close. Leaving the men to wonder where *Her Majesty* had gone." Lord Lennox winked at Esme.

Madoc looked between the two of them, like he couldn't understand how anyone could be foolish enough not to unravel the trickery. "That can't possibly have worked."

Harlow scoffed. "I assure you, men see what they want to see." She looked down at Esme. "I would suggest, Your Majesty, that you avoid wearing a blue cloak for the foreseeable future."

"What about her guards?" Madoc argued. "Did they really think the queen would be walking the grounds without an escort?"

"I believe your fellow guard has already explained the tendencies of tenacious men." Lord Lennox nodded toward Harlow. Esme smirked. She almost wished she'd been there to see it. Then realized that if she wasn't careful, those very men would soon be following *her* around.

It was a miracle she'd only encountered one stranger since returning to the palace.

Jarlath's likeness flashed in her mind. And with it the disenchanting notion that he might have been summoned to the palace not to deliver reports from his post in Isloran, but as a potential suitor.

Lord Lennox and Madoc continued to argue the merits of Keelin's ploys, while Esme's mind was consumed by thoughts of Jarlath. It was troubling to think he might have charmed her so completely that she'd been unable to see the underlying truth.

Then again…there was something about his voice, his words, the way he seemed so sincere. She was inclined to trust that his intentions were honorable.

She also couldn't deny that the more she thought of him, the more her interest grew. She wondered where he was at that moment. If he'd been able to sleep, or if the foreign sounds of Meallán had kept him tossing and turning all night.

One thing was certain; she wished to know him better. Because he was Tearlach's kin, or that he smiled and expressed himself so freely, she wasn't sure.

Perhaps it was the hostility Tearlach had shown Jarlath that had her impatient to see him again, to pepper him with questions about their shared past.

"Your Majesty?" Lord Lennox inquired.

She looked up to find the three of them watching her. "I'm sorry, what was that?"

"I asked if you were able to accomplish what you set out to do." Lord Lennox spoke quietly as Madoc and Harlow retreated a few paces to give them privacy.

"I was. Thank you. It was…a success." She nodded, expecting him to inquire further, but he merely responded with a meaningful nod of his own.

Esme wondered what all he knew. Tremaene's Minister of Trade, Aindreas, had helped locate the priestesses—or had at the very least known that someone had been working to keep the land alive in the north—yet hadn't revealed anything during their many council meetings. If Lord Lennox knew more than he was letting on, she was grateful for his discretion. She didn't have the same level of trust for every member of her council.

"I promise to provide a more detailed account soon."

"Only that which you feel is appropriate. Or enough to…appease," Lord Lennox advised.

"Precisely. Which reminds me..." Esme stepped closer. "Did word of my absence leave the palace?"

"Not that I'm aware. Your staff is very loyal, I assure you."

"It wasn't *my* staff I was worried about." Esme arched a brow.

"Even if a few strains of gossip escaped, I believe the arriving *horde* of noblemen"—Esme winced at his word choice. Just how many were there?—"reinforced the notion that you were no doubt here, welcoming them. As for the upcoming ball..." He trailed off, giving he a sympathetic look.

"Right." Esme ducked her head.

"She'll want to meet with you. Keelin."

"Yes. I know she will."

"Now." Lord Lennox offered his arm. "If you're set on walking about the lake, and you don't wish to cross paths with *Kenrich of Donellis*"—he gave her a warning look that made her chuckle as he escorted her toward the edge of the veranda—"might I suggest following the row of sycamores across the lawn to the woods." He glanced at Madoc and Harlow, then added, "Good the two of you aren't wearing the gold capes, though I recommend you keep a bit of distance so as not to attract much attention to Her Majesty."

Madoc stepped forward and crossed his arms over his broad chest. "I challenge this *Kenrich*, or any man"—he nodded adamantly; Harlow rolled her eyes—"to get within ten feet of Her Majesty." Madoc looked east, then west, as if the man in question might be caught lurking behind shrubbery, ready to spring forth.

Spring forth, and what? Bow to her? Esme bit back a grin.

Chapter Ten

ESME WOKE THE next morning to dozens of messages from her advisors. Keelin had evidently informed the council about the meeting with the priestesses, as several were requesting private appointments with her. Though she found it odd that Lord Torin's note merely—and surprisingly politely—invited her to approve his appeal for temporary access to the lumber in the Tamslo Mountains.

She was staring at the long, slanted letters of his request, trying to extract his intended use for the redwoods, when Keelin knocked.

Esme waved her in, finding Brighid waiting patiently behind her. She didn't have much time, then. They were set to inspect the nearest temple that morning. And judging by the hefty folio Keelin carried, her Minister of Communications had several items to discuss.

"Sit, sit. I need to ready myself, if you don't mind." Esme gestured to the sitting area.

"You're heading to the Arlais Temple this morning, isn't that right?"

She knew Keelin was only asking because every minute Esme spent away from the palace meant she fell further behind in reviewing items that required her approval.

There'd been nothing in the report about the orbs, the obstructed channels, or that the entirety of the Order had been fabricated. It had only included confirmation that there were unordained priestesses in the north who might be willing to summon the elements throughout the kingdom.

"The temple in the north was so opulent, so different from what I remember of the Arlais Temple. I thought I'd take a look for myself. It's been so long since I visited." Esme slipped into the bathing chamber, but not before catching sight of Keelin spreading out dozens of papers.

"As the memorial for the priestesses that were lost will be here in Meallán," Esme continued when she returned to the main room, toweling off her face, "I'd like to incorporate elements from each of the temples, taking care that we pay homage to all the women who perished." The lie about the memorial she'd given when Lady Audris had learned of her correspondence with the Triskele continued to serve as a believable cover for Esme's pursuits. "I plan to visit the Laurel, Junia, and Troya temples in the coming months as well," she added, knowing the odds weren't in her favor that they'd find all the items—or any at all—when they searched the Arlais Temple.

Keelin nodded, saying nothing about how an artisan could easily draw inspiration from each of the temples, or that such journeys took Esme unnecessarily away from the capital.

"May I go over some details regarding the ball while you dress?" she called out as Esme joined Brighid in the dressing room.

Esme must have given an affirmative response, for the following quarter hour was filled with questions she barely heard and mainly deferred to Keelin on.

Brighid was securing the last button on her dress when Esme glanced over at her midnight blue cloak hanging from a peg in the corner. *That won't do*, she thought. But Brighid seemed aware of the complication and went to retrieve a pale green cloak instead.

Out in the corridor, Roderick and Cahir were waiting. Esme accepted a pastry from Brighid, then turned to thank Keelin for keeping her apprised of everything regarding the upcoming ball. So very, *very* apprised.

Hoping to avoid any lurking noblemen, she led her guards around the corner. But the moment she stepped inside the stairwell, a conversation that ought to have been hushed drifted up from the floor below.

"Can you believe her?" one woman asked with obvious outrage.

The response was too muffled to make out, but Esme slowed her descent, suspecting the comment might have been about her.

"And with all these nobles to choose from, she still wants what's not hers."

"Milady would never," a quieter voice spoke up.

"Oh? *Milady*, is it? I've another name for that thieving—"

"And what name is that?" Esme rounded the last steps, coming into view.

Sheridan and Griselda both stiffened at her sudden appearance. Griselda dropped into one of the deepest curtsies Esme had ever seen. And while Sheridan took a moment longer, she too lowered herself.

Given Sheridan's tone and churlish words, Esme wondered if she'd forgotten something that had transpired between them. She couldn't say she minded if that particular memory had been lost—the few glimpses she'd had of her had involved Tearlach. The two of them standing rather... close. Esme would gladly forget those images as well, if she could.

"Griselda, I was hoping I might find you." She stepped past Sheridan, trying to ignore the echo of the woman's voice in her mind. *Thieving?* What had she meant by that?

"Your Majesty." Griselda hurried to catch up. "Please forgive me. I wasn't—"

Esme stayed her with a hand. "Think nothing of it," she assured the flustered young maid. "Gossip is nothing new to me. If anything, I should be thanking you for your loyalty."

"Always," Griselda rushed to reply.

"Loyalty, I've often thought..." A voice greeted. The same voice that had piqued Esme's interest such that it had lingered long after their encounter. "Speaks more to the recipient than the bestower. Only true leaders are deserving of genuine loyalty."

Jarlath's long, unhurried strides brought him close enough that she could smell the hints of honeysuckle and frankincense from his soap.

Seeing him again forced Esme to rearrange the pieces in her mind. Striking blue eyes aside, he looked nearly identical to his brother. But his voice—deep and rich—politely commanded respect, without the domineering quality Tearlach's possessed.

Nothing alike, Esme silently corrected.

Jarlath turned and offered a smile to Griselda. "Especially when that loyalty is given so ardently."

Usually the more exuberant of Esme's maids, Griselda appeared to have lost her ability to speak. When she curtsied lower and far longer than she had for her queen, Esme arched a brow, amused.

Returning her attention to Jarlath, Esme found him considering her with the same look of admiration he'd bestowed on her during their first encounter. His eyes dipped down briefly, taking notice of her traveling attire. "I apologize if I've kept you." He looked between her and Griselda, seeming genuinely repentant. "Could I escort you?"

Esme felt Cahir and Roderick move closer as she accepted Jarlath's offer, though they didn't intervene the way Killian had. She wondered again what Tearlach had said about him.

"Milady." Griselda finally found her voice. "You needed to speak with me?"

"Right..." Esme recalled how she'd selfishly pulled her maid away from her duties. For a moment, she considered having her deliver a message to Cadwyn about relocating a certain maid who seemed to think Esme had stolen something from her, but decided it might cause more harm than good. "Oh, it was nothing." She offered a smile as Griselda curtsied again, then scurried off.

"I wish I could assure you that friction among staff is uncommon." Jarlath winced apologetically as he gently placed his hand over hers.

"You heard all of that, did you?"

"Overheard. From down the hall."

Esme chuckled. "Subtle, that woman is not."

"Not in the slightest."

"If only I could recall how I'd made such an enemy in her," she mused, searching her mind for an altercation that must have occurred.

"There's rarely any truth to such comments. Best to ignore them altogether." His cheerful expression slipped for a fraction of a second, and Esme was reminded of all he surely had to endure—not only from years in the public eye, but in service to his father. Jarlath had been forced into a lifetime of responsibility, much like she had. To serve the people of Isloran instead of living for himself.

Esme thought of her simple life back in Debarrow, and how much she longed for that peace.

But even after so many years, Jarlath still had a smile and a kind word for everyone he met. Esme could only hope to one day possess such grace and humility.

The imposing front doors were eased open, revealing a waiting carriage.

At their approach, Tearlach stepped out from behind the cab, his eyes immediately locking on his brother. He folded his arms over his chest and blocked Esme's entrance. Or rather, Jarlath's.

Before another terse conversation could arise, Jarlath leaned in. His breath feathered against Esme's neck as he whispered, "Until I've the pleasure of seeing you again." Then he stepped back, casting a smile toward his brother that would disarm most. But not Tearlach.

The look Jarlath offered Esme was more sincere, as if he truly couldn't wait until their paths merged again. Admittedly, she was more than a little intrigued at the prospect.

"Your Majesty." He gave a slight bow, then took his leave.

Tearlach scowled as he moved aside and allowed her to step up into the carriage, as if she'd done something traitorous by simply being polite.

To her relief, Sully joined her in the cab, while Tearlach claimed the seat up top with the driver.

As they set off, her guards on horseback surrounded the carriage. Sully moved closer on the velvet bench to be heard over their hooves on the cobbled stones.

"Cadwyn informed me of everything," he said, though Esme knew it had likely been Tearlach. But she didn't want to think about him and how his interactions with her had shifted so drastically since their return.

"When you were eight or nine years..." Sully reminisced, his deep, calming voice drawing her back into the present. He glanced out at the banners strung up for the Festival of Tahra. "You were so enamored by the twirling streamers the Bilberry Theatre had posted outside their front doors."

Esme's eyes began to burn. She should have remembered. Only she didn't.

Sully stretched an arm around her shoulders and pulled her close. "Not to worry, my dear. I'll tell you all about it."

"Spare no detail."

"Do I ever?"

She laughed through the tears.

———————

They spent hours scouring the temple, but found nothing.

Worse, Tearlach had decided to ride inside the coach on the trip back to Meallán. Esme knew it'd been Sully's doing. He'd no doubt witnessed how carefully the two of them had avoided one another all day, and he'd had enough.

The horribly stilted silence only grew heavier as the sky darkened and the city wall drew nearer.

Finally, Esme could take no more of it. She readied herself by filling her lungs, then risked a glance at Tearlach.

"We should visit Athdara again."

"She won't know anything," Tearlach quickly dismissed.

"She might."

"If she does, I doubt she'll relinquish it."

Esme tightened her hands into fists in her lap, but didn't disagree.

After a moment, Tearlach sighed. He shifted to meet her eyes. The warm glow of the lantern swaying outside the small window broke up the shadows on his face.

"Fine. We'll go," he acquiesced before turning away again.

Chapter Eleven

ESME STOOD ENTRANCED by Shawndrell's magic as it swept across the training ring, caught in an endless battle against Cahir's earth magic. For a few moments, Esme was able to forget the reason she'd ventured outside that evening as she watched rocks and dirt take shape only to be whipped up into something new.

Since visiting the temple, her agitation had only increased. A bit of sparring, she hoped, would exhaust her enough for at least one night of restful sleep. And with her magic fully restored, she needed to release some of the pressure before her frayed emotions triggered something dangerous.

When Cahir seemed to give all he had—the ground buckling as a ragged peak rose up between them—Shawndrell tilted her head to take in the creation before bending down and sweeping her arms up to pulverize the hardened earth, exploding it into a glittering cloud of dust.

As she let her arms fall back to her sides, her joyful laughter rang out, like it'd all been a bit of fun. Cahir, though, was breathing so heavily Esme worried he might collapse.

Then Shawndrell spotted *her*.

The woman gripped the many layers of her skirts and rushed over.

But she didn't bow or launch into a lengthy story the way she had when Esme had first encountered her. Instead, Shawndrell reached for Esme's hand and pulled her into the ring.

"Ready?" the woman asked cheerfully.

Thrown off by the abruptness of the situation, Esme felt herself nod in reply. And it wasn't a fraction of a second later that she felt air magic nudge her fingers, coaxing her to engage. It reminded her of Tearlach's air magic, the way he'd first used it against her. Though she hardly believed Shawndrell would use her power to pin Esme against a tree.

Cahir's earth magic clearly hadn't been successful, but Esme was still inclined to test her own aspect of the element.

Thin tracks appeared in the churned dirt. Halfway between the two of them, Esme grew invisible vines upward, weaving them into a thick, defensive barrier.

Shawndrell's magic brushed against hers, but that was the only warning Esme was given.

Sharp tendrils sliced between her vines, cutting through them faster than she could rebuild.

Though Esme only moved a few steps to the left or to the right, it felt like they were sparring. Her brow prickled with perspiration as she tracked Shawndrell's fluid movements, mirroring her position to anticipate each attack. Her hands cramped with the effort to hold them still, to not reveal anything about her own intentions.

She wove vines as quickly as she could, but Shawndrell's magic kept shredding them to bits.

When she could no longer conceal them, color bloomed along the vines.

Shawndrell's eyes widened in delight, and her magic fell away as she clasped her hands together.

Esme dropped her shoulders and blew out a breath. What was left of her vines untangled and burrowed back into the ground.

"Wonderful!" Shawndrell proclaimed. Nothing about her appearance suggested that she'd exerted any energy at all. "Such a pleasure, Your Majesty!"

"Thank you. It was"—Esme took another breath—"exhilarating."

Shawndrell's boisterous laugh coaxed an exhausted smile from her.

"I'd like to see that storm magic I've heard so much about." Shawndrell looked up to where the Loinnir Lights had begun to brighten the evening sky. "Next time. Pallya will be wondering where I've gotten off to. Though, I suspect she knows quite well." Then, with a flick of her wrist and a twirl, she was off.

Esme stared after the woman as her breathing evened out. Only then did she realize that their mostly invisible sparring match had drawn quite a few spectators—several of whom seemed far too refined to be off-duty guards or curious palace staff.

"I can grab you a cloak," Cahir offered in a low voice, coming up beside her. They both glanced over as Quinlan easily thwarted a nobleman's attempt to cross the ring.

Esme's eyes widened. The man certainly wouldn't make that mistake again.

"That's presumably best," she agreed, following Cahir into the barracks.

Quinlan and Madoc were beside her the moment she returned to the yard with the hood of the borrowed cloak pulled low over her brow.

It appeared as though the crowd had dispersed. Yet, to be safe, they avoided the most direct route back to the palace, veering instead toward the edge of the woods that took up most of the southern grounds.

A lone figure was seated at a bench beneath one of the massive sycamores that lined the great lawn. Esme's guards moved to block her from view, though not quickly enough.

"Jarlath?" Though Esme was certain it was him, she was unable to keep the uncertainty from her voice. Her mind refused to reconcile how similar he looked to his brother.

He's not Tearlach, she reminded herself as Jarlath smiled and tucked his pencil into the book he'd been writing in. Esme's pulse quickened when he rose, the sensation not altogether unwelcome. It had been some time since her heart had reacted to something other than guilt or anger. Or heartache.

Jarlath tilted his head. "Almost didn't recognize you." He scanned the area, then looked back toward the palace. "Ah." Another smile played at his lips.

Madoc blocked his approach. "Her Majesty isn't—"

"It's all right." Esme stepped around her guard. "Jarlath and I are already acquainted."

Madoc lifted his chin, inspecting Jarlath through narrowed eyes. His response seemed one merely of protection, not of judgment. She hoped Tearlach wouldn't color everyone's view of his brother before they had a chance to know him.

To her, Jarlath seemed perfectly well-mannered and attentive.

"Your secret is safe with me," he promised, then leaned down, drawing her in with nothing more than his presence. "Though I must warn you, I saw a few impeccably dressed men pacing about the veranda not a half hour ago."

"Thank you for informing me." She allowed a smile.

"Perhaps you'd consider extending your journey a bit longer? I've been meaning to take in more of the gardens." He tucked the small book inside his jacket and offered his arm.

"Might I ask what you were writing?"

"Would you believe me if I said I'd been composing sonnets?"

She snuck a glance and saw his lips pressed together, as if he couldn't hide that he was jesting. Esme decided she liked that trait very much—a man who couldn't hide his true intent.

"Hmm," she mused. "If that's so, I'll insist you prove it."

Jarlath chuckled. "Alas, my mind is not so imaginative." He produced the book, turning it over in his hand. "I'm afraid the contents are rather dull." He slipped it back into his pocket. "Shipping schedules, trade routes. With increased demand, we've had to expand—Goodness, I warned you it was dull."

Esme grinned as Jarlath directed the conversation toward livelier topics. Not only was he well-versed in seemingly everything, he showed great interest in the various horticultural undertakings throughout the grounds, particularly the many types of night blooms that were beginning to open. And he had a delightful sense of humor about him, recounting a particularly comical fishing excursion as a young man that involved wresting from the river what had turned out to be a sunken log tangled in roots.

Jarlath's rich voice and spirited tales kept Esme's smile firmly in place until she returned to her room later that evening.

"Your Majesty." Winifred straightened from aligning numerous stacks of reports and requests that made Esme's sufficiently sized desk appear rather small.

"These are all from today?" Her smile fell, and the aches in her arms and shoulders returned in the span of a heartbeat. Her hand flexed, protesting the hours of signing that no doubt awaited.

"Indeed." Winifred stepped aside after adjusting one of the piles another fraction of an inch.

"Anything of note?" Esme asked reluctantly.

"Nothing out of sorts, Your Majesty. Aside from the earlier request from Lord Torin."

"Right," she sighed. "The lumber acquisition. I haven't been able to reconcile it myself."

"Assuring seaworthiness for ships is something of a necessity in Isloran," Winifred allowed.

"It's a reasonable request," Esme agreed, thinking of the book Jarlath had been making notes in about shipping schedules and routes along the coast. "But if it's pitch from the redwoods he seeks, why not state it so?" She met Winifred's concerned gaze. "Why lie about it?"

Chapter Twelve

STRONG ARMS LIFTED Esme. She curled into the embrace as if it were familiar, breathing in the scent of sandalwood soap and warm skin.

But at the crunch of paper beneath her boots, her mind registered her surroundings.

She shook out her arm, numb from cradling her head against the sofa cushion where she'd fallen asleep, as Tearlach led her slowly across the room.

She resisted opening her eyes, to awaken fully. Tearlach had been avoiding her. At first, she'd understood his desire to keep his distance. She didn't like it, but she understood it. He was the queen's personal guard, and he needed people to see him as such. But the unexpected arrival of his brother had driven a wedge between what was already a precarious relationship. Was his avoidance still to do with appearances, or was there more to it?

Perhaps it had nothing to do with her at all.

Even as groggy as her mind was, she couldn't convince herself of that. There was no denying that *she* was the reason he'd pulled away. Because of who she was. Who she'd always be.

She'd already made the decision not to confront him about it. Much as she desperately wanted to tear down the wall he'd built up between them, to go back to the way they'd been before, she couldn't bear the thought of hearing it confirmed. It would crush the remaining pieces of her already battered heart.

"We couldn't have done this another time?" Esme finally let her eyes drift open. Her fingers grazed the tauntingly soft blanket at the foot of her bed as Tearlach tugged her over to the concealed door in the corner.

"You'd rather wait?" His voice saturated the narrow passageway joining their rooms.

They couldn't very well wait. If Athdara knew anything about the missing pieces of the orbs, it was vital that they speak with her.

By the time they'd navigated the warren of tunnels beneath the city, and arrived at Athdara's unassuming door down a dark alleyway that was lit only by the glow of the lights in the night sky, Tearlach's jaw was set with so much tension that Esme's own had begun to ache. She felt his anticipation as keenly as her own. Though she'd wager his originated with the seer herself and not with the knowledge she might possess.

"She might know something," Esme offered weakly.

Tearlach grunted and rapped his knuckles against the door. "I'm sure she does. It's what she chooses to tell us." He glanced down at Esme. "Or anyone else who's willing to pay."

The seer had handed over nearly unfettered power when she'd offered up Alastar's identity to Lord Luxovious. Surely the woman had known she'd be sending an innocent young man to his death. Esme's throat tightened and her hands curled into fists as she considered—not for the first time—what else Athdara had revealed to Lord Luxovious. Or to others, for that matter. Anyone who could pay, as Tearlach had pointed out.

Finding the door unlocked didn't surprise either of them. Their arrival was clearly expected. And Esme would wager each of their questions would be as well.

In the sitting room down the narrow corridor was the same ermine they'd encountered during their previous visit, curled up on the footstool. It made soft squeaking sounds in its sleep. Esme watched the small creature, letting the peaceful sight soften the sharp edges of her mood.

Athdara didn't offer a word, or even a glance, when she pushed open the door to the small, dimly lit room where she met with clients.

Esme didn't bother with pleasantries either, depositing a stack of coins on the table between them as she eyed the woman. "Did you supply the names of the women Lord Luxovious used to begin the Order?"

Athdara appeared to consider the query. "It is not for me to decide one's path—"

"It is when you alter their fate by handing them over to a monster." Esme's voice quavered at the end and Tearlach placed a steadying hand on her knee where it was tucked beneath the table.

She redirected her attention to the weight of his hand, to the warmth seeping in.

"You knew what he was doing. The lies he would twist for his own gain. Did you know his end goal? Did you know—"

Easy, Tearlach cautioned.

Esme dragged in a breath, readying her next accusation.

Trap her in a cage of vines later, if you must. First, let's get what we came for.

"Can objects be imbued with magic?" Tearlach asked, removing his hand from Esme's knee. Athdara responded before Esme could fully register the loss.

"The vessels. Yes."

"You know of them," Esme accused.

"I know much."

If there were still gods above, she'd have prayed for restraint.

"Why not tell me?" Esme's tone was controlled, measured, even as she thought of the memories she'd sacrificed for that very piece of knowledge.

"This journey has many paths. And the choices are not mine to make."

"You will help," Esme ordered, infusing her words with all the authority she supposedly held as queen of Tremaene.

"If you ask the right questions."

Her anger swelled.

"How many pieces are there?" Tearlach asked before Esme could spit out the words he undoubtedly knew were on her tongue.

Athdara studied Tearlach for a moment, then closed her eyes and raised her chin.

Esme watched closely. It seemed as if images were appearing in the seer's mind. She wondered if Athdara's ability was similar to Esme's premonitory dreams. Only with control.

"There are several," she answered without opening her eyes.

"How many?" Tearlach's voice hardened.

"The vessels have been split into hundreds of pieces."

Esme's stomach dropped. She knew there were many, but having it confirmed made it all the more daunting. How would they ever track them all down?

"They are close," Athdara added, opening her eyes.

Esme shot a quick glance to Tearlach. He seemed equally amazed at the unprompted information.

"Where?" Esme hurried to ask, like the seer's benevolence might last a bit longer.

But Athdara seemed disinclined to offer more.

Esme shared another look with Tearlach, and saw something close to defeat flicker in his eyes. Not only were they facing the nearly impossible task of searching the entirety of the kingdom—

No. She squeezed her eyes shut, refusing to finish or even acknowledge the unsettling notion.

"If we…manage to find them all, will we be able to reopen the channels?" she asked instead.

Silence encircled them like a thick fog until Athdara's eyes met hers. The seer's words were clear and precise when she said, "You will."

Tearlach remained steady and unmoving beside her, though she could tell his muscles were as tight as hers as they waited for more. It couldn't be so simple.

"You will," Athdara repeated. "Though it may not come to pass as you see it."

As she saw it? *Would* she see it?

Her dreams had given warning of dangerous or deadly situations in the past. And *of course* it would be dangerous to unleash raw magic that had been confined for nearly a thousand years. She wasn't so naive as to think it wouldn't be. But it was necessary, and it *could* be done, as Athdara had attested. That was all that mattered.

Besides, anything was preferable to using her own body as a conduit.

"Must each channel be unobstructed individually?" Tearlach inquired.

Esme hadn't considered that. She hadn't witnessed Lord Luxovious sealing the channels, she'd only watched as the tiny bursts of light on the spherical map had winked out of existence, and had simply assumed that all of them had been blocked simultaneously.

"Once you gather the fragments and restore each vessel to its original form, the magic can then be released." Athdara paused before adding, "And your goal achieved."

My goal? Esme scoffed. As if restoring life to the land was some sort of frivolous personal undertaking instead of a critical mission.

"How do we…" She was almost too afraid to ask. "Combine the fragments? And release the magic?"

"Those paths have not yet been chosen."

Esme inhaled a strained breath at her vague response.

"But you will be shown," Athdara continued. "And you must"—the word reverberated through the small room—"keep the elements separate."

Separate.

"For it is not only natural magic the vessels contain. You mustn't merge them into a single power."

A shiver ran down Esme's spine, though she was grateful for the warning. "Keep the elements separate." She nodded.

A few moments passed as the significance of what was to come seemed to weigh upon them like a heavy cloak. Even Athdara appeared affected by it.

But before they concluded their session, there was another potential complication Esme needed to address.

"What about the mortal realm?" If Lord Luxovious had been able to block the channels in Tremaene, why had he left the human lands untouched? "If the fog can be crossed, why didn't he seek control of those lands as well?"

"The shield was once impenetrable, as you know. No Fae or human could breach it. Not even one who wielded dark magic."

"Has the fog always existed?"

Athdara didn't answer.

"Were you around when it was created?" Tearlach clarified.

The corner of her lip twitched at his speculation. "Yes, and no."

Yes, and no? Just how old was Athdara?

"The strong memories remain, though I've tried to vanquish them." She clasped her hands atop the table. "It is a curse to remember all one has seen."

That was the reason their kind chose to fade away after so long a life. For good or bad, living through so much made one weary. Or so Esme had been told. She wondered why Athdara had chosen to remain in the physical realm for as long as she had.

For a second, Esme almost pitied the woman for all she'd witnessed. Almost.

"The fog can be crossed now," Esme told her.

"Yes."

"How?"

"I believe your captain has a theory."

Esme tightened her jaw at the mention of Sully. She didn't like that Athdara had knowledge of so many people. Of her.

"He does," she hedged. "But I want to hear yours."

Athdara raised her chin, waiting.

Esme exhaled loudly. "He believes the dark magic from the war saturated the air, lingering long enough after it was summoned that it weakened the untethered magic of the barrier."

Athdara lifted a perfectly sculpted eyebrow a fraction of an inch.

"If we fail..." Esme didn't bother to enumerate the many ways in which that eventuality was possible. "If resources become scarcer, the human lands will be vulnerable."

The cloaked figure that had appeared at her bedside, ringed in black and purple flames, flashed in her mind, but Esme reminded herself that Lord Luxovious was trapped in an iron box and didn't pose a threat to Periwen. At least...not an immediate threat.

"Who else knows Periwen can be reached?"

Chapter Thirteen

ESME HAD BARELY slept after sneaking back into the palace. But the lights were beginning to fade into a pale blue morning sky, and sleep seemed long lost. She stumbled into the bathing chamber to draw a bath, hoping it would allow her at least another hour to herself before whatever tasks Keelin had planned before the ball were thrust upon her. But Tearlach's commanding voice put a stop to her plans.

Get dressed and meet me in the yard.

Esme whimpered and stared longingly down at the few inches of hot water swirling in at the bottom of the bath before reaching over to stop the stream.

The commotion below could be heard before she even reached the stairwell. It sounded as though the palace staff had multiplied in the hours since she and Tearlach had returned.

When Esme reached the main floor, she beheld a sort of organized chaos as servants scurried in and out of the great hall. Half a dozen hurried past with gilded chairs. Another followed with satin fabric piled so high Esme couldn't see the man's head.

The cool marble of the palace had been transformed into a warm, cheerful environment with silks and ribbons in pinks and oranges and reds swooping down from the ceiling. She took in the grandiose space, imagining what it would look like once the walls and windows were covered in the same shimmery fabrics, and the hall glowed with the flames of hundreds of candles.

Then her gaze caught on the throne set up on a dais at the far end. Without thought, Esme drifted closer.

Though the throne itself was newly crafted, it resembled her mother's so keenly she could practically feel her presence. Hear her laugh. See her welcoming smile as—

"Is it to your liking, Your Majesty?" Mairtín startled her.

Pressing a hand to her chest, Esme released a slow breath to calm her wild heartbeat before turning to him.

"Why..." She scanned the room once more. "Why is it here?"

"For the ball, of course."

"No." She shook her head.

Mairtín's eyes widened. "Is it not to your liking?" He looked horror-struck.

"No, no." She shook her head again, then offered the most genuine smile she could muster. "It's perfect."

"I see," he said, though it was clear he didn't. He cast a skeptical glare toward the throne, like he might be able to suss out the issue. "Then shall I..."

"The celebration isn't for me."

"But it is," he assured, straightening with a smile.

Esme closed her eyes, thinking how better to explain. "It's about the kingdom, our land and all it provides. Not the queen." She didn't mention the goddess they were supposedly honoring. Or the man who'd contrived the holy day.

Luckily, Keelin chose that moment to appear, striding over with open arms that looked ready to swallow the palace butler. "My mistake, Mairtín." She took him by the shoulders and turned him away, taking the blame herself.

———————

Tearlach met them near the western gardens on their way to the training yard. He was already lecturing Esme about what she needed to focus on the second he fell into step with her.

"More precise," he reiterated. "Not more powerful."

Esme nodded as if she hadn't already heard that advice from him before. The manner in which he discussed magic had her calling up the first time he'd *assisted* her. While his tactics back in Altan had consisted more of intentional provocation than traditional training, Tearlach had also explained that her magic had taken a very specific pathway when it had first manifested—the day she'd brought the dead wolf back to life. And due to that complication, she'd need to redirect her magic in order to take hold of it. To control it.

But Esme had never quite reconciled the theory that magic was to be directed purely by thought. She *felt* her magic. Felt it moving through her, rising from the deep well inside her, flowing through her veins, spreading out beneath her skin, until she could feel it tingling in her fingers and toes.

At least she'd learned to guide it without engaging her hands, which projected her intentions all too clearly.

When they reached the yard, Esme felt a jolt of anticipation that Tearlach might actually step into the ring with her. It had been so long since they'd worked together. Too long. Not since they'd returned to Meallán to take back the kingdom from Orianna.

But Tearlach stopped at the edge of the ring, and Hazel stepped into the center instead.

Esme's shoulders slumped, but she went to stand before her guard nonetheless, already feeling her lightning crackling in her fingertips.

Tearlach observed with the sort of keen focus she'd grown accustomed to, but had never been able to perform well under. So when Hazel at last deemed their session finished, Esme was prepared for Tearlach's critique. Yet when she searched the yard for him, she saw only a glimpse of his back as he strode toward the barracks.

Hiding her disappointment, she turned to Hazel. "Have you considered my offer any further?"

"I have." Hazel knelt down to unlace her shin plates.

"And?"

Her guard rose and stared down at her. "And I'll let you know my decision once I've reached it."

For the second time in a matter of days, Esme crossed paths with Jarlath. The more she saw him, the more differences she recognized between the two brothers. In that moment, it was the way Jarlath carried himself. One look at Tearlach and she could instantly sense the unending supply of power simmering just beneath the surface. And while Jarlath's build was similar to that of his brother's, he didn't seem to hide anything. He was open and welcoming. There was nothing concealed behind a carefully crafted facade.

"Are you having me followed?" she joked.

"Your Majesty." He swept into a bow. "I'd like to refute your claim, but it's nearly impossible not to take notice of the queen when she steps out of the privacy of her suite. And I must confess"—he moved closer, lowering his voice—"it's not the flowering trees that drew me out of doors this very day."

His words further separated him from the shadow Tearlach cast, and Esme felt herself warming to him even more.

She gave her guards a pointed look. Roderick's jaw tightened briefly, but the two of them slowed their pace and allowed her and Jarlath a semblance of privacy.

Jarlath remarked on the bounty of the fruit trees, then paused to offer his hand to a goat nosing against the vines that intertwined with the woven copper fence.

Esme took the brief opportunity to brush the dirt from her tunic. But Jarlath caught her as he straightened. His lips quirked into a smile.

"Seeing the queen in something other than a gown is refreshing." He glanced down at his vastly more proper wardrobe. "And I must admit, I rather envy your freedom."

"If only I could forgo the gown tonight." The words slipped out before she could think them through. "I didn't mean—That is, I'll be clothed." She winced.

Jarlath chuckled. "I understand, Your Majesty. A ball usually requires certain attire."

"It does." She sighed.

"Aside from the restrictive clothing, are you looking forward to the gathering this evening?"

"Yes," she lied.

Jarlath laughed heartily. "Deception is not your strong suit, I'm afraid."

"The food, I'm told, will be quite…inventive?" Gods, why did that sound like a question? She ducked her head, hoping to hide the blush heating her cheeks.

"Inventive, you say?" Jarlath grinned. "As in, it won't be recognizable as food or—"

Esme nudged him with her elbow. "Stop! It's all I could think of. I'm not exactly looking forward to the ball. Clearly."

"It wouldn't be the prospect of an endless string of eager men awaiting an introduction, would it?"

She bit back a groan.

Jarlath leaned in to whisper. "Or the dancing that may be asked of you?"

"Don't remind me."

"I suppose that's the reason so many noblemen have chosen to celebrate the festival in Meallán this year."

"Actually, the council…" Esme tried to take in a deep breath, but her chest constricted at the reminder. "They're pressuring me to…to…" She lowered her voice. "To marry."

Jarlath pulled her to a stop, then waited for her to look up at him. The concern in his eyes was almost more than she could bear. "I'm so sorry, Esme." Her given name on his lips, spoken with such reverence, nearly brought her to tears. "I didn't realize. Please forgive me for jesting at your expense. I truly didn't mean to—"

She placed her hand on his arm. "No, it's quite all right. After all, it's only a little dancing."

"Only a little dancing," he agreed with a sympathetic smile. "And perhaps you'll save one for me?" His voice held a hope she wished for herself.

"I'd like that," she answered honestly.

He grinned wider, then curled her hand around his elbow as they continued their stroll.

"It's times like these," Jarlath said after a moment, "that I envy my brother."

Esme glanced up at him. "Why is that?"

He met her gaze. "Because he gets to marry for love."

She hadn't thought of it that way. When Tearlach had been stripped of his title, he'd gained a kind of freedom his brother never would. Was that the reason she'd felt a sort of kinship with Jarlath, a man she'd only just met? They both lived with obligations few others understood.

"Wouldn't it be nice to have a chance at that?" he mused quietly, almost to himself.

It would, Esme agreed.

Chapter Fourteen

GRISELDA, BRIGHID, AND Marta were all waiting in Esme's room when she returned. They came to attention the moment the doors swung open, and judging by their expressions—not Marta's, as she seemed more adept at hiding true feelings than even Tearlach—Esme was rather late.

A quick glance at the clock confirmed it. Evidently, she'd let her encounter with Jarlath linger a bit longer than she'd intended.

Because she'd been distracted. Jarlath had distracted her. It certainly hadn't been intentional. Not at all.

She was beyond thrilled about the ball.

Even in her head, the lies sounded as if they'd been tortured out of her.

It was an effort not to dig her heels into the floorboards as Brighid hurried her into a waiting bath. Not four minutes later, Marta hurried her back out, wringing water from Esme's hair as she ushered her across the room to where Griselda waited with a chemise.

Brighid was busy smoothing the satin ribbons that would tie up the back of the cream-colored gown that had been delivered that morning. Tiny seedlike crystals were sewn into the bodice with golden thread. It was quite beautiful, if a bit boring. Or...expected, rather.

Griselda turned her around to pull the chemise into place before Marta quickly resumed toweling her hair. From her new position, Esme spotted several notes piled on her desk. They were smaller than the usual requests and council reports, with wax seals in an array of colors. Invitations, she assumed. As Keelin had explained, once formal introductions were made that evening, the noblemen were free to request private dining or outings with her.

It wasn't often that Esme enjoyed her persistent shadow of royal guards, but at that moment, she was quite glad for it.

Her eyes narrowed on something propped against the base of the lamp on her bedside table. The velvet pouch looked similar to a coin purse, though it was only large enough to hold a few silvers.

"A footman dropped it off earlier," Brighid supplied, noticing where her attention had strayed.

"From who?" Esme was almost afraid to ask. Was gift giving the next stage in the ridiculous arranged courtships she'd be forced into? Gifts she had no need of? And why had the footman left it on her bedside table instead of on the desk that was so clearly meant for missives and the like?

Cold sweat prickled at her brow as she feared the potentially private nature of the gift as Brighid rushed to retrieve it.

When it was placed in her hand, Esme was reassured that it was likely only a piece of jewelry, given its weight. She loosened the ties and let two small, teardrop-shaped rubies tumble into her palm.

She recognized them instantly.

They were for her? The earrings she'd seen Tearlach turning over in his large hands at the edge of the stream on the final day of their journey were *for her*? The small tokens that had enthralled Tearlach's mind so completely that he hadn't even sensed Esme's nearness that day *were for her*.

She thought back to the morning they'd left Juverna on their way to the temple, when she'd spotted Tearlach returning from a supply run with some of the guards. He'd avoided her eyes, but she'd seen him pocket a small parcel. Was that when he'd procured them? Only a day after Esme had discovered that his feelings went far deeper than his duty-bound role demanded?

She wouldn't fool herself into thinking he'd gone out of his way to find the beautiful, faceted stones. And yet...knowing that amid the single-mindedness of their mission, Tearlach had seen them and *known* that she'd treasure them...

A tingling warmth radiated through her body at the idea.

Because she *would* treasure them.

Because the small rubies, in their striking silver settings, were the only pieces of Tearlach that would ever be hers.

"You must have an admirer," Marta hummed.

"Yes," she breathed. Though she could hardly consider Tearlach an admirer. A forbidden love, perhaps. One who was set on avoiding her whenever possible, yet couldn't help but remind her that she was always on his mind.

"If I might say, milady. Those would match your scarlet gown perfectly."

Esme turned, finding Griselda, Brighid, and Marta all watching her, every urgent task forgotten. As if they, too, sensed the significance of the gift.

Might they know the sender? she wondered.

"Yes," she agreed. "I believe they will." A jolt of excitement made her shiver. Wearing a dress in such a brazen color would be wholly unexpected of a queen. And while she knew that Tearlach would never agree to a dance, by wearing the rubies—and a dress chosen specifically to accentuate them—it would feel like they were sharing something that night. Something unspoken and secret, yet on display for all to see.

A message, she thought, that while she was a queen, she was also a woman.

And her future was hers to decide.

Chapter Fifteen

GRISELDA FINISHED TYING the last of the ribbons that trailed down the back of the dress as Esme clasped the second earring, letting the delicate stone slip from her fingers. Marta gently nudged her to turn toward the mirror after securing another hairpin.

Esme's eyes fell on the reflection that stood before her. She took in the deep neckline of the scarlet gown, down to where both sides joined at the dozens of thin satin ribbons pulled taut just above her navel. The fabric twisted across her hips before sweeping down her legs in a fall of fabric that was a deeper, darker shade of red.

She felt beautiful, maybe even tantalizing. But more than that, for the first time, she felt *seen*. Like she wasn't dressing for a part she needed to play.

This is for me, she thought.

Esme glanced back to thank her maids, but found Tearlach standing outside her dressing room.

He stared at her for a long moment, taking her in. His eyes flicked to the earrings.

But before Esme could enjoy the precarious moment, a look of regret clouded his expression.

"Lord Torin has requested an audience."

Her lungs seized. "Now?" she forced out.

Tearlach clenched his jaw, giving a single nod.

She gave her maids a quick glance. They curtsied and left silently.

"Why can't he wait until—" Esme began, then shook her head. She didn't want to deal with Lord Torin during the ball either.

"I suspect a private meeting would be best."

"Do you know what this is about?" The more she knew going in, the better.

"No." Tearlach uttered the word so low and guttural she felt the vibration of it in the soles of her feet.

The uncertainty was far from ideal, but speaking privately seemed better than being put on the spot in the center of a crowded ballroom.

But Esme wasn't about to allow him anywhere near her bedchamber. And judging by the cacophony rising up from belowstairs, attendees were already arriving, which meant that any otherwise appropriate space on the main floor wouldn't be private.

"The suite beside my parents' rooms," she suggested, thinking of the space that mirrored her own on the opposite side of the grand staircase. It didn't hold any personal significance—had never been occupied in her youth. And being that it was part of the royal apartments, she hoped it would give her an advantage.

———

By the time Lord Torin was escorted into the room, Cadwyn, Sully, and Esme's entire royal guard—all dressed in their finery—had been alerted and were lining the corridor outside.

"I requested a private audience," he sneered at Esme without sparing a look toward his son.

When Esme didn't respond, Lord Torin huffed out a breath. Tearlach wasn't going anywhere. Even if she hadn't wanted him there, she knew well enough that his formidable presence would remain indefinitely.

"Leave us." Lord Torin flicked a wrist toward his attendant.

After the man slipped through the doors, Esme caught Cadwyn's eye. As the doors were pulled shut and the gap between them narrowed, her expression shifted, and she leveled Esme with a stare meant to harden her resolve against capitulating to anything Lord Torin might *suggest.*

Then it was just the three of them, standing alone in the empty room.

A look of disgust curled the corners of Lord Torin's mouth as he took in Esme's gown.

Good, she thought. She had no desire to please him, and wondered yet again when it would be appropriate to replace his seat on the council.

With a lift of her chin, she regarded him right back, refusing to speak first.

His expression transformed into something she suspected was intended to come off as fatherly. "My dear," he started. His brow furrowed like he might be concerned for her well-being. "I can tell that the arrival of so many noblemen has overwhelmed you."

Irritated her, was more like.

"I can't say that all these men are admirable or worthy of a queen's attention. I tried to warn Keelin off inviting Fergus's son." He shook his head, muttering the last part to himself.

Admittedly, he was giving quite a performance. If Esme didn't know what he was capable of, she might think he was actually trying to protect her.

"I do hope you'll be prudent about who you choose to spend your time with." He took a step closer and lowered his voice. "Just because a man is from a noble line does *not* mean he's honorable."

Esme furrowed her brow and nodded as if he offered sage counsel. "I see. And the honorable ones, who might they be?"

"It can be difficult to discern for someone so young an age."

Ah, they were back to that, then. Esme resisted the urge to roll her eyes.

"I wouldn't want you to wander down an unseemly path. Again." His eyes held pity. She wanted to gouge them out.

"And what path would you have me wander, milord?" She could hear the obvious brusqueness of her voice. She didn't care.

"My dear, I mean no disrespect," he assured.

"What *did* you mean?" The scarlet gown was making her bold, it seemed.

Lord Torin let out a sigh, as if her naivete exhausted him. "It is my sincere recommendation that you give strong consideration to the heirs of your most trusted advisors on the royal council."

Her stomach dropped. He meant Jarlath.

Had Jarlath been summoned to the palace for the sole purpose of winning her hand?

No, she decided. Lord Torin might have requested or even insisted upon his son's attendance at the ball, but in the short time Esme had known him, and with all Jarlath had confessed to her already, she found him to be incapable of insincerity.

Lord Torin was clearly in the dark about how much influence he held over the son who'd stayed.

"You mean for me to marry a lord's son?"

"Or a minister's, of course. Someone you can trust in matters of state."

"It seems you, yourself, have more than one son for me to choose from." She gave him a deceptively sweet smile.

Tearlach's presence in the room suddenly seemed larger. She could practically feel his gaze penetrating the skin at the nape of her neck. Slowly, she turned her attention toward him, lest there be any question as to whom she was referring.

Lord Torin was visibly seething when she faced him again.

"Is that all? Milord?"

Chapter Sixteen

SULLY LED ESME toward the rows her guards had formed at the top of the grand staircase. She'd decided to forget everything that had transpired with Lord Torin. *Tonight, I'll enjoy myself,* she resolved.

Straightening to her full height, she made to step forward, but realized someone was missing.

"Where's Hazel?" Just as the words left her mouth, the woman herself appeared. Wearing a gown.

Esme could only stare as Hazel approached. The gown was a purple so deep it was nearly black. But the flickering lights in the corridor revealed the fabric's rich, velvety color. The gown was fitted through the bodice and down the skirt, flaring only slightly where the hem of the dress grazed the floor. It was stunning. *Hazel* was stunning. And Esme knew she wasn't the only one thinking that.

In fact, it was possible that Hazel looked even more intimidating in a dress than in her royal guard uniform. No one would dare cross her.

Without turning her head, she offered Esme the briefest of sidelong glances and a barely perceptible shrug of her bare shoulders before moving to take her place next to Cadwyn.

It seemed Esme had a new lady-in-waiting. She suppressed a grin and walked past her guards toward the top of the stairs.

But Armel's attention was so arrested by the sight of Hazel that he failed to turn forward with the others. It was as if he was powerless to look away. For a man who rarely showed emotion—even when Esme had spat unkind words at him after a sparring match—it was quite endearing to see him so transfixed.

Only it wasn't a look of pure adoration for the woman he so clearly loved. It was shock. Shock that Hazel had taken her place beside Cadwyn, instead of with the guards. Shock at the realization that she was *leaving* him.

It was safe to assume that Hazel had hidden her intentions not only from Esme, but from everyone. Including Armel.

Esme gave him a discreet nudge, awakening him from the trance. He offered Esme a look that she couldn't decipher. She only hoped he wasn't silently cursing her for stealing Hazel away.

The great hall glittered. Flames from hundreds of candles shimmered like the Loinnir Lights against the richly dyed silks that covered the walls.

Murmurs about Esme's dress spread throughout the space like wildfire as the crowd parted for her.

She didn't meet anyone's eyes, though she caught sight of Audris and Pearce whispering to one another.

Esme ignored them, continuing on toward...well, she wasn't sure where she was going. There wasn't a dais or a throne waiting for her. She wouldn't be making a speech. As she'd told Mairtín, the ball was a celebration for everyone in Tremaene. It wasn't about her.

Once she'd made it nearly halfway through the great hall, she settled on a spot that was close to one of the many long tables weighed down by food and drink. When it became clear that Esme was simply another attendee, the musicians started up again, and dancing recommenced.

Her guards took up positions around the room, and Sully began his deceptively indifferent walk about the periphery, attentive to any valuable information he might hear.

Esme was pleasantly surprised by all the people she recognized. Winifred was listening intently to a man who wore the most intricately embroidered tunic she'd ever seen. Brighid was in attendance with her mother, Gwen. Esme hoped her other lady's maids were enjoying the night as well. She'd asked Keelin to be mindful of the schedules of everyone working in the palace that night, insisting that anyone who wished to attend the ball had the opportunity to do so. Abaigeal and Molly from the kitchens were dancing near the raised platform where the musicians played, and a footman whose name Esme had forgotten looked adoringly into a young man's eyes as they swayed to a rhythm only they seemed to hear.

Wealthy families and nobles stood out amid the crowd. They wore blatantly expensive fabrics, with jewels to match, and all seemed somewhat put out by the entire affair.

The majority of attendees, however, appeared cheerful. While they didn't likely have the means to waste on fancy clothing, they were enjoying themselves more fully than any of the well-dressed people in the room. Esme was heartened to see so many of them laughing and dancing together, their cheeks flushed with wine and good food.

She would've liked to participate in, or at least witness, the other festivities that had taken place in the past week, but with her journey north and seeking out Athdara the night prior, she'd missed nearly everything.

Next year, she promised herself. Even if the truth about Lord Luxovious and the false gods became public, there'd still be celebrations and festivals across the kingdom. She'd make sure of it.

The smile slipped from her face as two men passed by the table she'd claimed, speaking of recent brush fires out west.

Turning to Cadwyn, Esme asked, "Have you heard this?" Were her councilors keeping things from her?

"No. But I will," she vowed.

Before they could speak further, a man arrived at her side. A *noble*man.

So it begins, Esme groaned inwardly. She turned to face him fully, noticing that several more had taken to lingering nearby, awaiting their turns.

Cadwyn offered a look of solidarity, then stepped forward to make the first official introduction, while Hazel's look was a bit more...fierce. Annoyed, even. Esme hoped she'd scare a few of them off.

As the man led Esme away—she'd already forgotten his name—she remembered her conversation with Jarlath. *It's only a little dancing.*

Where was he, anyway?

She resisted the urge to search for him. He'd find her eventually. She'd promised him a dance, after all.

Several more introductions and dances followed. Some of the dancing felt stilted and awkward, though many of the men were quite skilled at it. All were perfectly pleasant, though she managed to find something marginally wrong with each suitor.

One hadn't been tall enough.

Another too tall.

One man had spoken too much.

Another's hair had been cut too short.

Face too clean-shaven.

Hands were broad, but not broad enough.

And the last one's eyes had been too...green?

She was grasping for excuses, she knew. The only thing that seemed to matter was that none of them were the person she truly wanted.

Cora interrupted one of the dances a moment before the music reached its finale, saving Esme from her next dance partner. "Some punch," she suggested, giving a pointed look *away* from the dance floor.

"That sounds wonderful," Esme accepted gratefully. "I'm quite parched." She thanked the man she'd been dancing with—*What was his name?*—then followed Cora.

Esme had been wanting to visit with Cora since she'd realized how badly she'd misinterpreted the woman's sudden appearance at the palace, and her relationship with Tearlach.

"You must feel"—Esme stifled a yawn, registering just how exhausted she was—"horribly neglected. You came here to see Tearlach, and I've kept him away from the palace for almost your entire visit." The truth was, *Esme* was the horribly neglectful one. She'd failed to make time to get to know the woman who was important to Tearlach—one of the few people who'd kept touch with him from his early life.

"Nonsense." Cora waved away her concern. "I've had time to explore." They each reached for a small crystal cup filled with a sparkling pink drink. "And my wife arrives in a few days' time."

"Oh, wonderful! I look forward to meeting her. Though, it's a shame she'll have missed the festival."

"Hardly a shame. Alpina isn't one to enjoy these sorts of things."

Nor am I, Esme thought, catching sight of Beglan making his way toward them.

When he reached her side, Beglan bowed, then lowered his already deep voice to ask, "Did you find the information you were seeking, Your Majesty?"

"I did. Thank you." Esme nodded, then introduced Cora to the bookshop owner.

"Are you enjoying yourself, my dear?"

"Very much. And you?" Cora asked in return.

"I'm delighted to be here," he answered with such sincerity. "So many years I've lived here in Meallán. And now, to be invited to such a grand celebration?" He glanced around the lavishly decorated ballroom with a hand to his chest like he couldn't believe his luck.

Esme noticed Winifred trying to edge past the crowd at the opposite end of the long table, and recalled the day the timid council secretary and Beglan had stumbled into one another outside the royal library.

"Beglan?" Esme pulled his attention back with a hand to his forearm. "I wonder if you might help me with something."

"Your Majesty?"

"I believe I saw Winifred just over there." She inclined her head. "She appears to be all alone." Beglan's eyes sought out the woman in question. "Perhaps...you could keep her company."

"Of course," Beglan assured readily, sketching a bow before turning away as if it were a royal command.

Cora gave her a knowing smirk. But uncertainty quickly stole the expression from her face.

"Your Majesty." Jarlath's voice caressed the back of Esme's neck. She inhaled a shaky breath as he stepped into view.

He offered Cora the type of greeting lifelong friends reserved for one another, but Cora's response seemed a bit forced.

Turning her back to him, Cora asked, "Shall we have tea tomorrow?"

"I'd like that very much," Esme agreed.

Then, after sparing a glance over her shoulder at Jarlath, Cora excused herself.

"Had I known she was visiting..." Jarlath stared after her, then faced Esme. "I must confess, I didn't know her all that well when we were young."

"Oh." He could have fooled her. Then again, in the short time she'd known Jarlath, she'd learned that he was nothing if not polite and friendly to everyone he encountered. Such a stark contrast from his brother.

"It wasn't long that she was betrothed to Tearlach, and it was so many years ago...Still—" He exhaled deeply. "I should have made a better effort at the time. I hope she finds herself well."

"I believe she does," Esme reassured him. "And it's not too late to get acquainted, now that you're both here."

"Right you are." Jarlath gave her a grin, then offered his arm in what Esme hoped was an offer to join him for a dance.

But as soon as he turned her toward the dance floor, he halted. "There you are," he exclaimed, guiding Esme instead toward a woman she quickly remembered to be Tearlach's mother. And Jarlath's.

"Your Majesty, may I present Lady Torin."

As if they'd never before met, the woman lowered herself into the most perfect curtsy Esme had ever beheld.

"A pleasure to meet you," Esme offered with equal innocence.

"Jarlath," his mother gently scolded. "When you said you'd promised a young lady a dance, I didn't expect—"

"Mother," Jarlath practically groaned as color bloomed on his cheeks.

Esme pressed her lips together, charmed by the closeness of their relationship.

But her good mood sank when she saw Tearlach watching from his position against the nearest wall.

He wasn't watching Esme. His eyes were fixed on Jarlath and their mother. On what he no longer had. A brief, secret meeting when Genvieve had managed to slip away from her husband was all Tearlach and his mother had shared in the years since he'd been forced to leave home.

When Tearlach's eyes changed from wistful to stormy, Esme turned back to see what had caused it.

His father.

Esme fought to keep her teeth from clenching and her hands from fisting the skirts of her gown. How dare he approach her after the way he'd spoken to her earlier.

"Perhaps you'll ask our queen for a dance," Lord Torin suggested, though it hardly sounded like one.

"Her Majesty can dance with whomever she chooses," Jarlath retorted, arching a brow. It was a look of defiance, and the only expression he'd made thus far that reminded her of Tearlach.

"Yes. She's made that clear," Lord Torin muttered, still refusing to meet Esme's eyes.

"Father," Jarlath warned.

Lord Torin huffed and turned to his wife. "Genvieve, come," he commanded. "Lady Audris is insistent on visiting with you this night."

The woman followed obediently, and Esme wondered how she survived such a life.

"It seems I must once again apologize for my father." Jarlath looked truly repentant about Lord Torin's lack of respect. "I assure you, his motives are his own."

Esme was heartened by his words, which only confirmed what she'd already suspected—that Jarlath had possessed no knowledge of or complacency in the scheme his father had devised.

"Be that as it may, I believe I *did* promise you a dance," she acquiesced.

Jarlath exhaled, clearly relieved by her response. "That you did. And if there's one thing I admire above all else"—he offered his arm once more, and Esme didn't hesitate to drape her hand over the crisp fabric that pulled tight around his muscular forearm—"it's a woman with integrity." He whispered the last part, his voice dropping so deep it sent a pleasant vibration across her already heated skin.

Chapter Seventeen

THE MUSICIANS FINISHED with a flourish, and Gorman bowed to Esme. She'd danced with eight other men before him, and her feet begged for reprieve. Her gown, while it certainly made a statement, seemed to cinch tighter around her midsection with each dance. It was her imagination, she knew, but the cool air out on the veranda beckoned.

She only managed to pivot a quarter turn before she was faced with yet another man. But he was someone she was glad to see.

"Can I tempt you into one more?" Killian asked with a mischievous grin as the lilting notes of a particularly slow and sensuous melody rose from the flautist.

After dancing too closely with so many strangers, Esme realized how much she needed the comfort of someone familiar holding her.

"A queen dancing with one of her guards..." she mused as he spun her slowly in a circle, then pulled her gently against the unyielding chest plate of his uniform. "What will they say?"

"Probably the same thing they're saying about that dress."
Killian winked.

———————

Finding Tearlach in the spot he'd been all night, Esme leaned against the wall next to him and let her head fall back.

"Not going to dance with anyone?" she asked, then felt the sidelong glare he aimed at her. "Harder to keep an eye on me, I suppose." Her fingers toyed with the edge of one of the hanging silk panels that covered the walls.

When he didn't answer, she looked up at him.

"I've managed to keep my eye on you all night, no matter how many men spun you around."

"You could keep better watch if you were the one holding me," she challenged in a whisper.

His nostrils flared, and for a moment she forgot why she'd thought it would be entertaining to provoke him. It only served as a reminder that he'd *never* hold her that way.

When the stare they were locked in became too much, they turned their attention back to the revelry of the ball.

Esme watched the people dancing, then let her gaze take in the rest of the merriment around the room. The crowds that were clustered near the drink tables never seemed to thin. She considered fetching another cup of punch when the memory of Tearlach sweeping her into his arms after she'd imbibed too much wine back in Altan overcame her.

Her eyes closed by their own volition as she once again felt those strong arms carrying her to bed the night the whole valley had come together the night before they were set to see the Northern Rebel army off. At the time, her thoughts had been hazy with wine, but as she stood there beside him, her mind was crystal clear.

She snuck another glance up at Tearlach, but for once his sights weren't on her.

She followed his gaze to find Hazel and Armel standing in each other's arms. Their bodies barely swayed with the music as they gazed into each other's eyes.

Esme's throat tightened. Her heart felt full at the sight, and broken at the stark reminder that she'd never feel something so all-encompassing.

"I...think I'll get some air," she murmured, pushing away from the wall.

The roar of the crowd followed her out into the night. She wanted to cover her ears, to disappear from it all, but she managed to keep her composure as she approached the stone wall of the veranda with measured steps.

"Lovely night," a calm voice commented from a few feet away.

Esme jerked her head toward the man. How had she not noticed him standing there?

He was gazing up at the Loinnir Lights, arms clasped behind his back. She wasn't sure he'd even recognized who she was.

"They're brighter here," he observed, as most did. The lights in the night sky were a reflection of the magic radiating across the land. And Meallán was one of the few places in Tremaene where the magic summoned by past priestesses—one in particular—still lingered.

"Yes, they are," she agreed, wishing that one night that she might look upon them without trepidation.

The man stepped a bit closer, though the move seemed to be only a courtesy so they might continue conversing.

"Where are you from?" She took in the cut of his overcoat and the gold chain of his pocket watch, though she didn't need to see what he wore to know he was a noble. There was something about his voice and the way he carried himself. Like he knew his place in the world.

Like he knew, and didn't particularly care for it.

"The Western Flats. Near Derval."

The brush fires, Esme remembered from earlier in the evening. But Derval was close to one of the temples; perhaps that area hadn't been afflicted by them.

"Are your lands, your people...Are they well? I've only just heard of the fires out west."

"There were some, yes. The water wielders have been..." He seemed to search the ribbons of lights in the sky for words. "Tireless?" He looked down at her. "Shall we say? For some time now. I'm grateful for their skill and resourcefulness."

"As am I," she offered. "I'm sorry I haven't been able to—"

He laid a hand on hers where it rested atop the low wall. "Do not worry," he assured, smiling down at her. "I'm not here to make demands of my queen."

He knew who she was, then. Esme studied him more closely. His eyes were kind. Even with the cool colors of the lights reflected in them, there was a warmth she could almost feel.

Before she could inquire as to what he *was* there for, he added, "Quite the statement you've made with that dress tonight." His smile widened, though there was nothing flirtatious about it. And when he politely excused himself with a bow, she watched him return to the great hall with bewilderment and a pinch of astonishment.

What an unexpectedly pleasant encounter.

By the time Esme reentered the hall herself, she felt lighter, less constricted by the bindings of her gown.

Spotting Abaigeal again, she made her way through the somehow even thicker crowds to greet her. Abaigeal was with someone who might have been her son, or perhaps her brother—there was no way to tell his age, but he looked similar enough with his auburn hair and spray of freckles across the bridge of his nose that Esme guessed they were related by blood.

"Abaigeal, I'm so glad you decided to attend!" Esme introduced herself to the man who turned out to be the woman's son.

"Thank you for having...well, all of us." She chuckled, stretching her arms out to encompass the entire room. Her freckled cheeks were pinker than Esme remembered from all the times she'd helped out in the kitchens, and made her wish she could enjoy the evening as much as Abaigeal clearly was.

"My mother insisted we dance." Her son, Niall, gave Esme a look that told her he wasn't all that keen on dancing with his mother.

"Well, if your father wasn't talking the ear off of..." Abaigeal waved her hand about when the name didn't come to her. "Then I wouldn't need you to dance with me." With a tug of his arm, she pulled her son along.

Esme smiled, watching them weave their way through the other dancing couples.

Across the hall stood Jaime. They seemed to catch each other's eyes at the same moment, and Esme worried that she'd attended the ball to relay additional revelations about her sister, Orianna.

Before she could find out, Lord Torin stepped in front of her.

Without a word, he took Esme by the wrist and led her into the throng of dancing guests.

"It wasn't enough that you invited these *common folk*," he sneered. "Now you have to sully yourself with the help."

Still stunned, Esme followed as Lord Torin guided them through the steps. His grip had shifted to her hand, and was tight enough that it probably appeared like she was a willing participant.

Deciding it was better to play the part than draw attention, she straightened and fixed her gaze on the collar of his coat over his right shoulder, refusing to look him in the face for fear of what she might say.

Her feet followed the dance as she surreptitiously attempted to catch the attention of someone she knew. But it was late, and the punch had been partaken liberally—so much so that few people seemed to even notice that their queen was dancing beside them.

"It's time to put an end to this foolishness." Lord Torin's voice was a deep rumble, meant only for her ears.

Esme clenched her teeth to suppress the shudder that threatened.

"Your plan with the wayward priestesses has been futile. As you well knew it would be."

She couldn't help but pull back to look up at him. "I assure you, it was not—"

"Save your hollow words for someone else. You know what must be done."

What was he getting at? Esme blinked up at him again, but Lord Torin was looking off toward something else.

"You've seen it for yourself." He pushed her back a step and turned her in time with the music.

The room spun. Her mind churned.

"Did you think to conceal the wealth of resources across the sea?"

Her steps faltered. *Across the sea?*

He knew about…He knew where she'd been living all those years?

"The lesser continent has enough to sustain the whole of Tremaene for decades to come."

At last, Lord Torin's gaze alighted on her.

"So I ask you, *my queen*. Why have you taken no steps to secure Tremaene's future, when the solution is so clearly within our grasp?"

Chapter Eighteen

"YOU SPEAK OF Periwen," Esme allowed once she found her voice.

A low growl came from Lord Torin's throat, and she wondered at his ability to contain his temper if pushed too far.

"You know what I speak of," he said through gritted teeth. "I only question why you chose to keep the salvation of our kingdom secret from your council."

Esme took a breath, tamping down the rage that burned in her belly.

"You claim," she began calmly, all too aware—and grateful—that they weren't alone, "that there are vast resources for the taking across the sea, milord."

His grip on her waist tightened, and Esme fought the urge to stomp down on the instep of his foot, the way Killian had taught her.

"I will remind you, *Torin*, that Periwen is not an uninhabited wilderness."

He huffed out an exasperated breath, as if that detail mattered little.

"And that Tremaene has no claim on another's sovereign territory."

She expected a harsh comment about her weakness as a ruler, but saw only a look of disdain in Lord Torin's eyes.

For all that she admired and respected her father, she couldn't reconcile his reasoning in placing such a man on his council. Had Lord Torin always been so unkind and arrogant, or was it Esme's gender, her youth, that brought it forth?

"I see now that so much time spent with inferior peoples has clouded your mind," he dismissed with clear disgust.

She doubted it was her time in the mortal realm that Lord Torin disliked, or that she'd rebuffed the established hierarchy and tradition of privileged assemblies. It was *her* he found so offensive. And while she yearned to enlighten him on many issues, the implications he'd made about Periwen were beyond alarming.

"Your Majesty." Killian's voice rescued her. "I wonder if I might—"

"Yes," she replied breathlessly as she spun toward him, letting him shield her.

Esme heard Lord Torin's grunt behind her, but she didn't look back.

Killian held her up. He didn't say a word, acting as though nothing were amiss. She felt him sway, turning her about when she couldn't control her legs enough to follow the steps.

After another melody finished, Killian ducked his head. "You all right?"

"I…" She looked up, and the concern in Killian's eyes nearly made her weep. She was so tired. "I think I'll retire." Her voice sounded thin.

With a tight nod, Killian slowly pulled back, keeping a firm grip on her upper arms until he was certain she was steady. Then he tucked her arm around his.

Two steps later, Tearlach was flanking Esme from the other side. She reached out to grip his arm too, then risked a glance up at him. He looked furious.

She dropped her gaze. If she didn't, she'd tell Tearlach right then and there what his father had implied. What he'd *threatened*. And that sort of confession was best delivered in private.

Cadwyn and Sully stood near the doors that opened into the main corridor. Their conversation seemed serious, which Esme would normally worry about, but all she could manage was a weak nod as Killian and Tearlach guided her out of the hall.

Killian did his best to distract her, complimenting the decor, the food, the music. Esme didn't hear any of it, but his voice was soothing.

When they reached her chamber, both men stepped back.

Esme wasn't ready to be alone. And truth be told, she was a little surprised that Tearlach hadn't already marched inside with her.

He knows Periwen can be reached, she told him quickly, then thanked Killian for seeing her to her room.

Tearlach pulled out his watch as if nothing had passed between them. "Tell Quinlan and Madoc their shift is starting early."

Killian hesitated only a moment before leaning in to kiss Esme's cheek. "You looked stunning tonight. Nice choice." He smirked. "Get some sleep."

Esme managed a tired smile as Killian strode off to summon her guards.

Tearlach waited until he was out of sight, then ushered her inside and latched the doors.

Esme toed off her shoes and collapsed on the nearest sofa.

"What were his exact words?"

With effort, she opened her eyes, finding Tearlach standing over her with a cup of tea. There were few things that would tempt her upright at that moment. Tea was one of them.

After accepting it, she noticed the tea service her maids had sent up. And on the floor beside her sat a basin of hot water with iridescent swirls of bath oils for the aching feet. She nearly whimpered at the sight. Bless her maids for always knowing exactly what she needed.

Cradling the teacup as if it were a tether to a less complicated reality than the one she found herself in, Esme watched Tearlach settle onto the sofa across from her.

He waited while she took a sip, then another. She wanted to reach up and touch the rubies he'd given her. Oh, how she'd wished to be alone with him that night. Where no one could see.

Instead, they were alone because Lord Torin had not-so-subtly suggested that she wage war against the mortal realm. And if she refused…

That was why he wanted the pitch from the redwoods in the Tamslo Mountains. She'd been right not to grant his request. Though she didn't think her inaction would halt his efforts for long.

After setting the cup back on the saucer, Esme shifted over and lifted the hem of her gown, then slid her feet into the steaming water and bit back a groan of utter relief.

Once the pain in her arches eased slightly, she told Tearlach everything his father had said.

The whole while, Tearlach held so deathly still that Esme was convinced he hadn't taken a breath since she'd started speaking.

"If Lord Torin knows, others might," she finished.

Tearlach offered a slight dip of his chin—the first reaction he'd allowed.

"We need to alert the guards," she continued. "Tell Sully and Cadwyn. Find out how Torin learned that the fog can be crossed. If it's no longer a secret that the mortal realm can be reached…" Her breath hitched. "If others know…" She searched Tearlach's eyes imploringly. It wasn't just Tremaene she needed to save; Periwen needed her protection as well.

"I'll tell them." Tearlach's voice was steady, but she could feel the ferocity resonating beneath the words. Their mutual disgust for his father gave her an odd sort of comfort.

"Sully and Cadwyn...they might have overheard something tonight," Esme said softly, speaking mostly to herself. She reached for her tea. Its calming properties seemed to be waning, so she simply stared down at the dark liquid and the pale milk swirling through it.

"If the priestesses fail..." She blinked in quick succession, like it might ward off the weariness creeping in. "And if we can't stop your father..." A yawn overtook her. "He knows I won't do as he implied, which means he's already planning to do something himself. That's why he wanted the pitch. The moment he has what he needs, he'll set sail for the mortal realm. He'll take everything, exploit every last resource they have. And that's the best-case scenario"—Esme's voice cracked—"given the way he spoke of them. The entire population...they're all in danger."

The mortal realm would be no match against whatever army Lord Torin amassed. They had no defense against magic. Except...perhaps, iron. "But what good is iron as a weapon if you don't know the enemy's weakness toward it?" she said to herself. "Or that the enemy even exists?" And if Torin managed to keep it all quiet? If he was able to thieve everything Tremaene needed from Periwen without anyone but his underlings knowing? He'd look like a savior.

How selfish to worry about that detail, she scolded, then felt the weight of Tearlach's hand coming to rest atop hers. He knelt down before her and, with a gentle touch, eased the cup from her hands and placed it on the table behind him.

"He can't do anything tonight."

Esme nodded weakly.

"You should get some rest."

"I should," she agreed, though made no move to rise.

Neither did Tearlach.

His gaze shifted to the bodice of her gown. "Do you need help with..." He met her eyes again, and a tendril of heat unfurled in her belly. "Shall I call for one of your maids?"

Her heart sank. "No." She cleared her throat. "I can manage."

Tearlach regarded her a moment longer, making Esme desperate to know what he was thinking.

But all he offered was a nod before rising and stepping away.

"Tearlach?" she asked quietly, her grip tightening in the layers of silk draped across her legs. "What if he wakes?"

It took him only a second to realize her mind had strayed to Lord Luxovious.

"Impossible," he told her.

"Is it? He managed to reach Orianna, to coerce her into doing heinous things. Tearlach, what if he finds me? What if he discovers that the only woman powerful enough to trap him—to *free* him—had a daughter?"

Slowly, Tearlach reclaimed the seat across from her, but she could tell from the tension in each movement that he wanted to come closer.

"*He will not touch you,*" Tearlach swore, his voice weighed down by the fierce protectiveness he'd always had for her—the one thing he couldn't conceal. "Do you understand me, Esme?"

She gave a shaky nod.

"He will not touch you," he vowed again. "Not ever."

Chapter Nineteen

"ARE YOU SURE you're in the right place?" Esme teased, unable to hide her smirk.

There was a lengthy pause before Hazel sighed and claimed the chair on Cadwyn's right.

"I'm sure."

Cadwyn poured tea and Esme offered up a plate of scones. It couldn't really be called breakfast, as it was practically midday. But with the stack of requests that had arrived sometime before Esme had rolled out of bed, she was more than happy to pretend the day had only just begun.

"Was it the dress?" Cadwyn asked with a flick of her brow.

Hazel nearly choked on her tea. It was the first time Esme had seen her flustered. Did Hazel really think they'd ignore the fact that she'd danced with Armel the night before? Or that the poor man had practically swallowed his own tongue when he'd first set eyes on her wearing that exquisite gown?

Slowly, Hazel lowered her cup, then spooned some brambleberry jam onto a scone.

Esme shared a look with Cadwyn as they waited.

"It wasn't the dress." Hazel's lips tipped up at the corners.

Esme had been right, then. It wasn't the dress, but what the dress represented. Armel could no longer rely on their forced proximity to ensure he'd always be close to her.

"And *I* asked him to dance," Hazel informed them, then waved off Esme's look of utter delight. "I knew he'd never get up the courage to cross that ridiculous line he drew back when we first met."

"And you neglected to tell him about your new position," Cadwyn pointed out.

"Perhaps," she admitted. "But I'm not going to give up being a guard."

Esme could live with that. She wanted Hazel as a lady-in-waiting *because* of the woman's fierce convictions, not despite them.

"Though I'll admit, I'm looking forward to larger accommodations. And softer linens."

The three of them spent the following hours sharing stories from the previous night. Most centered around a certain male guard who'd finally realized what he was about to lose if he didn't make his feelings for Hazel known, and Esme was grateful that the conversation wasn't focused on her and her many dance partners.

She was fairly certain that Tearlach had informed Cadwyn and Sully—perhaps even Hazel, Armel, and Killian—about what Lord Torin had threatened. Thankfully, though, Cadwyn and Hazel didn't bring that up either.

But Esme's responsibilities could only be put off for so long.

"Ladies," Tearlach greeted as he strode in.

Hazel did a terrible job of hiding her distaste for her new honorific.

Did you read Jaime's letter? Tearlach asked. Of course he knew about the letter. It had been set aside from the others—likely his doing—and was therefore the only one she'd taken the time to read that morning.

"You're here about Jaime's letter, I presume," Esme answered aloud as she went to retrieve it, deciding it needn't be kept secret.

The note from Jaime, herself, was fairly brief. It explained that she'd forgotten about a letter that had been delivered shortly after Orianna had taken the throne. Jaime claimed that its contents had never seemed significant, yet she hoped it might assist Esme in better understanding Orianna's motivations.

Unfortunately, Jaime's assessment had been accurate; Orianna's words didn't reveal much.

Handing the letter over to Cadwyn, Esme recalled some of the woman's words, and the humility of her tone when she'd expressed sadness at the tragic accident that had claimed the lives of the late king and queen.

It had nearly convinced Esme that she hadn't been responsible for the tragic accident. But Orianna's handwriting had become increasingly hurried toward the end of the letter. She'd repeatedly mentioned her crown, and the power it held. Of course, wearing the crown gave her power, but the way she'd referred to it as a physical object rather than what it represented struck Esme as strange.

She'd long assumed that Orianna had never worn her mother's crown. The one she remembered from the night in the throne room had been almost as intimidating as the high-priestess herself—a monstrosity of sharpened crystals and silver spikes, connected by a web of delicate chains.

"Remind me to write a reply to Jaime," Esme requested of Cadwyn as she scrubbed the image of Orianna from her mind. Cadwyn nodded in reply, handing the letter over for Hazel to read.

Based on what Esme had seen in Lord Luxovious's memories, Orianna wasn't *completely* to blame for the atrocities she'd inflicted. And though Esme couldn't divulge Lord Luxovious's role in all of it, she could at least assure Jaime that other powers had been at work. It would put her mind at ease, Esme hoped.

When the clock chimed, alerting her of the lateness of the day, Esme slipped past Tearlach and into her dressing room.

"Where are you going?" he called after her.

"I'm having afternoon tea with Cora." Esme pulled a deep green tunic with silver beadwork over her head, grinning at the silence that followed.

Honestly, she was nervous about her visit with Cora, unsure of what the two of them would discuss if not Tearlach's early life. But his obvious bewilderment at learning of their social call gave her an unexpected flutter of excitement.

She emerged, pinning her hair into a hasty updo. "I'm sorry to cut our time short," she told Cadwyn and Hazel. "But I—"

"Cora?" Tearlach finally asked. "Why?"

Cadwyn and Hazel shared a look, and Esme wondered how much they suspected about her relationship with Tearlach.

"Are you sure...that's wise?" he asked carefully. Too carefully.

"Wise?" She blinked at him. *Are you worried about me or yourself?*

Esme wished she could relish in his loss for words, but it only made her anger rise anew. He kept so much from her. Even someone he clearly trusted and considered a dear friend was apparently off-limits.

Her eyes held his a moment longer before she walked out.

Chapter Twenty

TEARLACH EYED ESME as she approached the training yard with Harlow and Hazel. He'd want to hear everything about her tea with Cora the day before. And if Cora chose to divulge everything they'd discussed, she was welcome to, but Esme wasn't inclined to offer him anything. She was still too incensed that he'd tried to control yet another aspect of her life.

Cora had been a lovely companion, despite the knowing glint that would appear in her eyes every time Esme mentioned Tearlach's name. She clearly assumed that they were more than a queen and her guard.

Though Esme couldn't very well fault someone else for her inability to hide her reactions. It was highly probable that she'd confess everything to Cora one day. It was eating her up inside, especially since Cora's endearing stories about her former fiancé had only added to Esme's inconvenient feelings toward Tearlach. It'd been clear in the wistfulness of the woman's voice that she'd missed her childhood friend very much in the years since they'd broken their engagement.

Tearlach didn't take his eyes off of Esme as she drew near. From the intensity of his stare, she knew he was holding back an interrogation.

But his voice didn't come through. Instead, he adopted his usual stance at the edge of the central ring—arms crossed, legs set apart, eyes narrowed, jaw locked—as Esme spent the following hour fending off frozen spikes that Armel hurtled at her and sudden bursts of fireballs from Killian. When she was already shivering and sweating from icy fragments and searing heat, Cahir and Shawndrell joined their threesome, weaving their earth and air magic together to erect pillars of sand and dirt and swirling dust that made Armel and Killian's weapons all the harder to anticipate.

At some point, Sully had turned up to watch. And he wasn't the only one.

Noticing Jarlath in her periphery, Esme turned her head at the exact moment he spotted her. Their eyes met, and his entire face lit up.

But when she caught sight of Tearlach's arm sweeping out, she spun back around.

A colossal, icy spear was careening toward her. Esme dove for the ground right before it exploded into a million sparkling bits of ice.

She stayed down, glaring up at Tearlach as he stormed over. "I had it. Did you really need to—"

"Save you again? Evidently."

He reached down a hand for her, but she refused, getting to her feet as shards of ice melted into the dirt coating her skin. She could feel muddy rivulets tracking down her arms and cheeks.

"I had it," she repeated through gritted teeth.

"You didn't," he informed in his most condescending tone. "Go again. Only this time, try to remember where you are and what you're doing. A battle is made up of distractions—enemies coming at you from every direction. You can't let even a single one steal your focus, even for a second. It's not worth it."

It's not worth it. The words echoed in Esme's mind, and she struggled not to look over at Jarlath.

She was acutely aware that everyone was watching their interaction.

Because Tearlach wanted them to.

You shouldn't have done that.

Yes. I should have. His eyes darkened.

Esme straightened, readying herself for whatever verbal barb would come next, but Tearlach turned and stalked back across the ring.

"Go easy on her," she heard Jarlath reproach with obvious concern.

Tearlach turned to glare at his brother. "Leave," he growled.

Jarlath backed up a step, lifting his hands in a placating manner. But Tearlach wasn't done.

He matched his brother's retreat. "And if you don't, you can step into the ring with me."

Jarlath raised his hands again. "Fighting isn't my forte."

"No," Tearlach agreed. "Your power lies in manipulation. Betrayal."

Esme's breath hitched. It wasn't much, it wasn't even anything specific, but it was the first time Tearlach had revealed even a hint as to what had torn them apart. At least, as he saw it.

Jarlath dropped his arms and bowed his head, shaking it slightly as if he felt sorry for his brother.

Tearlach's eyes flared, but he only managed one more menacing step before Hazel and Killian got between them.

Jarlath backed away with a look of concern on his face, like he was saddened by what Tearlach had become.

Not for the first time, Esme wondered what he'd been like before, what he might've become had he not been forced to leave home after his broken engagement. If not for the Dark War. If not for Sully asking him to bind himself to a young woman he'd never met, to leave behind the life he'd built for one of secrecy. If his honor hadn't demanded that he stay on as her personal guard after they'd defeated Orianna.

What might his life have been if he'd been able to choose his own path?

Chapter Twenty-One

SULLY AND ESME rode in silence as the wide-stretching city wall slipped beneath the horizon. Lord Lennox's home wasn't too far outside of Meallán. He'd invited Esme and her retinue to dine, and she was glad to take an evening away from making sense of reports—which were only comprehensible because of Winifred's notes.

"Do you remember Jarlath? From...before?" she asked Sully.

"Not particularly. It was seldom that Lord Torin traveled to the city with more than one attendant."

"So...you didn't know him well?" Esme pressed.

Sully chuckled. "I believe I only spoke with Genvieve once or twice in all the years that Lord Torin has held the title. As for Jarlath...I can't recall whether or not we were ever properly introduced."

Esme made a sound of disappointment, returning her sights to the hills in the distance.

"I hear you've been spending time with him."

She glanced over, but Sully's expression showed curiosity, nothing more.

"I can't understand why people seem so hostile toward him."

"He's Torin's son."

"So is Tearlach."

Sully raised his brow at the sharpness of her retort. "Have you spoken with him about it?"

She knew he meant Tearlach. "I have not," she replied succinctly.

Sully hummed as if in contemplation, but Esme wasn't naive enough to think he'd only just considered the situation.

She didn't offer anything more. Truth be told, she wasn't sure how she should feel. After the confrontation between Tearlach and Jarlath the other day, she hadn't spoken with either of them. Correspondences continued piling up on her desk, so she'd busied herself with replies instead.

Esme rested her head against the tufted fabric and looked up at the roof of the carriage like she could see Tearlach riding up there with the driver. She'd anticipated that things would be different between them after their visit to the sacred pool. Had assumed that they'd dance around one another for a time, but would ultimately grow closer as friends. Because...well, they'd understand each other better, knowing that each of them desired something beyond their grasp.

At least, that was what Esme had hoped. And for a short time, it seemed as though they were moving in that direction.

But when they'd returned to the palace, Jarlath had been there, and something shifted. Not just between her and Tearlach. Others could feel it too.

Esme stared out the small window, watching the vegetation fade.

A faint pulse of raw magic tugged at her, but it wasn't enough to cause pain. Spotting their destination between two stands of tall oaks up ahead, she felt assured that she wouldn't need Tearlach to siphon any of her magic.

The sun was just setting when they pulled around a circular drive. Lord Lennox's home wasn't overly lavish, though neither was it understated. The stonework framing the front doors and the windows was etched with scrolls and what appeared to be woodland creatures. Two modest rows of hedges were trimmed neatly, lining the front walkway.

Hazel and Cadwyn emerged from the other carriage as Lord Lennox's wife bustled out to greet them.

Ellison was a lively woman who seemed to keep Lennox on his toes. She ushered everyone inside, insisting that all of Esme's guards take dinner at the main table. When Sully politely explained that several would need to remain on duty, she assured them that everyone would be fed well and good before the night was through.

Esme was seated beside the hostess, and they were only partway through the first course before Ellison began inquiring about all the noblemen she'd danced with at the ball.

Esme could feel everyone's eyes on her, especially Tearlach's. "There were many guests in attendance," she answered deftly. "I wish I'd had the chance to meet them all."

Ellison was undeterred. "Well, you needn't worry. You'll find a suitable match; I'm sure of it."

Thankfully, Hazel took that moment to ask about the wine, and Lord Lennox leaned over to quietly inform Esme that he had news for her.

"Later?" he asked.

She gave a discreet nod.

"Out in the gardens, when the tea is brought out?"

Another nod.

It wasn't easy to slip away without Tearlach following, but Esme's excuse of needing to freshen up seemed to keep him in his seat—even as his eyes tracked her movements when she left the room. She knew he'd be only a few steps behind once he sensed her heading in another direction.

The gardens looked wintered over—a disconcerting sight that was all too common in the smaller towns and villages throughout the kingdom. There was a small stone fountain in the center of a shallow pool, with a few tufts of lilyturf growing along its edges.

"I wondered why some of the councilors seemed so lax about our need to restore the land," Lord Lennox said once Esme reached his side. He clasped his arms behind his back and gazed up at the dwindling lights in the sky.

"I'd wondered that myself," she agreed, knowing she wouldn't like what he was about to say.

"I've always prided myself on being a man who could start up a conversation with a rock."

A laugh tumbled from Esme's lips. She turned to gape at him.

Lord Lennox smiled down at her. "So, naturally, people from all walks feel comfortable conversing with me. With me, near me..." He waved his hand like the distinction didn't matter.

Gossip. Lord Lennox was a gossip. She almost couldn't picture it.

"And what I've heard"—he adopted a more serious tone—"is that some members of the council believe there are other *means* with which to restore our lands."

"Is that so?" Esme felt the fine hairs on the back of her neck rise.

"I couldn't say who, specifically—those who were whispering about it were palace staff. But even they pieced together enough to know it involves resources that lie beyond our shores."

"Beyond our shores?" she asked as if it were the first she was hearing of it.

Lord Lennox rocked back on his heels and furrowed his brow. "All I can think is that it must involve the mortal realm. Though, I can't understand how that would even be feasible."

"It does seem…a bit outlandish. How would they cross the barrier?" Esme moderated her intonation, careful not to give anything away. She wasn't sure how much or little he knew.

"Precisely. You can see why I thought it was nothing but hearsay. Then I heard it a second time, and feared it may not be. And if things get any worse, here in Tremaene…"

Esme watched Lord Lennox scan the gardens like he was imagining what they'd once been, lush and bountiful.

"If things get worse, then who knows what some might attempt," she concluded.

Still in a contemplative state, Lord Lennox offered a somewhat distracted nod.

If others had heard similar rumors, then word was spreading. But by whom? It couldn't have been Lord Torin. If people knew that Periwen's resources were within reach, then he couldn't very well threaten her about it.

She recalled seeing Neala at the ball. The general knew about Periwen—all three of the generals in Altan had been made aware before Esme had even returned. Might she have mentioned something? Certainly Neala wouldn't propose invading the smaller continent, especially when the valley in Altan was relatively well stocked. Fulton, however…

Esme made a mental note to ask Keelin if he'd been in attendance as well. If even one of the generals was involved in Lord Torin's plan, it would be difficult to stop them.

———————

Esme felt the confines of the carriage more acutely than ever with Tearlach taking up more than half of the bench they shared and the threat Periwen faced consuming the remainder of her thoughts.

When they finally passed through the gates on the north side of town, she reached up and pounded her fist on the roof of the cab, halting their procession immediately.

"What's wrong?" Tearlach demanded.

So many things, Esme wanted to say. "Nothing. I just need some air. Let's walk back to the palace." She was surprised when he acquiesced with a quick nod.

The warm hues of the lanterns set the cobbled streets aglow, melding with the cool tones of the shifting lights in the sky to create a sort of eeriness that Esme felt in her bones.

Two of her guards took their horses on ahead, checking the route before circling back. Hazel and Tearlach walked several paces in front of Esme and Cadwyn, with Sully and the rest of her guards following with the empty carriages.

As they approached an alleyway like any other, just beyond one of the larger town squares that featured an octagonal pool and an elaborate fountain, Esme felt it again—the eeriness that couldn't have been from the ominous lighting alone.

A chill inched up her spine, and she turned to look down the alley.

It was darker than it should've been. Like an unending chasm had opened in their world and swallowed all the light.

Her vision focused on the only thing visible.

Cadwyn sucked in a breath and yanked Esme away, seeing it as well.

Seeing *him*.

Madoc, Roderick, and Quinlan surrounded her in a heartbeat. She could hear the agitation in the horses as the drivers tried to bring the carriages closer.

Esme was quickly ushered into the nearest one. Cadwyn and Hazel hurried inside as Quinlan and Madoc physically blocked the doors. She could hear Tearlach's clipped tones just outside, demanding what

Roderick and another of her guards had seen. Their responses were low enough that she couldn't make them out, but Tearlach turned to look through the small window, catching Esme's eye. Assured that she was as safe as she could be, he scanned the empty street once more, then hauled himself inside.

Hazel and Cadwyn pressed closer together, trying to accommodate more people than the carriage was intended for as Quinlan and Madoc piled in, bracketing Esme. It didn't just feel cramped—Esme could barely draw half a breath, squeezed between the two of them.

Tearlach stared at her from the opposite bench. The lantern swung violently as they sped through the streets, flickering against the already harsh planes of his face, and making his eyes appear more enraged than she'd seen in a long time.

Suddenly, Esme felt foolish. What if she'd imagined the whole thing? Causing so much commotion and panic over nothing was...

"I'm fine." Her voice broke the silence. "It was nothing. I must have...seen..."

"It wasn't nothing," Cadwyn cut in.

Tearlach jerked his head toward her. "You saw?"

Cadwyn nodded.

It's not a big deal, it wasn't—

Not now. The voice he used to speak with her silently possessed more restraint. It almost sounded reassuring.

Tearlach rested his head back so his eyes were fixed on the carriage roof. He didn't demand further explanation from Cadwyn, and she didn't seem inclined to offer any.

The silence was nearly suffocating by the time they reached the stables. It wasn't until Esme was alone in her room with Tearlach that she spoke again.

"It wasn't really him," she said, hoisting herself up to sit on the end of the bed.

"*Him?*" Tearlach asked like he knew exactly who she was speaking of, while hoping he was wrong.

She stared at him for a second before repeating, "Him."

Tearlach exhaled roughly, then closed his eyes for several measured breaths.

When he started pacing down the center of the room, Esme tried to reassure him. "He wasn't *there*. Not really."

Without pausing his strides, he turned his head sharply toward her. "Explain."

"It was..." Esme wrung her hands on her lap, then wrapped her cloak tighter around her legs. As if it might hold her together.

"It was only a...*projection*." She could still see Lord Luxovious standing in the dark alleyway between the buildings, his seemingly corporeal form silhouetted by the glow of black flames tinged with purple, undulating along the hem of his obsidian cloak.

Tearlach came to a stop in front of her, knowing there was more she wasn't telling him.

"I've seen him—*it*—before."

A flash of hurt shone in his eyes—there and gone in an instant. "Why didn't you tell me?" His body had gone taut, and she knew he wanted to reach for her, to protect her in a way a guard couldn't. In a way he'd never allow himself to.

For a moment, Esme let herself remember—let herself *feel*—the fierce possessiveness he'd expressed when she'd first told him about the things she'd seen in Lord Luxovious's memories.

But Tearlach had better control over the emotions that had overtaken him back in the secluded oasis in the mountains. He widened his stance and folded his arms over his chest, then raised his chin as he stared down at her.

"Tell me everything," he ordered, his voice even and free of emotion.

Esme took a breath and began with the morning at the inn in Juverna, when Lord Luxovious had first appeared to her.

Chapter Twenty-Two

ESME REACHED FOR the blanket that had fallen away in the night. It was cold, as if it were a night in late autumn back in Periwen, when the days were warm but the mornings were coated with frost.

Something shifted in the darkness, and Esme's grip on the blanket tightened.

There, standing before the tall windows, silhouetted by the lights in the night sky, was Lord Luxovious.

Her heart started to beat violently in her chest as she forced a slow breath from between her lips. She thought of slipping out of bed and escaping through the secret passageway to Tearlach's room, but her body refused to move. Even if she did manage to escape, the figure standing across the room would certainly find her again.

After he'd appeared in the alleyway two nights prior, Esme had feared his return. She just hadn't expected him to find her again so soon.

The hood of his dark cloak was pulled low, though she could see deep shadows under his eyes that hadn't been there before. There was a severe jut of a chin and a sharp line of a nose that had once belonged to the man he'd been. Black flames ringed the hem of his cloak, but the garment that had seemed almost smokelike when he'd appeared back in Juverna instead seemed heavier, more tangible. As if he were no longer an illusion, but fully formed.

"I've been searching for you."

Esme trembled at the statement. His voice was rough from disuse, yet layered with a thousand years of secrets. Did he know hers too? Did he know who she was, that she was Erena's daughter? That she might have the ability to free him?

Did he know what she'd seen, that she'd witnessed the things he'd done? That she knew the truth he'd tried so hard to conceal?

"The daughter of the great and powerful Erena," he declared.

He'd come for *her*, then. He needed her.

She didn't want to think about what his dark magic might do to her—take from her—in his quest to gain his freedom. All she could hope for was that it would be a less dreadful outcome than if Lord Luxovious had come to silence her for all she'd seen.

Esme remained silent, even though she desperately wanted to summon Tearlach, to see him burst through the door adjoining their rooms and vanquish the specter. But she couldn't risk him too. Lord Luxovious wanted her, and only her. So it was her alone that he would get.

Slowly, the figure tilted his head, and Esme had the strange feeling that he was looking at her with what might have been admiration— either for her or for her mother. Recalling the few words he'd voiced, she had to admit they hadn't *necessarily* been malevolent.

Even where he stood—several paces from the foot of the bed, bracketed by the tall windows—could have been taken as a sign that he wasn't there to harm her. He hadn't positioned himself between her and where her guards were stationed on the other side of the main doors. And his posture seemed as nonthreatening as it could, given the gnarled bones and joints she'd caught sight of before.

If only she could convince her thundering heart and the chill of perspiration prickling her skin that she wasn't in immediate danger.

"You've seen things you shouldn't have."

He knew. He knew everything.

Esme held her breath. Her assessment suddenly seemed overly generous. Of course he didn't have a strange sort of admiration for her mother—for the woman who'd *trapped* him. He was there to punish her for invading his mind. To take back the memories Esme had stolen.

It was all she could do to keep her grip on the blanket rather than shield her head protectively the way her instincts would have her do. As if it would stop the wicked power she knew he possessed—the same power Orianna had used on her, hooking her claws into Esme's skull, dragging them through her mind.

Again, she considered calling out to Tearlach. But what would he do? What *could* he do? Could a blade pierce a being who wasn't fully formed? Would Tearlach's magic work against the apparition? Would hers?

"Terrible things," Lord Luxovious went on.

Esme braced herself.

Help. The word was poised at the precipice of her consciousness. Still, she held it back, held back the summons.

"Things I did as an overly ambitious young man. Things I'm ashamed of," he finished, with an exhale so heavy his shoulders seemed to release the weight they'd been carrying.

"Things that I must"—his eyes seemed to focus more intently on her—"atone for."

Atone for?

Esme's body told her to be afraid of the man—*the creature*—standing before her. But her rational, foolish mind wanted him to keep talking.

Curiosity won out. If he revealed even the slightest clue about how she might unblock the channels, she needed to hear it. He was the best source they had, after all.

With great effort, Esme convinced her body to relax. When she felt her muscles slacken, she pushed herself up slowly, then leaned back against the headboard.

"I wasn't always that way, you know." His voice softened with the admission, and Esme found herself wondering what kind of man he'd been before he'd become the lord of Kearney.

Suddenly, it wasn't just about the information he might bestow, she wanted to *understand* him. She wanted to know how one came to be corrupted by dark magic, to succumb to it. Were all who held power vulnerable to such temptation? Was she?

"At first, it was only a few fields of barley. The farmers burned the yield and prepared to plant anew the following season."

Esme's mind tripped over the word *season*. He was speaking of a time long ago, then. When the Wastes had been a thriving territory like any other in Tremaene.

"But when the wheat darkened and withered, I knew it was the blight. Nothing could be done. Soon, every swath of farmland had been charred. Attempts were made to sow the arid plains in the south. Every drop of water was diverted, until the riverbeds had all but run dry. I allowed it, hoping it would stave off starvation. But the blight couldn't be stopped."

He bowed his head, and Esme realized her forehead was creased with concern.

"I knew it was dangerous to meddle with the magic, but at the time... I couldn't let it spread. Couldn't allow it. The entirety of Tremaene was in peril. And all because of a sickness that had begun on my lands." He paused for a breath, then looked up, meeting Esme's eyes. "I did what had to be done."

He waited, as if he needed her to connect the pieces. Needed her to understand.

"Athdara," she guessed. "The Order."

He nodded. "I wanted to protect the rest of the kingdom. My land was finished, but Tremaene was not."

Esme wanted to believe him. It all made sense. The memories she'd seen of his earlier ministrations hadn't been corrupt, not really. She'd assumed his goal had always been ultimate power. But what if that had been a consequence of dealing in dark magic? What if he'd become a victim because he'd risked exposing himself to the only thing he believed would save Tremaene?

But even if the dark magic *had* ruled him in all his awful deeds, was that any reason to trust the man standing before her? Corruption didn't fade over time, didn't lessen its hold. If anything, Esme suspected it would grow stronger.

"We can right things. Together."

Esme stared back at him. Ignoring what she hoped wasn't a plea for her to free him, she asked, "How?"

"I've had much time to ponder things in my...restful state. I know there is a way. But it will require your power and mine."

Esme couldn't help but consider what he was suggesting.

"I've an eternity. You and your people do not," he reminded. "I will return, daughter of Erena."

And with that, he was gone.

She stared at the spot where he'd stood, wondering if any of it had been real. Or only a dream. She hated that everything he'd said seemed... reasonable. As if the same could have happened to anyone, even her. Was she willing to go to the lengths Lord Luxovious had in order to save her people, her homeland?

The answer was like a brand burned into her mind.

Yes.

Chapter Twenty-Three

ESME DECIDED TO take breakfast in the dining hall the following morning. She told herself it had nothing to do with the darkened ring on the floor where Lord Luxovious had appeared the night before, but that was a lie.

When first she'd woken, she'd felt encouraged. Somewhat. If Lord Luxovious was truly repentant for the harm he'd inflicted, the damage he'd caused, then perhaps he'd provide insight into how the dark magic had been used to choke off the flow of raw magic.

It had taken less than a minute for Esme to reject the optimistic notion and accept that it'd all been a manipulation. A ploy.

She didn't need him; he needed her. To free him.

How better to do that than to prey on the weakness she held for the well-being of her people.

By the time she dressed, her hunger was battling relentlessly for her attention over her rekindled wrath for Lord Luxovious.

Given that most of the palace staff ate rather early, the hall would likely be empty. Cahir and Madoc descended the stairwell ahead of her, rounding the steps quickly. Esme hurried to catch up and, with her eyes downcast, nearly collided with someone when she reached the main floor.

Strong arms reached out to steady her, as a book slid across the marble floor.

"Apologies, Your Majesty."

Esme looked up into Jarlath's apologetic eyes.

"I'm afraid I get a little"—he glanced at where his book had slowed to a stop several feet away—"in my head when I'm reading." His cheeks blushed an endearing shade of pink as he retrieved the book and tucked it behind his back.

"We seem to run into one another quite often," she noted, wanting to give him a moment of reprieve.

Jarlath huffed out a breath of relief. "Guess I'm just lucky." He looked over at her guards. "Late as it is, I was on my way to the dining hall. Time got away from me this morning."

"I'm headed to breakfast as well. If there's anything left. I...had a late night, myself."

"Might I join you?" Jarlath offered his arm. "I can almost guarantee we're the only two who still desire breakfast at this hour."

"On one condition." She took his arm.

"Anything."

"Tell me what you were reading."

The blush reappeared as he chuckled. "You drive a hard bargain, Your Majesty. But I find it difficult to deny you anything."

It was Esme's turn to blush.

"The book is quite juvenile, I assure you." He angled the cover so Esme could see it.

It was worn, the cloth binding frayed at the edges, as if Jarlath had read it a hundred times. She wasn't familiar with that particular collection of short stories, but given the faded gold illustration on the cover, she guessed it was a book of children's fables.

It was almost too sweetly innocent to be true. If she hadn't laid eyes on the book herself, she might not have believed he read such things. And seeing how much he clearly treasured it only endeared him to her more.

"There are times when I find myself seeking the familiarity of the stories and the lyrical prose. And times when the words offer new meaning," he explained, though he didn't need to. Esme understood just fine.

"I wish I still had the book my mother read to me when I was young. The stories from our childhood have a way of...shaping us, helping us become who we're meant to be."

Jarlath gave her a lopsided grin as if he'd found the only other person in all of Tremaene who felt the same way. "That they do. I suppose sometimes...I need the reminder."

After sharing a meal made up of leftovers from the picked-over assortment, Jarlath accompanied Esme for a stroll around the lake. When they reached the southernmost side, where the shore was rocky, she eyed one of the giant willows.

Without allowing a moment to second-guess herself, Esme gave Madoc and Cahir a pointed look, then grabbed Jarlath's hand and tugged him through the curtain of fronds.

His laughter followed. "I'd ask what you were up to, but I think I can guess."

"I don't get much privacy," she admitted before realizing how that sounded. "Not that—I didn't mean...I just..." Her face felt like it might catch fire as she gestured to where her guards waited beyond the canopy. It was only conversation she was after. Truly. To have an honest moment with someone whose company she genuinely appreciated, without her guards hovering nearby. They *were* nearby, she knew. But beneath the willow, there was at least the illusion that she and Jarlath were alone.

"Esme," he said in a soft voice, taking one of her hands. Her mind quieted instantly. "You needn't explain. I don't get all that much privacy myself."

He released her hand far sooner than she would've liked, and shrugged out of his coat, laying it on the mossy ground between them.

Time passed easily then. Jarlath shared a few of his favorite stories from his book, and Esme told him of her childhood, how she'd climbed trees or swum in the lake after dark, when the Loinnir Lights would dance across the surface of the water.

Eventually, the conversation meandered into Jarlath's life on the coast. It was a stark reminder that Esme needed to figure out Lord Torin's plans. And whether it even was a plan, or just an empty threat.

"The biggest boat I've ever been on wasn't built to seat more than a few people. I can't imagine what it would be like on one of those giant vessels with dozens of rowers."

Jarlath chuckled. "Oarsmen," he corrected.

Esme forced a scowl. "And what if the *rower* isn't a man?"

Jarlath made a show of looking comically apologetic, which had Esme biting back a grin. "I'm afraid we still call them oarsmen." He winced.

Esme shook her head. "What a shame. I hereby order you to think up a more inclusive title."

"If my queen demands it." His voice dropped low, and his smile became more heated than the playful one he'd previously allowed.

Esme swallowed as she stared at his smile, at what it seemed to suggest.

She thought about what it would be like to close the distance between them, to indulge in a moment of physical affection. Even if her heart knew he wasn't the man she desired, her body didn't seem very concerned by that detail. Because he looked so much like the person she *did* want.

Because a part of her desperately craved touch, connection. And Esme was fairly certain Jarlath was offering precisely that.

In the recesses of her mind, she remembered her plan to learn more about the ships in Isloran, but then Jarlath's blue eyes darkened, and he leaned in.

"What else does my queen demand?"

Esme inhaled a quick breath. "She wonders if you might—"

The branches were ripped aside by Tearlach.

Chapter Twenty-Four

ESME SCRAMBLED AWAY, putting as much distance as she could between herself and Jarlath.

"You're needed," Tearlach said without unclenching his jaw. His nostrils flared with each inhale.

"For what?" she managed as her heart continued to spasm against her rib cage.

I wasn't doing anything wrong, she told herself firmly.

Then why did she feel ashamed at being caught about to…

About to *what*? What *had* they been about to do? It no longer mattered, yet she couldn't help but feel like the moment had gotten away from her, like she'd been about to cross some imaginary line she could never come back from.

"A meeting," Tearlach answered.

"With whom?" She was stalling. She knew she was stalling. But some foolish part of her mind believed that if she kept Tearlach talking, it might distract him from what he'd almost witnessed.

"That's private." Tearlach shot a look of disgust toward his brother, though it only caused Jarlath to share a companionable smile with Esme.

Instead of arguing with Tearlach, he rose gracefully, then offered Esme a hand. He retrieved his jacket, brushing bits of dirt and moss from it.

Before he took his leave, Jarlath bent to press a kiss against Esme's hand, then whispered, "Your queenly responsibilities demand your attention. Until next time."

All Esme could do was nod as he turned, leaving her alone with Tearlach.

Tearlach. Her anger at his interruption returned fully.

Pulling her shoulders back, Esme raised her chin and asked, "What's this important meeting about?"

"Your safety," he replied, which told her exactly nothing.

She'd wager there was no meeting at all, and matched his seemingly permanent glare with one of her own.

"He's your brother. He's no intention of hurting me."

Impossible as it seemed, Tearlach's glare hardened. He jerked his head, indicating that she follow, then whipped aside the fronds.

Of course, she followed. Her guards fell in a good many paces behind her.

"If you don't trust him, don't you at least trust me?" She tried to keep up with Tearlach.

"You don't know what he's capable of." His response hinted at a tarnished history that Esme suspected was only one-sided.

She hurried in front of him and grabbed his upper arms, forcing him to stop.

"Then tell me," she demanded.

For a moment, he seemed to consider her request. The muscles straining in his neck relaxed, and his eyes softened as he stared down at her.

Then he looked toward the palace. "We're late."

Esme let her hands drop, and Tearlach stepped around her.

She stood there a moment, trying to summon a breath.

Then Cahir was beside her, offering his arm. She took it. Madoc's too.

———————

As it turned out, there *was* a meeting. Esme wasn't altogether surprised. Tearlach clearly didn't want her anywhere near Jarlath, but she didn't believe he'd outright lie to lure her away from him.

Everyone had gathered in Esme's suite—her entire royal guard, Sully, Cadwyn, Tearlach, even Myles. They crowded what usually seemed like a rather large space. But after what Lord Torin had threatened, and what Lord Lennox had partly confirmed, they needed to be especially careful in keeping their discussions private.

Tearlach began by reiterating the need to find the fragmented pieces of the orbs that had been used to seal off the channels. Having already visited the Iola and Arlais temples, there were three left to search. Esme tried to remain optimistic that the pieces would be found, though none of the memories she'd witnessed had been from the fall of the Order. The most likely scenarios involved some of the late priestesses hiding the sacred garments and adornments away when their Sisters had started "falling ill," or the distressing reality that everything in the temples had been looted.

Which was why Esme needed to visit each of the remaining temples. She didn't expect to find much, but perhaps something at one of the sites would look familiar to her based on what she'd seen in Lord Luxovious's memories. Or maybe being in those locations would trigger a premonitory dream. It might even be worth the frustration to visit Athdara before they left to see if she might offer—

"Hazel and Roderick have agreed to visit the Laurel, Junia, and Troya temples alone, allowing the majority of the guard to remain here with our queen."

Esme blinked at Tearlach. *Remain here?*

"Wait." She stood, ignoring the confirmation that Roderick was also a sensor, and gauged the reactions around the room. Once again, it appeared she was the only one who hadn't been aware of the plans Tearlach had laid out.

"I'm going," she informed him.

Tearlach was clearly anticipating her claim. Calm as ever, he told her, "No. You're not going anywhere."

When Esme sucked in a breath, prepared to explain that *she* was the queen and that *she* would decide where she went, Tearlach held up a hand.

"The threats are too great." He didn't elaborate, and Esme wondered how much he'd divulged to the others about the sighting in the alleyway.

"That's not your call to make."

"It is when you're about to put yourself in danger."

"If I might…" Sully risked wading into what was more to do with her and Tearlach than a journey to a neighboring territory. "I'd advise against taking part in this venture, my queen. After leaving for so long to travel north, the council could begin to question your motives, and may become suspicious of the true direness of the situation."

"And if you wish to keep secret," Cadwyn took over, "everything involving the creation of the Order, as well as everything…that *man* did, then I must agree with Tearlach and Sully. You should stay here. Maintain the guise that all is well and is being remedied with the assistance of the unordained priestesses you met with."

She made a good point. And Esme held out hope that it wouldn't be merely a guise much longer. She'd sent the women of the Triskele a missive immediately upon returning to Meallán, deciding it was best that they know the truth. She'd reasoned that by trusting them with such secret and dangerous information they'd offer their assistance in locating the missing articles.

She'd yet to receive a response.

Esme turned to Tearlach. The look of determination on his face was different, defiant. Challenging, even. Like he was daring her to question him again. Like it was about far more than whether she'd accompany Hazel or Roderick in their search.

"Leave us," Esme ordered. She didn't need an audience.

There was a moment of hesitation, but soon everyone filed out of the room.

Esme slowly walked over to Tearlach. "What's this really about? Cadwyn and Sully gave compelling reasons for me not to leave Meallán. But that's not why you want me to remain here, is it? You know better than anyone that I'm no safer here than I am out there. If anything, I've more enemies inside these walls."

She waited, fully expecting a refutation to her claims, or insistence that she follow his orders when it came to her protection.

Instead, Tearlach dropped his head. "Esme," he sighed, letting weariness seep into his voice. "I need to keep you safe." When he raised his head again, there were shadows marring his eyes that hadn't been there earlier. "Please. Let me do my job."

His *job*. Another reminder of what she was to him.

She almost asked where he'd been the night before. If it was *his job* to protect her, then where had he been when Lord Luxovious had stood in that very room, only a few paces away from her?

Esme wanted him—*needed* him—to accept that danger could find her anywhere. That Lord Luxovious would continue coming to her until he got what he wanted.

She needed Tearlach to feel the same urgency she felt about locating the fragments of the orbs and any scrap of evidence that might be found at the abandoned temples—not only to restore their land, but to sever at least one of the holds Lord Luxovious had on her.

She didn't say any of that.

Because she felt as weary as Tearlach looked.

So she agreed.

"Send Hazel and Roderick, then."

Chapter Twenty-Five

ESME LAUGHED AS she blocked the wooden sword with her own.

"Grip it with both hands," she instructed with a smile, twirling the bulky weapon around her wrist. "Haven't you ever held a sword?"

"Like this?" Jarlath asked as he adjusted his grip and swung the sword aimlessly about.

Esme shook her head. Surely he was pretending.

The training rings were aglow with the cool-colored lights in the night sky, ringed in darkness by the tall trees that surrounded the yard. It was quiet; the sounds of sparring and laughter that usually drifted through her open windows at night were absent. And the whispered conversation between Quinlan and Cahir barely reached her.

It hadn't been her intention to avoid any of the guards when she'd asked Jarlath to meet her at such a late hour. She'd hoped only to circumvent the persistent suitors who wouldn't leave despite her clear lack of interest.

"More like this?" Jarlath shifted his grip to an awkward hold and furrowed his brow in such an exaggerated way that Esme nearly snorted.

"Not even close. The good news is, you can't possibly get any worse."

"Can't I?" he challenged, his eyes alight with mirth.

Esme moved to his side and gently tugged his hands from the wooden blade. "Like this." She positioned them properly, and felt his soft hum of agreement. But before the warmth of his hands could seep into her skin, she retreated. No matter how similar in appearance he might be, Jarlath wasn't the person her foolishly stubborn heart wanted.

"Playing with toys is beneath Her Majesty," came Tearlach's voice.

Esme turned just as a sword arced through the air, its hilt aimed at her.

The wooden replica she'd been holding thudded to the ground a second before she caught the other, far more deadly one.

She gaped at Tearlach, then down at the blade in her hand. Had he actually *tossed* a sword at her?

It was beyond reckless. She might have been seriously injured. Or worse, if she hadn't turned in time to catch it.

Tearlach rotated his own blade effortlessly, then arched a brow at her. It was then that she realized he could've easily used his magic to direct the sword, had it not sailed through the air as intended, or if she hadn't been so quick to react.

Esme's shock quickly turned to anger.

Tearlach waited.

Stifling an exasperated sigh, Esme turned her back to Tearlach and offered an apology to her preferred sparring partner.

Thankfully, Jarlath didn't seem put out. In fact, he looked almost entertained by Tearlach's show of prowess.

That's what this is, right? Esme asked herself.

Jarlath retrieved her discarded wooden sword, then bowed. When he straightened, he leaned in close to whisper good night before leaving Esme alone with Tearlach.

Quinlan and Cahir were suddenly—suspiciously—absent as well.

Esme willed herself to channel her irritation into whatever sort of fight Tearlach sought.

She adopted a casual stance like his, then mirrored Tearlach's steps, crossing left over right as they circled one another. When he tossed his blade between his hands, Esme matched the movement as if it were the most natural thing.

Only it shouldn't have felt that way. They'd never sparred before. Not with anything tangible anyway.

His steps changed direction. Esme matched them. It was like a dance—the purpose of which she still couldn't decipher.

Was he making some kind of point? Certainly he was, but for whom? Jarlath had left. Her guards were nowhere to be seen. If his goal was simply to run off his brother, then why were they facing off against one another?

Tearlach cocked his head to the side, and Esme narrowed her eyes.

Fine, she conceded, then swung her blade. The edge grazed the front of Tearlach's shirt, leaving a slit across his chest.

"Why—" she stammered as he circled her like nothing had happened.

When she attacked again, Tearlach parried, but didn't riposte.

"What are we doing?" Esme demanded.

"Sparring."

"No, we're not. *I'm* sparring. You're—"

Tearlach advanced.

Esme blocked the attack.

"Why now?" she asked.

"Why what?"

"I thought Killian was better with a sword." She tossed the ridiculous claim back at him as their blades clashed. Even back in Altan, she'd known that no one could match Tearlach's skill. It was one of the reasons Sully had selected him for the Lifeblood Oath.

"He is," Tearlach lied effortlessly. "But you're stuck with me."

Esme couldn't help but hear the underlying meaning in the words. There wasn't a day when guilt didn't claw at her heart. Tearlach might have willingly pledged himself to her after they'd defeated Orianna, but she'd accepted. She'd taken away his freedom, the life he might have had.

"Is that so?" She forced levity into her voice.

"There's no getting rid of me," he promised, angling to strike a blow to her shin plate.

Esme jumped quickly to avoid the blade, even as her thoughts strayed to her mother's journal and the page where Erena had penned instructions for creating a Lifeblood Oath. Esme hadn't looked at that particular page since she'd first uncovered the journal. Couldn't bring herself to.

Still, she wondered...

What would they be to one another if they were no longer bound together?

Silence closed in around them as they continued to methodically mirror one another's movements.

It was odd, Esme thought, without Tearlach's usual direction or critique. For a moment, it felt like they were on equal footing. Not a student and her teacher. Not a queen and her guard.

Her frustration melted. All she wanted was to stay locked in that strange dance forever.

But dawn was hovering just below the horizon, and her arms were beginning to tremble with fatigue.

"Fight for it," Tearlach urged.

Esme's steps faltered. She recovered clumsily, her eyes finding his as she blocked the next attack.

"Fight for it. Fight for what you want." Ferocity bled into his words, and Esme could have sworn she saw a flicker of desperation in his eyes.

Her breathing sped up. She no longer knew if she was mimicking his movements or the other way around.

Instead of focusing on the muscles in his arms as they contracted, or trying to gauge how much weight he shifted onto his right foot or left, she watched the way his chest expanded with each breath, watched the pulse pounding at the side of the throat. She searched for fractures in his armor. For the smallest flare of emotion.

"Is this all you've got?" Tearlach taunted.

Esme's eyes snapped to his. The words might have been about her handling of the blade, but her mind couldn't help hearing the other implication—that *she* was the one standing in the way of them being together.

"Are you just going to—"

She lunged.

The point of her sword ricocheted off the broadside of his blade. It was an easy maneuver to block, but the momentum allowed her to swing her back leg forward. And what appeared to be nothing more than a pivot brought her close enough to hook the heel of her boot behind his knee.

It was a poor excuse for a feint, and one Tearlach would certainly see coming.

Yet, he stumbled.

And dragged her down with him.

Feeling Tearlach's breath against her neck, Esme suppressed a shiver. She wrested the blade from his grip, then pinned his shoulder with her elbow before daring to look down at him.

Tearlach stared back for a breath. Two.

Then he curled his leg around the backs of her thighs. Esme was on her back a fraction of a second later, with Tearlach looking down at her.

He held her wrists above her head, but his grip wasn't tight. She could have easily pulled free. Could have pulled her knee up and twisted out of the hold.

But the fight drained out of her, soaking into the packed earth like spilled wine.

"Fight back," he said softly. "Fight for what you want, Esme."

"It's not a fair fight. You don't fight for what you want," she accused in an equally hushed tone, though the words felt like daggers as they left her lips.

Tearlach blinked. His jaw slackened.

Esme felt moisture gathering along her lashes. A single tear seared a path down her temple, and the heat of embarrassment burned in her throat.

She couldn't be there. Couldn't bear to have him looking at her... like that.

She needed to be *anywhere else* but near him.

"Get off me."

"Make me."

"Get off me. Now," she growled.

The weight of his hands bracketing her wrists vanished instantly.

Esme shoved at him, pushing him away easily.

Tearlach didn't get up as she clambered to her feet.

"Esme," he pleaded quietly.

"Don't follow me," she warned.

Cold rain pelted her skin as Quinlan and Cahir emerged from the barracks to escort her back.

And as much as she tried to rein in her emotions on the long walk back to the palace, the rain refused to let up.

Chapter Twenty-Six

ESME WAS STARING out at the songbirds that'd gathered along the railing like they might impart wisdom as to how she could realign everything that seemed askew in her life when her skin prickled with awareness, alerting her that she was no longer alone.

"About last night..." Tearlach began as he came to stand behind her.

Esme closed her eyes, like it might ward off the shiver his deep voice always seemed to evoke.

"I'm truly sorry." His inhale was slow and deliberate, and Esme turned to face him. Tearlach's eyes locked with hers. "It was wrong of me to..." He swallowed roughly. "I shouldn't have—"

A knock at the door fractured their tenuous connection. And without waiting for a response, Cadwyn and Hazel walked into the room with clear purpose.

"Your Majesty, we—" Cadwyn stopped. "Apologies. Are we...interrupting?"

"I'm truly sorry," Tearlach repeated softly before averting his gaze and slipping past them.

Hazel aimed a vexed look toward him, but Tearlach didn't offer so much as a greeting to either of them. Or a farewell to Esme.

Cadwyn pressed her lips together and lowered her brow in concern.

But Esme was thoroughly uninterested in hearing whatever platitude she might offer, so she addressed Hazel instead. "I thought you'd left."

"Delayed."

"We just received word from the priestesses," Cadwyn informed her.

"A letter?" Esme glanced between them, her heart beating wildly in an instant. "Where is it? What did they say?"

"Not a letter. They're here."

"They're *here?*" Her voice rose. Surely she'd misheard.

"At the Arlais temple."

"We have to—" She ran to the door, only to spin back around. But Cadwyn had already retrieved one of her cloaks. Esme tossed it over her shoulders and pulled the hood into place as they made their way down the corridor toward the stairwell. "Tell Mairtín to—"

"I've already told him to prepare rooms in the east wing."

"Good. That's good. Wait." Esme halted halfway down the stairs. "There are unoccupied rooms in the east wing?" Hadn't it been overrun by noblemen?

"Keelin sent them away," Hazel said, nudging her to keep moving. She did, but as soon as they reached the main floor, Esme shot her an inquiring look.

"What?" Hazel demanded. "Fine. I might have...*encouraged* it."

"Encouraged their departure? How?" Esme cocked her head, wondering why she hadn't enlisted her new lady-in-waiting's talents sooner.

Hazel merely shrugged. "Does it matter?"

"I…suppose not," Esme admitted, then glanced around the main floor, finding it surprisingly empty. She pulled back her hood as there was no longer reason to hide. No need to sneak out through the kitchens either.

But her relief was joined by an unsettling thought. If all the noblemen were gone, had Jarlath been shooed away as well? She knew he hadn't been summoned for the same purpose as the others, but Keelin might not have made an exception for him. Had he left without saying goodbye?

Her throat tightened, wondering if their blossoming friendship had only been that to her.

Outside, the three of them hurried into a waiting carriage. Cadwyn reached over to pull the door shut, but a large hand caught it, and Tearlach climbed in.

He claimed the seat beside Esme, and for several unbearably long seconds, the four of them sat in stilted silence.

When the carriage lurched forward, Esme forced herself to ask why Sully hadn't come along.

"He's up top," Tearlach explained before the weighty silence settled around them again.

Cadwyn pulled out a small book and focused her attention on the page she opened to so intently Esme was almost convinced that it contained all the secrets of their world. Hazel, however, glared at Tearlach. Not until they left the city behind did she seem to give up and close her eyes, resting her head against the upholstered panel.

Esme chose to stare out the small window and pretend she was alone in the carriage. But try as she might, she could still sense the man sitting beside her. Could feel his heat and the press of his thigh against hers.

What happened last night? she asked when she could no longer bear the tension crackling between them.

Seconds ticked by, marked only by the jostling of the carriage and the quickening of her pulse.

I'm sorry, Tearlach offered once again. *I wasn't thinking.*

Wasn't thinking? She didn't believe that one bit. There was little—if *anything*—Tearlach did without thinking it through.

Then why... she started. *Is it—Was it Jarlath? You didn't want me spending time with him, is that it?*

It wasn't an issue anymore, she supposed, given his unannounced departure.

When Tearlach didn't answer, Esme strained her neck fighting not to look over at him. It was bad enough they weren't alone for that particular—Could she even *call* it a conversation?—she didn't want to draw attention to the invisible connection they had.

He doesn't possess the same antipathy as you do for him, she stressed, knowing full well that whatever she said about his brother wouldn't matter.

Still, she tried. *You should have spoken to him.*

When he again didn't respond, Esme followed Hazel's example and closed her eyes, hoping the rocking of the carriage would lull her into a false sense of peacefulness.

———

Roderick offered Esme a hand once they pulled to a stop. Evidently, he'd delayed his departure as well.

"Thank you," she murmured distractedly, already taking in the temple.

The women of the Triskele had already met Hazel and Myles. And they'd...well, they'd *encountered* Tearlach.

Esme surveyed her guards. She couldn't very well bring them all inside.

"I'll wait here," Cadwyn offered as Tearlach instructed four of the guards to scout the perimeter, then motioned for Roderick, Hazel, and Myles to follow him inside.

"No." Esme held up a hand. "Only Hazel and Myles."

Tearlach inhaled deeply, holding her stare. *What are you doing? This isn't—*

Now you're talking to me? For a moment there, I thought our delightful little connection had been severed.

His eyes hardened, but he said nothing more.

"Sully?" she asked once the guards who'd scouted had returned. "Is the area secure?"

"It is, my dear."

"Good, then." Esme didn't spare another glance at Tearlach before she marched toward the steps of the temple.

She came to a stop as soon as she entered the rotunda, unable to hide her shock at seeing every member of the Triskele waiting for her. Part of her hadn't truly believed that any of them would actually be there.

But there they were. All of them.

And it was already a far better reception than the last time they'd met. Esme cast a knowing look to Myles. Surely he was thinking the same.

"And where is your personal guard?" Moira inquired.

"Unless you decide to hold a blade to my guide's throat again, I don't see the need."

"Yet your *attendant* is once again present." The woman clearly knew Hazel's role wasn't merely that.

"Lady-in-waiting," Hazel corrected easily. It was the first time Esme had heard her say it without a hint of reluctance.

"Can I assume you've read my letter?" Esme turned the questioning on Moira.

"You may."

"And you all," Esme paused as she looked to each of the women, "understand that the Order was created under the premise of—"

"We do," Moira said, stopping her.

Esme nodded slowly. "To be clear, you—"

"We have reasons of our own to believe that your claims are accurate, Your Majesty."

"I see," Esme replied, though she didn't really. What else did they know?

Unfortunately, none seemed inclined to elaborate, and her attempt to inquire further was thwarted as Moira continued.

"We've come to assist in restoring the damaged channels."

"Damaged?" Hazel responded harshly. Esme cut her a look. One misstep and they'd lose their greatest resource.

"We may not agree with every one of your assertions, but we will help nonetheless."

The urge to explain precisely why her assertions were more than mere speculation was strong—Esme had intentionally omitted the means by which she'd acquired the truth about how the Order had come to be in her letter. But their offer of assistance was more than she'd expected, so she bit her tongue.

Learning that one's beliefs were based on lies wasn't easily accepted. After witnessing Lord Luxovious's memories, she'd felt unmoored for days. Still did. She could hardly presume to understand how difficult it was for the women who stood before her, who'd devoted their lives to serving baseless beliefs.

Myles caught her attention and flicked his left eyebrow, indicating that he'd detected no falsehoods in Moira's statement.

Very well, then. She supposed it didn't matter overmuch, so long as they were willing to help.

"Have you secured the items you need?" Ceridwen asked.

"Not as of yet."

Esme didn't ask whether they'd brought Sister Firinne's vestments. Hazel hadn't given any indication that she'd sensed the dark magic. They'd likely keep them hidden until the other missing articles were found. Even with their willingness to assist, Esme had no doubt they'd hold tight to any advantage they had.

"What is your plan, then, Majesty?" Moira's voice had an edge of impatience to it.

Hazel answered before Esme could, claiming that parties had already been dispatched to search the remaining temples. It wasn't precisely true, though it would be in a matter of days.

"I can assure you there's nothing more to be found at the Iola Temple," Moira told them. "And, I'm afraid it's not likely anything will be found at the others," she added in a softer tone.

Esme nodded. She worried the same. But Hazel and Roderick would still go. They needed to be absolutely certain.

And if nothing was found at the temples, then—

No. She'd worry over that later.

"When they are found"—Catriona spoke up, and Esme appreciated that she hadn't said *if*—"how is it that the magic within the silver pieces will be released?"

"They'll need to be destroyed." She didn't know how else to phrase it. Athdara had been vague, but Esme couldn't fathom a method that managed to release only the raw magic, while somehow keeping the dark magic contained within the orbs. They'd *need* to be destroyed. It was the safest way to ensure that the dark magic didn't fall into the wrong hands. In addition, she strongly suspected that the manner in which the orbs needed to be destroyed would have to mirror their creation—by someone who could wield all of the elements. Someone like her.

But her newly formed partnership with the unordained priestesses would surely unravel if they learned that her magic might, with time, become as powerful as Orianna's.

"And how, exactly, is that to be done?" Keva pressed.

"I...I'm not really sure," Esme admitted, hoping her honesty might work in her favor.

The women passed knowing looks between themselves before Moira gave Vevila a subtle nod. The woman retreated, disappearing behind one of the massive pillars at the far side of the rotunda, then returned carrying a medium-sized chest made of what appeared to be the same wood Tearlach had used to contain the poisonous effects of his iron weapons. *Elder wood.*

Her eyes darted to Hazel, who seemed equally taken aback. She hadn't sensed anything, then. Were the adornments inside? Could elder wood conceal magic as well? Even dark magic?

"Our sacred vestments, Your Majesty." Moira lifted the lid. Catriona stepped forward and reached inside, producing a white robe.

Esme watched Hazel out of the corner of her eye for any sort of reaction. Yet even as the heavy garment was carefully unfolded, revealing intricate, knotted whorls of silver thread, Hazel showed no signs that she'd sensed anything amiss.

But by the time all the items had been removed from the chest, Hazel had gone tense. Her gaze wasn't fixed on any one item in particular. It seemed unfocused, like she was no longer seeing what was before her, only sensing the magic, trying to detect from where it was originating.

Esme looked at each of the articles, like she might be able to assist in some way. There was a midnight blue silk headscarf with small, seed-sized gems sewn along its edges, a silver circlet with a strikingly reflective clear crystal, an amulet with a black, nearly opaque gemstone nestled in the center, a silver ring with a sapphire so blue she wondered at its origins, and a silver wrist cuff, adorned with an opalescent crystal, surrounded by intricate etchings.

Four rather large gemstones, Esme noted. But she suspected they were only meant to look valuable, important.

The sacred book that had been mentioned at their first meeting wasn't among the articles, though Esme was fairly certain that the text contained nothing more than the propaganda she'd read in one of Beglan's ancient tomes.

"May I?" She inclined her head, seeking permission to inspect each of the items more closely.

Moira acquiesced with a dip of her chin.

Hazel stepped forward too, approaching Vevila first, who held the amulet. Her breathing had become unsteady, but even as she ran her finger along the silver setting, it didn't appear as though she'd detected the source of the dark magic.

Esme wondered what it felt like. Even the small amount she knew Hazel must be sensing was undoubtedly pulling her mind back to the battlefields.

Wanting to give her space, Esme moved to inspect the cuff, then the circlet. The adornments looked similar enough to the ones she'd seen in Lord Luxovious's memories, but she knew the man wouldn't have hidden powerful objects in such obvious places.

Esme reached for the white robe Catriona was holding next. The silk was smooth and cool beneath her fingertips, but the stitching was rough. Her nail caught on the jagged silver beading along the hem and she sucked in a breath.

A pulse jumped in her finger. It arced across her palm, then fluttered up her arm.

When the sensation faded, she slowly lifted her gaze to Catriona.

The woman stared back with something akin to knowing in her pale blue eyes.

Chapter Twenty-Seven

DESPITE ASSURANCES OF safety and secrecy from Sully, Tearlach, and every one of her guards, the priestesses declined Esme's offer of accommodations at the palace.

"At least allow me to provide protection during your stay."

"Not necessary," Moira maintained.

"Very well. And if I should have need to speak with you?"

Moira lifted her chin. "I'm sure *someone* can find us."

Esme merely bowed her head and, after expressing her gratitude once again for allowing her to take possession of Sister Firinne's sacred articles, retreated to the carriage.

Tearlach's nearness on the bench beside her for once didn't overwhelm her senses. Because there was a single, incessant thought consuming all of Esme's awareness. And her hands prickled with a sensation she wanted to forget. She could still feel the catch of the silver beading, like it had pierced her skin and embedded something inside her that she couldn't seem to shake.

When the rhythm of her heart finally returned to a normal canter, she noticed a new, subtle thrumming buried beneath. Like a second heartbeat.

And all she could think was how much she wanted to touch the silver again.

It's not me. It's him. His memories.

He craves it, not me.

Then again, maybe it was only Alastar's magic that called to her. He'd been able to wield each of the elements, just as she could. Perhaps it was no different than how raw magic recognized her as a match, wanting to flow through her.

That was all it was. She'd felt a connection to Alastar's magic.

It was a reasonable conclusion, one that Esme repeated to herself over and over while wringing her hands, trying to scrub the imprint from her skin.

––––––––––––

Esme stirred, but she ignored whatever had woken her and nestled deeper under the covers.

The faint scent of scorched wood was only in her mind. The remnants of a dream, she told herself.

Still, she opened her eyes a slit. The familiar glow in her room flickered. Like flames.

Not the Loinnir Lights, then.

She wasn't alone.

Esme tightened the muscles around her ribs, like it might help control the breath she took in. It still came out shaky as she sat up and faced Lord Luxovious.

He stood closer than he had previously, only an arm's length from the foot of her bed.

With a slow tilt of his head, he seemed to consider her.

"Have you told them all your secrets? All of *my* secrets?"

He knew. Of course he knew. The question was, did he have a way of communicating with the unordained priestesses, or did he know because of his connection to her?

"They're aware that the Order was...fabricated," she said carefully.

He chuckled. "And did you tell them why?" There was a disturbingly cheerful note to his query.

Why? *She* didn't even understand the why of it. Power? Control? Esme wasn't sure she wanted to know what his intentions had been. After the glimpses she'd witnessed, she wanted to know as little as possible about the workings of Lord Luxovious's mind.

The only thing she cared about was learning how to undo everything he'd done to Tremaene.

"That I created a means by which to save a dying kingdom? That I sacrificed myself"—he gestured to the cloak that covered what Esme knew was a gnarled, twisted figure—"for the good of all Faekind?"

Esme could only stare at him. Was he really trying to convince her that—

"Worthy as your kind may be of the magic that's been bestowed upon them, this world cannot be maintained properly without strict discipline and regulation."

Your kind? He spoke of Fae as though he were something...different. She supposed he was. But there seemed to be more to it, something buried beneath the words that hinted at a larger picture she couldn't quite make out.

"Without me, without the necessary steps I took to ensure a sustainable future, your kingdom would have perished."

Esme absently rubbed her hands together, trying to dissect his words.

He noticed the movement and hummed, looking her over with a more scrutinizing eye. Like he could see the residue of the dark magic coating her skin like oil.

Could he sense it? See it surrounding her like a glowing, undulating aura?

"It is not something to fear," he told her in a soothing tone. "So-called *dark magic* isn't nefarious. It is only different. More complex. Common magic has limitations. It can create or manipulate the elements. *Great magic*, however, reconstructs, reshapes. Under the right master, that is."

He looked at Esme's hands again, lying still and limp on her lap.

"Not all have the prowess to harness great magic." He lifted his chin as if seeing her with a newfound respect. "Not all are worthy."

The words had barely met her ears before he vanished.

Esme scrambled to the edge of the bed. The black flames that had ringed the hem of his cloak lingered for a moment—a hint of purple flickering deep inside them.

The desire to reach out and touch them was nearly overpowering. Would the flames burn her skin? Would the strange fire feel the same as the silver beading on the robe?

She held herself back, gripping handfuls of the bedclothes as she watched the flames die out.

Chapter Twenty-Eight

"ALPINA," ESME CALLED out, surprised to see her at the palace.

The woman turned her head slightly to give Esme a sidelong glance. "Your Majesty?"

"I'm sorry, it's just..." Esme chuckled. "Cora's told me all about you, and shared a few likenesses as well. I feel as though we've already met."

"She's always forgetting what I look like," Alpina jested with a lilt one didn't often hear.

"Perhaps it's because I've seen you take on more personas than a play actor," Cora replied as she came to join them, reminding Esme that Alpina was not only a shapeshifter capable of taking other Fae forms, but was also rather talented at stepping into various roles.

Cora welcomed her wife with a kiss.

"What can I say?" Alpina gazed down at her adoringly. "I'm very good at what I do."

"That you are," Cora practically purred, causing Esme to blush. "And now, if you don't mind, Your Majesty, I think I'll steal her away for a bit."

"Of course. I'm afraid I'm needed in the council chamber anyway." She nearly groaned at the reminder.

Alpina shared a look with Cora before stepping away from her to take Esme's hand.

For a split second, she was delighted at the woman's informality, until a small folded note was pressed into her palm.

"A pleasure, Your Majesty. I hope we'll have time to visit more when time allows."

"My hope as well," Esme agreed, closing her fingers around the folded scrap of paper as she watched Cora steer Alpina away.

Before Harlow and Cahir could escort her to the council chamber, Esme ducked back into the stairwell to read the note.

Eight constructed.

Twenty more commissioned.

Materials will be acquired through any means necessary.

Alpina's latest role was easy enough to surmise. She'd managed to gain access to Lord Torin's enterprise. Esme couldn't imagine how trying the undertaking must have been, what with how he'd discarded and maligned Cora so. It made Esme even more grateful for the information Alpina had been able to obtain.

As she feared, Lord Torin wouldn't await her approval on lumber rights. And she already knew he wasn't inclined to support any levelheaded, lasting solutions. If Esme didn't thwart his pursuit, and soon, he'd seize Periwen and devastate their resources the moment his ships were ready.

———————

Yet another nobleman was discussed as if Esme weren't even present in the meeting. They expected her to choose a person she barely knew to share the responsibility of ruling the entire kingdom. *And* share her bed. The latter of which seemed inconsequential to her councilors.

I'm not going to marry, Esme reminded herself, even as she thought through the implication that a marriage—especially a political one— needn't have anything to do with love. Which she supposed was true. Love wasn't necessary. *Trusting* someone was. It was perhaps the most crucial piece of the partnership her councilors were campaigning for. But how did they expect her to trust someone she'd shared a single dance with?

It was preposterous.

Everything would be so much easier if she could simply marry the person she already trusted most in the world. Who also happened to be the person she loved.

Since that wasn't bound to happen, she'd strive to build stronger relationships with her advisors. Lord Lennox had proven himself reliable. He'd repeatedly put the good of the kingdom above personal interests. Or so she'd assumed.

Lady Pallya seemed committed to the needs of her territory most, which was reasonable. But Esme wondered if that sense of purpose and protectiveness extended to the kingdom at large.

Keelin, Gwen, and Aindreas had all impressed upon her the devotion they had to their roles, and seemed impartial in their assessments and recommendations.

Esme didn't bother giving further consideration to Lord Torin, Lady Audris, or Pearce's allegiances. If they'd any intention of proving their loyalty to her or Tremaene, they'd yet to do so.

She glanced over at Sully, thankful that one of the people she trusted served as her Minister of Defense. How different might it be if she had an entire council of advisors she could hold in such high regard? People she trusted to put the good of the kingdom above all else? People she trusted to tell her the truth?

Lord Torin shot her a glare that said he knew she wasn't paying attention.

Someone who respects my position, Esme added to her mental list with a sigh. If only her guards could be—

"Are we boring you, Your Majesty?" Lord Torin's voice was hard, and Esme wondered how much he'd censored himself.

If her lack of interest in the discussion hadn't been evident enough by her silence, her exasperated sigh had surely clued them in.

Esme blinked slowly and turned her attention to Lord Torin as if it cost her a great deal of effort.

"Very much," she told him with a curt nod. "Perhaps we should move on."

"Perhaps we should." He cocked his head a fraction of an inch. Just enough for Esme to dread what he would say next. "What progress has been made by the women you *believe* have the ability to summon magic as our priestesses once did?"

It was a near thing, but Esme managed to keep her expression disinterested, even as her entire body went taut. Did Torin know they were nearby, perhaps even in the city? She should have insisted they take some of her guards for protection.

"Any at all?" he prompted when Esme didn't immediately respond. "As we suspected..." He shook his head in the way a disappointed tutor might.

"As a matter of fact, they've been exceedingly helpful thus far. Our goals are one and the same, after all," she reminded Torin.

"Hmm." He seemed to consider her claim, though his expression was more of a sneer. "How long will their *cooperation* last, I wonder? Perhaps it's time for us to—"

"Progress has already been made," Esme asserted. If he mentioned anything about his plans toward Periwen, she feared others might find merit in the conquest.

"Is that so?" He leaned back in his chair.

"While I don't expect *everyone* to fully grasp the physical and mental toll an undertaking of this magnitude entails, or the complexity and preparation the sacred summoning ritual requires, I have absolute confidence in the abilities of these women to restore our land. I will also remind you"—Esme glanced around the table, letting her warning look fall last on Torin—"that while these methods may not be the most expedient, we mustn't be hasty by searching for short-term fixes. I realize that the hardships plaguing much of Tremaene will endure a while longer, but it's imperative that the solutions we implement be sustainable. Foolish, shortsighted alternatives tend to have far more consequences than benefits."

For a moment, it seemed no one would refute *or agree* with her. Then Lady Pallya, Lord Lennox, Sully, and Aindreas nodded their agreement. Gwen and Keelin seemed to accept Esme's plea, though it was clear they weren't altogether convinced.

Torin's disdain, as expected, was nearly palpable as he shared a look with Lady Audris.

Esme took a deep breath, hoping that whatever he had up his sleeve could quickly be countervailed.

"What idealism you have, Your Majesty," Lady Audris commented without an ounce of sincerity. "But might we turn our attention to something that's long overdue? You've yet to name a lord or lady of the Tamslo Mountains territory. Surely, it's slipped your mind—what with all these excursions you keep taking—but we must have…"

Esme wished she could plug her ears with wool as Lady Audris yammered on. The not-so-subtle digs were no doubt her own words, but the intention reeked of Lord Torin. He wanted—*needed*—access to the redwoods for the pitch they would provide if he was to continue construction of his ships. Esme hadn't granted his request, but if the lordship went to someone under his thumb, he could circumvent her authority.

As each of her councilors made cases for noblemen Esme had no care for knowing, she realized she already had the perfect person for the job.

"Actually..." She rose from her seat to address the room. "I've selected a new lord for the Tamslo Mountains."

The silence that followed lasted a mere second before Lord Torin, Lady Audris, and Pearce erupted with anger.

Gwen and Keelin seemed surprised at the announcement, yet not unwelcoming toward it. Winifred, who'd studiously maintained her usual impartial demeanor throughout the entire meeting, allowed an impressed expression to momentarily break through her facade.

Esme gave a hint of a smile as she received similar looks from her remaining councilors. Even better, when objections were voiced, they defended their queen's right on the matter.

"You *cannot* do this," Lady Audris exclaimed, cutting through the noise.

Esme clenched her teeth. Oh, how she wanted to leave them to their bickering. But she remained where she stood, offering only a challenging stare to Lady Audris.

"This is unacceptable!" Pearce shouted from across the table. Reason, it seemed, would not get through to him either.

Easy. Tearlach's calm warning rumbled through her.

Esme ignored how that single word felt like a soothing balm as she surreptitiously glanced around until she noticed that vines were spiraling down the chains of the chandelier, inching ever closer to the flickering flames.

That...wasn't ideal, she contended, reining in the magic that had slipped her grasp.

"We cannot abide by this." Lord Torin stood, silencing the room with a threatening tone he seemed all too comfortable using. He looked to each of the other councilors, disregarding Esme's authority completely. "*This* is not how things are done."

"*Torin*," Lord Lennox cautioned, rising from his seat as well. Even Sully, who always kept his composure when tensions were high, tightened his grip on the arms of his chair.

"You can't *possibly* think she's even slightly capable of managing this kingdom," Lord Torin snapped at Lord Lennox. "She's just as inept and weak willed as Rion was."

There was a collective intake of breath as the late king's name echoed through the council chamber.

Chapter Twenty-Nine

TEARLACH WAS AT Esme's side in an instant, angling himself between her and Torin.

Sully stood from his seat slowly, and she could tell from the set of his jaw that he was prepared to defend her and her father alike.

"*She* is Your Majesty," Esme spoke before Sully could tell Torin exactly what he could do with his insults. "And you will do well to refer to my father with the same respect." She glared at him in a way she hoped projected the true meaning of her words—that his position on the council was not guaranteed.

Tell Regan to fetch Myles, Esme told Tearlach.

Tearlach tore his unyielding stare away from his father and directed it down at her. *What?* he demanded.

The page outside, tell him to bring Myles here. Now, Tearlach, she ordered.

He shifted a quick glance at the double doors across the room, as if the distance were a great expanse.

"If you would," Esme said aloud with a lift of her chin and a wave of her wrist, so the others would perceive it as an anticipated request.

That Tearlach couldn't very well deny her order in front of her council also helped maintain what little respect her title still granted her.

"Right away." With a stiff nod, Tearlach stepped around her.

Every person in the room watched him with blatant curiosity as he strode over to the doors.

"And now"—Esme set her shoulders back and exhaled deeply enough to expel some of the tightness in her muscles—"if the members of this council can refrain from any outbursts, I'll allow this session to continue. If not, I've no doubt Captain Sullivan will happily see you out."

Sully's answering grunt as he reclaimed his seat spoke to his lingering fury.

Torin was lucky he hadn't spoken ill of Esme's mother instead, or there was a strong chance he'd no longer be standing.

When Tearlach sauntered back to his station behind her, it did little to mitigate the tension that had the room practically vibrating. He said nothing to Esme and, more importantly, had returned alone.

Where's Myles?

Before Tearlach could respond, Regan eased open one of the doors an inch, just wide enough to catch Esme's eye. The fraction of his face that she could see appeared...uncertain.

Myles was probably waiting outside the chamber. He wasn't the type to stride into a room and claim everyone's attention. Which...Esme probably should have considered.

Her objective was more of an idea—a musing—than a carefully thought-out plan. But there wasn't time to second-guess herself.

After gripping Tearlach's arm firmly enough to warn him that he stay put, she hastened toward the door, ignoring the murmurs and questioning looks that followed her out of the chamber.

"Myles." The slight exclamation in her voice as the doors shut behind her did nothing to soothe the panicked look on his face. "I've a job for you."

He raised his eyebrows, like he too was recalling the late-night dinner they'd shared down in the kitchens, and was suddenly regretting what he'd confessed about wanting to contribute somehow.

Still, he replied, "Anything, Your Majesty."

"Lord of the Tamslo Mountains."

Myles stared at her like she'd misspoke. When she didn't say anything more, he looked over at the footmen, then to Regan, like the page might offer some sort of explanation.

"Apologies, Your Majesty, but I don't follow."

"Esme," she corrected. "I want to name you Lord of the Tamslo Mountains."

"But, I'm not—I don't...I'm not of noble lineage."

"All the better." Esme smiled.

Myles continued to give her a bewildered look.

"Will you accept?"

"Of course, I...would..." He looked around the antechamber.

"Myles." She took his hands in hers, drawing his focus back to her. "I need someone I can trust. Someone who will put the needs of his people above his own self-interests. And I believe that person is you."

"But...Cahir—"

"Can go with you, whenever you need to be there. And if he decides that his attentions should be there instead, I'll understand. You're his priority, and I've no intention of challenging that."

When he still didn't seem convinced, Esme sighed. "Myles? Do you want this? Do you want to represent the interests of the people in the mountains—*your* people? To make sure their voices are heard? To make sure they're taken care of?"

"I do," he admitted, though his voice was uncertain. Then, finally, his brow unfurrowed. "I...accept."

"Excellent." Esme smiled wide, feeling like she'd finally gotten something right.

Releasing his hands, she signaled for the footmen to open the doors. "If you would."

When Myles retreated a step, Esme grabbed the sleeve of his shirt. "Nope. We're doing this now."

"But I..." He looked down at his plain clothes.

"Myles." She waited for him to meet her gaze, wanting him to see the confidence she had in him, the certainty she felt in her decision. "You're the right person for this. That's all that matters."

He took a ragged breath, ran a hand through his unruly auburn hair, then pulled himself up to his full height and nodded.

***

A letter from Lady Pallya sat atop a fresh stack of requests on Esme's desk. It was an invitation to dine with the lady and her wife. Evidently, Lady Pallya had been impressed with Esme's actions earlier that day. She even went so far as to write that Esme had the acumen of a true leader.

Leader. She stared at the word, written in such a neat hand that it couldn't possibly have been a hollow compliment. She hadn't realized how much she needed to hear that. Or...see it, rather.

Esme was still thinking on it later that night when she opened to a blank page in her notebook and began a letter of her own.

Dear Mama, she wrote, the scratch of the nib against the rough paper harsh as her pen strokes tried to keep up with her thoughts.

Chapter Thirty

DINING WITH LADY Pallya and her wife turned out to be surprisingly pleasant, due mostly to Shawndrell's infectious laughter and the genuine enthusiasm she expressed while telling even the most mundane stories.

Esme could see why Lady Pallya had been drawn to her. Which was also how Esme found herself sparring with Shawndrell later on, in the early morning hours.

"Another splendid match, Your Majesty," Shawndrell exclaimed as Esme fought to catch her breath.

"Splendid for you, perhaps," she panted. "I hardly—"

"Pish! You put up a good fight. And we had fun, didn't we?"

Esme chuckled. "Yes, we did. It was quite enjoyable."

"That's all that matters. Now, let's see what the kitchen has ready at this hour." Shawndrell turned and strode off like she knew Esme would follow.

With the sparring over, there was nothing left to distract Esme from the tingling sensation in her fingertips. A sensation that didn't feel like her own magic. She tried to convince herself that it was simply the remnants of Shawndrell's air magic that had swept along her skin during the match.

Esme scrubbed her hands against her pants and refused to think about the other, far more likely origins of the strange sensations.

When the sun began to rise, and the two of them parted ways, Esme returned to her room and found her troublesome thoughts there waiting for her. But rather than ruminate about dark magic, or allow herself to speculate what it might indicate that she could *still* feel it beneath her skin, she decided to practice separating the elements of her storm magic.

Because Athdara had insinuated that her magic mirrored Alastar's, the young man Lord Luxovious had used to draw up the raw magic and funnel it into each of the orbs, Esme worried that the task of reversing what Alastar had done might fall to her. It hadn't been clear from Lord Luxovious's memories whether Alastar had used his combined magic or only one element for each of the orbs. And given Athdara's warning about keeping the elements separate, Esme decided it was best to be prepared.

But while Alastar might have been well-versed in wielding each aspect of his magic independently, Esme was not. And so, she would practice.

Hours later, she was still attempting to isolate the water from her storm magic. She'd been careful to keep the cloud compact, hovering it just above the empty bath, reasoning that by using only a little of her magic, there'd be less risk of damage. Though really, Esme was afraid of what might happen if she let too much of her magic flow through her without restraint.

She shook out her hands as her concentration on the cloud slipped. It dissolved into a fine blanket of mist that clung to her skin.

Maybe it was all in her head. Maybe she hadn't felt anything more than the raw magic when she'd touched the silver beads on the ceremonial robe. The orbs had contained a fair amount of elemental magic, not just dark magic. And they'd been split into hundreds of tiny slivers, then encased in silver. Had she really felt the smallest traces of dark magic beneath all that?

Yes.

What would it feel like when they tracked down the remaining pieces? Would she be able to stomach it? Resist the dark magic's pull?

Esme blinked her focus back into the bathing chamber, finding that a new storm cloud had gathered, darkening with the direction of her thoughts. She narrowed her eyes and stretched the churning mass as she pulled some of the water from it. But her mind wandered back to the adornments the priestesses had entrusted her with—wrapped in wool and locked in the elder-wood chest down in the dungeons.

Knowing they were there in the palace, only a few floors away, made her feel uneasy.

You can't feel them, she told herself. *It's only your imagination.*

Still, her pulse sped up and she hurried out of the bathing chamber, hearing the sound of water crashing into the empty basin as she released her hold on the magic.

Yanking open her bedside table, she pulled out her mother's journal and flipped to the second half of the book. The titles of each spell were scribed in the Old Language, without any sort of translation or indication as to their purpose. Even if she asked Beglan, he likely wouldn't know the entirety of any one phrase.

It was foolish. A waste of time. Esme knew that.

Nevertheless, she scoured each set of instructions and the seemingly unrelated combinations of herbs, elements, and lunar cycles, trying to guess at each spell's objective. Hoping there'd be something that might remove the residue of the dark magic she'd encountered.

A spell to make her forget how it made her feel.

Or a spell to protect her from it, make her immune to its draw. Its power.

Her search was fruitless, as she suspected it would be. There was only one spell she knew the purpose of, and it wouldn't help with dark magic.

She gently closed the book and returned it to its keeping place.

Her stomach rumbled with hunger, reminding her just how long she'd been toying with her magic. After dressing for an early dinner, she stepped out into the corridor and stumbled to a stop.

Standing there, with his fist raised to knock on her door was someone she'd thought she wouldn't see again. At least not for some time.

"Jarlath. You're still here."

"That I am," he said with a crooked smile.

Chapter Thirty-One

"STOP THE KNOCKING," Esme groaned, turning her face into the pillow. Her head felt like it weighed a thousand pounds.

The night before had been fun, but she was certainly paying the price that morning. She and Jarlath had talked into the evening and through the night. So late that the Loinnir Lights had begun to fade when he'd insisted she retire to her bed.

Yes, there'd been wine. And Esme had been glad to be free of her endless responsibilities and tormenting thoughts for just a little while that she'd likely imbibed too much, laughed too loud, and smiled so wide her cheeks hurt. It'd felt good to let go for just one night.

Tearlach's scowl greeted her when she finally dragged herself out of bed and opened one of the doors a crack. The sight was such a stark contrast to the man who'd come to see her the evening before.

Jarlath always seemed so open. It wasn't that he couldn't hide his emotions or inner thoughts. It was more that he didn't try to. Didn't want to.

Tearlach, inversely, wouldn't reveal a flicker of emotion unless he wished to.

Esme opened the door all the way and tugged her robe more tightly around her, already counting down the seconds until she could slink back to bed.

Tearlach marched in, clearly intent on speaking with her about something he deemed important.

His eyes strayed to the empty bottles of wine and the two nearly empty glasses.

Surely he already knew. Even if he hadn't been informed by the guards on the night shift, she and Jarlath hadn't kept their voices particularly quiet out on the balcony. And Tearlach's window wasn't far.

Thankfully, Cadwyn and Hazel chose that moment to seek her out as well, cutting off whatever opinions Tearlach might've had on the matter. Esme wasn't sure how measured her reaction would've been if he decided to pass judgment on her.

"Oof. Rough night?" Hazel looked her over.

Esme groaned. "No. Just a late one."

Cadwyn was already eying her with concern as Hazel took notice of Tearlach's stony expression.

In the foggy part of her mind, Esme wondered why Hazel was even at the palace. Hadn't she left to search the Laurel temple?

"We'll come back later. I'll have Marta come by with breakfast and some headache tonic," Cadwyn insisted.

"Just some tea. Thank you."

"And breakfast." Cadwyn's voice was stern enough to convince Esme that breakfast *would* be had, whether she wanted it or not.

But when Cadwyn turned to go, Hazel seemed reluctant to leave. She glanced at the wineglasses, then back to Esme.

Was she set to give the same warning that would no doubt be issued by Tearlach as soon as the two of them were alone? How much did Hazel know of the brothers' feud anyway? Had she sided with Tearlach like the other guards, without question?

Only...there was something different about the slight lift of Hazel's eyebrows. It wasn't a look of warning or of condemnation, but of loyalty. To *her*.

Esme gave a subtle shake of her head, indicating that she'd be fine speaking with Tearlach alone.

When Hazel finally left them, Tearlach watched her go, like he too realized that her allegiances had shifted.

Though it took less than a second for his ire to return.

"Not him," he told Esme harshly.

"Really? This again?" She threw up her hands and went to change, knowing he wouldn't leave anytime soon. Besides, Cadwyn was right; she needed to eat something if she wanted to feel better.

"Why not him?" she shouted from the dressing room, immediately regretting it when her head throbbed in protest.

Tearlach didn't respond. Of course he didn't.

"What is it? You've seen something your brother's taken an interest in and you don't want him to have it?" She winced. Jarlath didn't *have* her. But she was tired of Tearlach's prejudice and wanted to provoke him enough that he might give her a real answer.

If there was something that she should've been genuinely concerned about, she wanted to know. Though she suspected it was a slight that Tearlach had simply held on to for far too long.

Jarlath offered the kind of companionship Esme hadn't realized she'd been longing for. He was easy to talk to, his adorable wit had her smiling more often than not, and laughing alongside him just felt...good.

Furthermore, she couldn't deny how refreshing it was to be in the company of someone who wasn't charged with protecting or serving her.

Esme knew it would be infinitely harder to get past the ill-conceived feelings she had for Tearlach if she kept up a friendship with someone who looked so much like him. Or rather...a smiling, open version of him.

There'd been brief moments the night before when Jarlath would get a serious look on his face as he stared up at the lights or off toward the countryside past the city walls when Esme could almost imagine it was Tearlach sitting there beside her. Perhaps it'd been the silence of those moments. And oh, how she'd wished she could have moments like that with Tearlach.

"You know that's not it," came his gruff reply as she tugged on the loosest fitting shirt she could find.

"Do I? Because you won't tell me why you and Jarlath don't get along." She emerged from the dressing room feeling mildly more alive with a fresh set of clothes, then immediately held up a hand to stop Tearlach's excuse. "Don't try to deny it."

He huffed out a breath.

"What is it about him? Is it because he's heading down the path that was meant for you? He's living the life that was your birthright?"

"Hardly."

"Then what? He's not your father. He's not the one who—"

"Just—" He stopped her. "Not him."

"You don't get to decide who I spend time with. Why is it so hard for you to accept that I want someone in my life who doesn't just see my title when they look at me? Don't I deserve that? Don't I deserve someone who'll let me be...*not* the queen for a few hours? Someone who lets me forget, just for a moment, everything I'm suddenly responsible for? Don't I deserve to just be *me* every once in a while?"

"Of course you do," Tearlach admitted quietly, though his breathing had become more ragged, like her words had caused him physical pain.

"That's right. I do." She stabbed a finger at his chest.

He caught her hand when she tried to pull back. "Esme, please. Not him. He's not worthy—"

"Of a queen?" She yanked her hand away.

"Of *you.*"

She couldn't disguise her quick inhale.

He stared down at her with an intensity that made the throbbing pain inside her skull fade from her awareness.

She risked a step closer.

But Tearlach dropped his gaze.

"Esme..." His voice sounded pained. "I can't. I can't...be that for you." He slowly met her eyes again. "I need to protect you. That's my job. That's...all I can be...for you."

Esme turned away, squeezing her eyes shut tight against the sting of tears. Bile rose in her throat and she swallowed hard. Why did she keep letting herself believe that he'd—

Her teeth ground together. "Really?" She spun back around, channeling her hurt into something she could wield. "Is it your *job* to avoid me whenever possible?"

Indignation flared in his eyes, and he took a step toward her, closing the distance between them.

Esme's heart hammered against her ribs when he reached for her.

Then he dropped his hand to his side and hung his head.

I'm sorry. I can't.

Chapter Thirty-Two

"YOUR MAJESTY?" HARLOW called through the closed door.

Esme eyed the stacks of requests that had left little more than a letter-sized work surface on her desk. If whoever was at the door had even more—or worse, letters from nobles which she'd hoped had been sent from their own homes and not from somewhere in Meallán—she'd seriously consider not accepting them.

Mairtín had been by twice in the previous two days. At least he'd been understanding when she'd declined his request for her to see something he wished to gain her feedback on.

With a reluctant sigh, Esme rose and crossed the room.

Finding Myles standing just outside of the door, she couldn't help but smile.

"Myles! Come in. Come in." She gestured him toward the sitting area. Seeing him was a bright spot in the dull and dreary world Esme found herself in.

"Or perhaps I should refer to you as *Lord* Myles." She grinned even as he cringed at the new title. "You'll get used to it." She patted his shoulder when he took a seat. It had only been a matter of days since she'd irrevocably changed the trajectory of his life.

"I'm sure you're right on that account. And thank you for... the opportunity."

Esme halted at the hesitancy in his voice. "You've not changed your mind, have you?"

"No. No. I just...I wanted to be sure *you* hadn't changed your mind."

She took the seat across from him. "Certainly not."

He gave a stilted nod. "It's evident that the other councilors don't share your...confidence in my appointment."

"Ah. Let me assure you that their reluctance is more about me than it is about you. Half of them would've objected to anyone I chose."

Myles nodded again as he studied his clasped hands.

"Is that your only concern?"

"The thing is...I don't exactly know what's expected of me." A blush spread along the tops of his cheeks. "I should have asked before, but I was...well, you'd taken me by surprise that day."

"The truth is, Myles..." She leaned back, hoping her relaxed posture would put him more at ease. "I'm not quite sure myself." Luckily, she knew someone who was.

When Winifred arrived a short time later, Esme wasn't the least bit surprised at the council secretary's preparedness. Even without being told, Winifred knew exactly why she'd been summoned.

Unfortunately, as she laid out several documents and ledgers on the table between them, Myles looked even more overwhelmed. She couldn't blame him. Cadwyn and Sully's efforts to prepare her for her first couple of council meetings had felt much the same.

Hoping to give him a moment to adjust, Esme asked Winifred about the matter they kept coming back to.

"Did you learn anything new?"

Winifred glanced over at Myles.

"Say what you need to. He's about to come up against Lord Torin anyway, especially if he doesn't let go of his ruse about needing the lumber in the mountains."

Myles's brow furrowed, and Esme wondered whether he could sense a lie by proxy.

"Alpina informed me about the ships he's already built and the ones he's commissioned. Tell me you have something substantial. A document of..." Esme wasn't sure what sort of evidence she'd need to convince the rest of her council of Torin's plans, but she'd need more than hearsay.

"Nothing that can't be explained away as something else," Winifred told her regretfully. "What will you do, Your Majesty?"

Esme closed her eyes for a moment. "Nothing yet. I don't want to draw attention to his plans until I can be certain the council will support me."

"You could propose a decree to preserve the redwoods," Winifred suggested. "Given the current conditions, protecting what's left of our forests would be seen as prudent."

"I fear that won't stop him."

"If I may, Your Majesty," Myles spoke up. He hadn't asked what Lord Torin's purpose was for building a fleet of ships, but it seemed he'd pieced together enough. "Might I suggest a false report from Minister Aindreas. Perhaps a blight or an infestation of insects. Something that could easily spread. Aindreas could even go so far as to recommend burning the trees in order to stop it and preserve the remaining vegetation in the mountains."

"Smart," Winifred commended. "Torin won't want to risk infecting the rest of his lumber."

"It'll certainly hold him off for a time," Esme agreed, giving Myles an appreciative smile.

Chapter Thirty-Three

THE FOLLOWING DAY, Mairtín convinced Esme to follow him across the corridor to the room opposite hers that had once been intended for a sibling.

The breath left her the moment he opened the doors. It had been redesigned as an office. *Her* office.

"How did you...Mairtín, I don't know what to say. This is..."

Mairtín gave a pleased smile, straightening even more than his already perfect posture would seemingly allow. "Your first lady-in-waiting and the captain are the people to thank, Your Majesty."

Esme chuckled. "Then I shall thank them as well. But what you've done here..." She turned in a circle, taking in the changes that had been made to the layout that mirrored her bedchamber. One wall was lined with bookshelves that reached high enough to warrant a ladder. The other three walls were painted a glossy midnight blue. The white marble of the hearth had been kept the same, offset by gold accents. And above the hearth...

Her eyes welled with tears.

The painting of her parents was one she'd never seen before. Recently commissioned, she guessed.

She turned to Mairtín and reached up to capture him in an embrace. "Thank you, Mairtín," she whispered. And despite his rigid code of conduct, he hugged her back.

"My pleasure, Your Majesty."

Esme dashed the tears from her cheeks as they pulled apart. Mairtín's eyes were a bit glassy as well, but he bowed as he always did, and left without turning his back to her.

When the door clicked shut, Esme shut her eyes and let herself simply *feel* for a moment.

Shaking out her hands, she exhaled loudly, then set about exploring the new space. Small lamps had been placed throughout the room, casting a warm glow across the smooth, glossy surface of the dark walls. It felt less open and airy than her bedchamber. *Calmer*, she realized, trying out one of the two deep-cushioned chairs angled toward the hearth. They'd be perfect for reading or taking afternoon tea. That there were only two additional seats beside the one behind the desk, and no tables other than the small ones that held lamps, meant there'd be no meetings in there. The room was just for her, much like the office that adjoined the council chamber. Only the new space didn't contain memories of her father that were too heartbreaking to remember.

The bathing chamber was much the same as her own, but the dressing room had been transformed into a reading hideaway, complete with dark wood bookcases, lamps, and a cozy, overstuffed chair. It was already her favorite spot. So much so, she considered asking Mairtín if he could convert the double doors to a single, concealed one, so she might hide herself away when she felt like escaping.

Esme didn't think about how quickly the massive desk centered in front of the glass doors would be covered in requests. Instead, she tried out the chair and turned it to look out at the balcony, where several potted junipers were spaced evenly in front of the railing, lending another layer of seclusion.

Perhaps what she'd needed was a change of scenery, because the longer she sat there, gazing out through the narrow gaps between the junipers, she felt more at ease. Or maybe it was the distance—however small, as she was only across the corridor from her bedchamber—that had her shoulders releasing the tension she'd been holding on to for days. Weeks, really.

It wasn't until a knock sounded and Marta's voice called through the doors that Esme realized she'd been staring off into the distance for quite some time.

Her stomach grumbled as Marta wheeled in a cart.

"Shall I?" She gestured to the small side table near the hearth, then paused as she took in the painting.

"True likenesses, don't you think?" Esme asked. The painting of her parents didn't look like any of the official portraits she'd seen in her youth. They weren't in their regalia. Instead, her mother was wearing a simple dress, her hand cupping her husband's cheek. Her father was gazing back at her like she was his entire world. He was dressed in the type of clothing Esme had only ever seen him wear when the three of them would venture down to the lake for a picnic and he'd allow himself to remove his coat.

"Yes," Marta agreed with a slight catch in her voice. She looked over at Esme and smiled. "Captures them perfectly."

The quick, double rap of knuckles that came in the afternoon wasn't unexpected. Esme knew Tearlach would show up sooner or later. Either to inspect the new space—though he'd likely already done so—or to continue the *discussion* they'd begun the other day.

"Enter," she called out.

Tearlach stepped into her new office and eased the door shut behind him. His strides were unhurried as he crossed the room and came to stand in front of her desk.

"Roderick returned an hour ago."

"And?"

"He found nothing."

"I see." Esme leaned back in her chair and looked up at the ceiling like it might provide a map to the objects they sought.

"He'll leave for the Troya temple in Donellis in the morning."

Roderick really was searching all the temples himself, then. Had Hazel decided to remain at the palace because of her? Something about that felt rather like friendship, she decided.

When Tearlach offered nothing more, Esme cocked her head to the side. "Is that all?"

He regarded her for a moment before answering. "No."

She gestured for him to continue.

"I know you don't believe my...*reservations* about my brother."

Esme stood, but Tearlach held up a hand.

"Just, be careful. Please."

"He's not out to hurt me." She sighed. "Tearlach, your brother is a good, decent man. Why can't you see that?"

"A good man?" His expression morphed into fury so fast, Esme almost staggered back.

"Yes. He is." She recovered and rounded the desk. "He's good and kind and he's only ever been respectful and polite to me."

Tearlach glared at her in a way that was so unlike his brother. Had they always been so dissimilar? Or had life and war and the breaking of his betrothal with Cora damaged Tearlach so much that he'd become a completely different person?

Yes, she admitted silently. Coming out the other side of the Dark War unchanged seemed nearly impossible.

Still, that didn't give him reason to treat her the way he had since they'd returned—casting her off on the other guards, warning her about getting involved with Jarlath without offering an ounce of explanation as to why.

"But that's not the reason I enjoy his company."

Tearlach's nostrils flared.

"It's because I'm not *his job*."

He reared back as if she'd struck him. And for a protracted moment, they only stared at one another.

"I have enough people who want to advise me, who'll fight for me— *kill* for me. I need someone who won't treat me like an object that needs to be protected or safeguarded."

Jarlath felt like that sort of person. The way Carrick had felt when life had been simple and uncomplicated back in Debarrow. Jarlath was a friend, and he treated her as such. Treated her as an equal.

The silence that stretched between her and Tearlach was almost unbearable.

He exhaled an exhausted breath, then closed his eyes as he shook his head.

When he looked back at her, his features had hardened. "You're one of the smartest people I know, Esme. You understand the needs of your people. You won't accept anything other than what's best for this kingdom."

She blinked at the sudden compliment, though she suspected he wasn't finished.

"But when it comes to him..." Tearlach shook his head again, in an almost pitying way. "I never thought you'd be foolish enough to trust someone who's so clearly using you."

Esme clenched her jaw. "Get out."

———————

Esme hated how much space Tearlach's words had taken up in her mind.

She wanted to trust her instincts. Needed to. And Jarlath had only ever shown himself to be honest and considerate. Even when they'd spent most of the night out on the balcony, under the stars and the dancing lights, he'd never made her feel as if he expected more from her. Hadn't pressured her in any way. He'd made her feel safe and comfortable.

She'd actually been contemplating appointing Jarlath to take over his father's seat on the council. It wouldn't appear like she was ousting someone she disagreed with if the person she named as their replacement was the current lord's son.

As she picked her way through the woods—preferring to follow her own meandering path over the cultivated one—she wasn't surprised when she reached the lakeshore and found Jarlath standing at the western edge, gazing out at the still water with his hands clasped loosely behind his back. He clearly enjoyed his strolls around the lake as much as she did.

Just the sight of him summoned a sense of peace in her. He had that effect, and Esme couldn't deny how much she liked it. How much she needed it right then.

But when Jarlath caught sight of her and made his way over, she could tell by the worry pinching his brow that she hadn't been successful in hiding her inner turmoil.

"Your Majesty, is everything all right?"

"I..." She couldn't break eye contact while he looked at her with such raw concern. "I'm fine. I just...No, I'm fine. Everything's fine."

Jarlath's mouth flattened into a stern line. He was clearly unconvinced by her assertion, though he didn't press her about what was bothering her.

"I heard you stood up to my father in a meeting the other day."

"I suppose I did." She chuckled lightly, appreciating the distraction. When Jarlath offered his arm, she didn't hesitate to loop her own around his.

"I'm impressed. Though I really shouldn't be. You've shown yourself to be a formidable woman, Esme. I'm...proud. Is it appropriate for me to say that?" He huffed a self-deprecating laugh as color blossomed along the tops of his cheeks.

"*Proud* of me?" She couldn't help but challenge. "For what? Putting him in his place after he insulted my father? Insulted *me*? That was self-preservation, nothing more. And if I hadn't, Sully or—Sully would have done far more than I did."

"I was always afraid of him when I was a boy. Even now, I struggle to assert myself when our...*opinions* vary."

"I'm betting your opinions vary quite often."

"You'd win that bet. I'm more of the accommodating one in my family. Sometimes even more so than my mother, and she rarely speaks a word against Torin."

"Being accommodating isn't such a bad thing. I'm sure it serves you far better than being argumentative or stubborn-minded about anything you vaguely disagree with."

"I suppose you're right. Though it didn't always seem like a positive trait growing up. My brother was better suited to the sort of verbal sparring my father was so well-versed at."

"Figures," she muttered.

Jarlath pulled her to a stop. "Did something happen?"

"No" was her immediate reply. "Well, yes. We..." She shook her head.

"He didn't...*hurt* you, did he?" His eyes widened at the thought.

Esme couldn't help but chuckle. "No. He's not like that," she assured him before her thoughts reminded her that not all hurt was physical.

"Did he say something to upset you?"

"Your brother is a man of few words."

"Quite true. But sometimes it only takes a few."

Esme studied him for a moment, weighing how much she should say.

"And oftentimes silence can be just as harsh," he furthered.

"It can," she agreed softly.

"I know it's not my place, but if you'll allow me, I'd like to remind you that you're not alone here, Esme."

When he said her name like that, with such care and reverence, her heart ached.

"You're surrounded by people who love and support you. And if... *someone* is making you feel less than...Well, all I'm saying is that I don't like seeing you this way. If this *someone* is making you feel anything less than cherished and respected, then maybe they shouldn't be in your life."

Except Tearlach would always be in her life. There was little she could do about that. Whether at the palace or far away, they'd always be bound together.

She'd never be free of their bond.

And he'd never be free of her.

Chapter Thirty-Four

ESME STARED AT the blank page of her notebook. She'd intended to write to her mother again, to tell her everything she was contemplating, the confusion she felt, the guilt, the heartache. But there was permanency in writing down her feelings, committing them in ink. And she couldn't quite bring herself to do that yet.

Closing the notebook, she curled on her side.

"I don't know what to do," she whispered into the empty room.

She understood that her mother had wanted Esme protected, and why Sully had chosen Tearlach to be that person. But the protection she'd needed from Orianna was no longer necessary.

Tearlach clearly wasn't happy there. And with each passing day, Esme found it more and more painful to be around him, to think about him.

To want him.

It wasn't until long after the palace had fallen quiet that Esme decided her best option was to talk things through with Tearlach. She'd present her plan as a rational course of action that would benefit both of them.

After confirming that Tearlach had retired to his chamber, Esme stuffed the items she'd gathered into the pockets of her pants, eased open the concealed door, then crept through the passageway to his room.

She raised her fist to knock softly, not wanting to wake him if he'd already gone to sleep, but the door swung open before she could.

Everything'll be fine, she tried to convince herself as she looked up at Tearlach. *He can go back to his life in Altan. He isn't happy here.*

Tearlach stared down at her, but didn't ask why she was there, or if something was wrong. He knew she wasn't there because of a safety concern or because she wanted to visit Athdara again.

When he stepped aside, allowing her in, Esme let out a ragged breath, and reminded herself that the Lifeblood Oath wasn't necessary anymore.

I'm setting him free. I no longer need that kind of protection. I'm surrounded by guards, day and night.

But memories tugged at the fragile threads of her logic. Every time Tearlach had been alerted that she was in danger. When he'd rescued her from Orianna's scouts. And how, after Killian had been killed by an iron-tipped arrow, Tearlach's voice had demanded—*begged*—that she use her magic to bring him back. Would she have attempted it otherwise? Would Killian still be with them?

She tried not to think of all the nights traumatic memories had consumed her mind and haunted her sleep. How many nightmares Tearlach had saved her from. How many nights he'd kept watch by her bedside, to make sure even the memory of Orianna couldn't touch her.

He'd been with her through all of it. Before she even knew who the glowering, taciturn metalsmith was.

I didn't leave her behind.

Esme clenched her eyes shut at the unwelcome echo of Tearlach's confession.

It doesn't matter anymore, she told herself, easing farther into his room. The contents in her pockets brushed against her thighs with each step, reminding her of why she was there.

Tearlach stood in the center of the flatwoven rug that took up nearly the entire length and width of his small quarters. She glanced at the comfortable-looking chair tucked into the corner beside his bed, then to the set of wooden ones flanking the small table near the window. Even if she chose one of them, she knew Tearlach would remain standing. So she did as well.

"I want to break the oath," Esme said in a rush of breath.

"What?" Tearlach glared at her, lowering his brow in a manner that made him look primed for a challenge.

For battle.

"I've been thinking…" Esme shifted from foot to foot as she looked down at the intricate pattern of the rug. "It isn't right, you giving up your freedom to—"

Her head snapped up at how quickly Tearlach advanced on her.

"Who put you up to this?" he demanded.

"Who?" She scrunched her brow. "What do you…No one *put me up to this*. I'm doing this for you. So you can—"

"Was it him?"

The calm facade Esme had striven for crumbled. She bit back a growl, turning her own glare on him.

"It *can't* be him, Esme. He's not—You can't trust him."

"And if I choose to trust him? What then?"

Tearlach exhaled hotly and yielded a step. He folded his arms over his chest. "Then it won't be long before you find your own throne *behind* the one he's erected for himself. Or before Tremaene is no longer in your hands."

Esme scowled and inhaled a slow, measured breath, ready to tell him exactly what she thought of his assumptions. But Tearlach wasn't finished.

"Are you willing to toss your birthright into the fire over some frivolous flirtation? He isn't worth it. You need—"

"What *I* need? What *Tremaene* needs, that's what you mean. What a queen needs. Not me. This...*issue* you have with your brother has nothing to do with me. Nothing to do with what *I need*."

"It has everything to do with you. You *are* Tremaene. And when someone poses a threat to—"

"I'm not Tremaene! I'm not just a crown. I'm not something to be manipulated or...or protected or married off to someone the council thinks will do a better job at ruling than me." Esme shook her head to clear it; that wasn't the direction she needed the conversation to go. "You didn't swear your life to Tremaene, Tearlach. You swore it to me. Not to Tremaene. Not to the crown. To *me*. Or have you forgotten?"

His breathing quickened as he glared down at her. And somehow the distance between them lessened.

"When are you going to see that I'm more than just a queen? That I know my own mind, know what I want? What I need." Her eyes darted between his, looking for a flicker of understanding, contrition...something.

"I'm more than just a crown, Tearlach."

"You don't think I know that?" he shouted, visibly shaking.

She gasped, and for several seconds could only stare at him as he fought to control the emotions he always kept so tightly locked down.

He looked as wrecked as she felt, having convinced himself that he couldn't be with her. That he *shouldn't*. She hated that word, almost as much as she hated the word honor. Nothing but shackles, that's all they were.

And Esme knew that Tearlach would never loosen those shackles on his own, so she risked a step, knowing that in all likelihood it would only fracture the already broken pieces of her heart. But she had to try. Couldn't bear not to.

She might've gone to his room that night because she needed more space from him. Endless space. She needed him on the other side of the kingdom if she wanted any semblance of emotional stability. Or sanity.

But it hurt. It physically hurt when he pushed her away, when he kept her at arm's length.

Much as she wanted—*needed*—him far away, they were drawn to each other, like a force that couldn't be overcome.

And being as close as they were in that moment...

So close, and yet not touching.

She vibrated with the need to touch him, to be touched. To feel him breathing her in, consuming her in every way.

"Then why don't you do something about it?" Her voice trembled, but she didn't try to hide it. Even as she rooted herself in place and fisted her hands at her sides, she couldn't dispel the jagged edge of her breaths.

"You don't *need* to be the queen's guard."

Tearlach swallowed. She watched the muscles along his throat work, knowing he was holding back words, and wanting desperately to know what they were.

Fearing the ones he'd eventually force himself to say.

"I can't."

"You can't be that for me, or you can't be that for anyone?" she challenged.

Tearlach closed his eyes. "Esme," he pleaded, voice raw.

"You refuse to even *try*."

His jaw clenched, and she knew he wouldn't refute her claim. They'd never be anything more than charge and protector. A queen and her loyal guard. But even that was no longer feasible.

Impossible. It was impossible.

Esme couldn't continue on as if the confusing, tormenting, heartrending feelings weren't consuming her entire being, stalking her waking hours and haunting her dreams.

"You're a coward," she said in a harsh whisper, knowing the accusation wouldn't matter. Once Tearlach's mind was made up, there was no changing it. Had she really been so foolish to think he might be swayed?

She stepped back, suddenly needing room to breathe. If she was truly going to follow through, she needed her mind clear. Or at the very least, less muddled.

And as much as that small stretch of space between them made her heart clench, she knew what needed to be done.

Tearlach stiffened as she pulled the pouch of ashes from her pocket and set it on the table behind her. When she produced the dagger he'd given her, he jerked forward, like he wanted to stop her. But he held himself back.

Closing her hand around the wooden hilt, her thumb stroked the impression of the carved letter *E.* She tried not to imagine the note Tearlach had written along with it. Or the note that had accompanied the chest plate she'd given him when he'd pledged his life to her yet again, and how he'd kept it in his breast pocket.

There'd been no note with the earrings he'd gifted her before the ball, but everything that had gone unsaid that night—before that night, and since—she felt in every breath she took. In every beat of her heart. In the blood coursing through every inch of her body. She felt him *everywhere.*

Esme flexed her hand, stifled the sob that was lodged in the back of her throat, and drew the blade across her palm.

Chapter Thirty-Five

BLOOD WELLED FROM the gash, hot and red.

She didn't feel the pain. Not really. Not the way Tearlach seemed to.

Every muscle in his body looked like it'd been pulled taut. And from the anguish in his eyes, Esme wondered how much, or little, control she had over the emotions flowing through their connection at that moment.

But all he did was stare down at her.

It wasn't shock. He seemed more...lost than anything.

That he'd lost her? That he knew he was about to?

Or could he already feel their bond fraying?

Her breath sawed in and out. She didn't try to slow it. Couldn't.

Folding three of her fingers over the cut, she reached out to take Tearlach's wrist with her thumb and forefinger—ignoring the slight tremor in the hand holding the blade.

It was difficult enough to inflict pain on herself; she didn't want to think too much about doing it to another.

For a protracted moment, she only held his wrist, giving him time to pull away. When he didn't, Esme turned his palm up, inhaled a bracing breath, and slid the edge of the dagger across his skin.

Her mind blanked as she looked at the blood spilling from the cut. His blood. Tearlach's blood.

The blood that bound them together.

Her vision blurred.

She heard the soft thud of the dagger landing on the rug as she reached back for the pouch on the table.

The Lifeblood Oath had been forged in fire; ash would rend it.

With shaking hands, she loosened the strings, smelling the remnants of the sandalwood, sage, and mugwort she'd burned earlier.

Tearlach hadn't shifted an inch. His hand remained stretched out where she held it between them. But the tension coming off him was like nothing she'd ever experienced. It made her feel lightheaded. Weak. Like she might collapse into his arms at any moment.

She couldn't surrender to the temptation.

You've come this far. Just keep...keep going. Keep going.

Thunder rumbled in the distance as she emptied the contents of the pouch along the small river of blood in the center of Tearlach's palm.

Then their hands were pressed together. She couldn't remember doing it. Her mind was a jumble of tormenting thoughts.

The thunder grew louder. A booming crack shook the floor beneath Esme's feet as rain lashed against the window.

None of it mattered, because she felt something deep inside her unravel.

Then slip away.

It was as if a corset tied too tightly had finally come undone.

She inhaled, feeling her chest expand with the breath. But with it came the sensation of being untethered. It was dizzying. Like she might float away. Like she'd never touch the ground again.

That's what Tearlach was to her. He was the solid ground beneath her feet. A safe place for her to land.

He was her safe place.

He was *hers.*

Was hers.

Without him, how would she...Would she ever feel safe? Be safe?

She tightened her grip on him as her palm started to burn, trying to hold on.

But the fire burned through her, searing every trace of Tearlach from her blood. Until there was nothing left of him.

When the pain threatened to overwhelm her, Esme wrenched her hand away.

The burning vanished instantly, but the crash of emotions filling in its wake was even more painful.

Everything Tearlach felt for her assailed her body, her senses, her thoughts. Her heart.

They were the last, she realized. The last things she'd ever feel through their connection.

Companionship, frustration, pride, protectiveness, anger, devotion, tension, fondness. Love. So much love.

It felt like she'd been struck in the chest, the breath forced from her lungs.

She gasped, her body trembling with the all-consuming devotion and adoration Tearlach had for her.

Her hands fisted at her sides, like the small action might stave off the inevitable. Spare her from knowing—*feeling*—the rest.

But it came anyway.

The heartbreak.

The constriction around her own heart tightened.

And she felt the moment *his* heart broke.

"Esme," Tearlach pleaded softly, trying to reach for her. His eyes were glassy, pained. Full of anguish.

She looked away.

Those eyes. *His eyes.*

The dark eyes that were so much like her own.

She'd see her own heartbreak reflected back at her.

It was too much. She couldn't—

Squeezing her eyes shut, she clenched her fists tighter. The dried blood and ash cracked and crumbled.

Peering down at her palm, she found the cut already healed—a raised scar that would likely be gone in a matter of minutes, dark from the ash. Forever sealed within.

A reminder of what they'd shared.

Of what she'd done.

A memory she'd never forget.

Stumbling back, she scrambled for purchase along the wall until she found the latch for the door. Yanking it open, she hurried back through the passageway, feeling her way to her room as her vision blurred.

Chapter Thirty-Six

ESME KNEW SHE'D made a mistake the moment she'd drawn the blade across her flesh. Even before that, when she'd burned the herbs and carefully swept them into the pouch. But she'd told herself it was a last resort if they couldn't find a way to move forward.

Even when she'd gathered up the pouch and her dagger, she still hadn't believed she'd use them. Not really.

But it was done. Their connection broken.

Then again, maybe...Maybe *they* weren't broken. She'd give him time to realize that what she'd done was necessary. That it would strengthen what they had. *Maybe...*

Esme stopped her pacing in front of the hearth and looked down at her palm. Her tears had long since dried, and the scar had all but vanished, leaving only a black line across her palm. She traced it with her finger. Her natural ability to heal quickly had never before felt like a curse. She didn't deserve relief from the pain. She needed it. Needed something to focus on.

It'd been hours, but the thundering of Esme's heart finally slowed enough that exhaustion threatened to take hold.

But she didn't retreat to her bed, much as the escape of sleep tempted her. Instead, she went to splash water on her face, changed into something that didn't have blood streaked across one of the pant legs, then crept through the passageway to Tearlach's room.

"Just...talk to him," she whispered a moment before she knocked.

There was no answer.

She considered pushing her way into his room, but there was no reason to. Even without their connection, she knew he wasn't behind the door.

Armel was on duty. Esme didn't give him a chance to question why she was awake at such a late hour before she inquired as to Tearlach's whereabouts.

"I assumed he'd retired for the night." When Esme didn't respond, he added, "Shall I find him for you?"

"No." She shook her head. "It's...will you...if you see him, will you tell him I need to speak with him?"

Armel nodded, his face etched with worry.

"On second thought, morning will suffice. I'm rather tired." She faked a yawn and hurried to shut the door, then rested the back of her head against it for several seconds to make sure Armel wouldn't come to check on her.

Switching out her soft-soled shoes for boots, Esme grabbed one of her cloaks, then snuck into Tearlach's room.

It was dark. Even the curtain hanging above the single window had been drawn shut. She crept over to the door and eased it open, then made for the stairwell.

She rounded the steps quickly, pausing before the main floor came into view. The unguarded kitchen doors would be the easiest places to sneak out, but the main level of the palace never seemed to sleep.

Strangely, though, the only footfalls and muffled voices she heard were distant.

Gripping the curved handrail, she leapt over the remaining steps, landing somewhat gracefully.

Then slammed right into Jarlath's chest. Again.

His arms steadied her as Esme fought to hide the surprise on her face. Not at his sudden appearance, but at not having heard his approach.

He'd likely come from the kitchens, Esme reasoned as she untangled her arm from her twisted cloak. She'd never noticed him to be as stealthy as his brother, but she supposed there was nothing unusual about it.

More likely, he'd been lost in thought and had—

Why was she spinning her thoughts over Jarlath's sure-footedness? Apparently she'd latch on to anything other than what she planned to say to Tearlach once she found him.

"Couldn't sleep?" Jarlath asked.

"No, I...Yes, trouble sleeping." Esme nodded one too many times, and it didn't escape Jarlath's notice.

Instead of questioning further, though, he offered his arm. "Herbal tea always helps me."

She threaded her arm with his and let him lead her down to the kitchens.

But as much as she wanted to enjoy a cup of tea with him, she needed to find Tearlach more. She pulled him to a stop. "Jarlath, I..." Her mind struggled with an excuse that would convince him to leave her alone down there.

"Esme, is...is everything all right?" He guided her toward the wall beneath one of the sconces and peered down at her more closely. "You can tell me anything, you know."

She knew that, even without the sincerity in his eyes. But she didn't want to tell him what had happened between her and Tearlach. Couldn't tell him. Not without divulging the secret of the Lifeblood Oath that bound them. That *had* bound them.

Her eyelids felt heavy. Exhaustion was trying hard to claim her. But she wouldn't let herself sleep until she found Tearlach. Until she set things right.

When she failed to respond, Jarlath leaned closer. "What can I do?" Gently, he tucked a lock of hair behind her ear.

Esme shivered at the contact and swayed toward him. She couldn't help it. Her body was oversensitized and any form of comfort felt a thousand times better than it should have.

The kitchen doors swung open, and even in her weary state, Esme glanced toward the sound.

Tearlach stood with his arms holding open the doors, staring at her and Jarlath. The gutted look in his eyes quickly became one of fury. Toward her or his brother, she wasn't sure.

Jarlath straightened beside her, but didn't step away. Given that Tearlach's stance made him appear ready for battle, she knew Jarlath was only trying to protect her.

Tearlach flicked his gaze to Jarlath's hand that had landed so softly on Esme's shoulder she hadn't noticed it. His eyes narrowed, meeting hers once more before he released the doors, letting them swing shut as he strode down the opposite corridor.

"Tearlach! Wait!" Esme pushed away from the wall, but Jarlath's hand was suddenly on her upper arm.

His grip tightened for a fraction of a second, and her eyes darted to the point of contact. He released her immediately.

"Esme," Jarlath soothed. The sincerity in his expression seemed slightly forced. "Are you sure you want to—"

"Your Majesty," Armel exhaled as he rushed over. He gave her a look that told her how displeased he was at her attempted escape. But the one he aimed at Jarlath was far worse.

Esme didn't waste the momentary stare-off between them. She ducked under Jarlath's arm and bolted over to the stairwell Tearlach had taken.

Armel called after her, but she'd already reached the main floor.

"There you are." Killian's relieved voice sounded from somewhere behind her as she scanned the nearly vacant space for Tearlach.

Spotting him, she took off toward the main doors just as they were closing. The footmen hurried back over as she slid to a stop. Armel got there first, yanking the massive doors open.

Across the gravel drive, she saw Tearlach. But a hand took hold of hers before she could run after him. She looked up at Killian, then Armel. At the footmen and the palace guards who were all watching from the top of the steps.

"Give him some time," Killian said gently.

Esme sucked in a breath, set to argue, but it came out as a shaky breath. Her hand tightened on Killian's as she looked back at the gate. Where Tearlach had disappeared into the dimly lit streets of Meallán.

———————————

When the morning light spilled into her room, and Esme still hadn't managed any sleep, she decided that Tearlach had had enough time.

"Find out where he went," she said as way of greeting when she opened her doors to find Killian on duty.

He didn't hesitate. In fact, he seemed to be expecting the request.

Cahir watched as Killian stalked off, then turned to Esme. "Everything...okay, Your Majesty?"

"Perfectly fine," she grumbled, retreating back into her room.

As soon as she'd finished dressing for the day, a soft knock came. She opened the door to find Cahir balancing a small tray with tea and biscuits.

"Thank you." She forced a gentle tone.

He offered a smile, which she returned as she took the tray from him.

"Has Killian..." She tilted her head to look past him.

"Not yet."

Esme huffed out a breath, setting the tray down on the table beside the door. She splashed some of the hot liquid into a cup, then drank it in a single swallow. It burned, but she didn't much care. Cahir winced.

She gestured for him to help himself to the other cup, then went to find her riding boots. If Killian wasn't able to locate Tearlach, she'd track him down herself.

Her *plan* lacked any sort of strategy. And she knew Cahir would insist on escorting her—or sticking her in a carriage.

Might as well take him with.

"Come on," she said as she brushed past him.

At the bottom of the grand staircase, she noticed Beglan and Winifred at the entrance of the royal library. She tried to muster a smile at the sight of the two of them standing rather close together, but what little energy she had left was needed for her tired legs to carry her out to the stables.

"Your Majesty," Keelin called out to her at the same moment Killian appeared with a palace guard whose name Esme had no hope of remembering without at least a few hours of sleep.

She was vaguely aware of the hand she held up to Keelin as the woman joined them—her attention solely on the guard who looked far too contrite for Esme's liking.

"Tell her." Killian nudged the man.

"Your Majesty, your guard—"

"Tearlach?"

He nodded.

"Where is he?"

"He...He returned in the early morning hours."

Esme shot a look to Killian. If Tearlach was back, then why—

"Then left again a short time later, heading down to the stables."

"Did you speak with him?"

"No, Your Majesty. But one of the stablehands said he retrieved a sack from the loft."

"I don't..." Esme shook her head, trying to make sense of what he was telling her. "I don't understand. Where did he go after that?"

"Not sure, Your Majesty."

She closed her eyes. How was it that *no one* seemed to know where Tearlach had gone?

"But the stablehand said he offered him a horse. Only...your guard refused. Said he..."

"He refused? Why?" Esme snapped.

The man swallowed and shifted a glance to Killian. "He said he wasn't returning."

"He what? He's not...coming back?" Her voice broke on the last word.

"I don't believe so, Your Majesty," he finished, ducking his head.

Esme dropped to her knees, unsure if even the marble floor would hold her up.

Then Killian's arms were around her, and a chorus of concerned voices surrounded them. Armel was there too, kneeling down beside her to take one of her hands.

When Killian gently lifted her head off of his shoulder, Esme opened her eyes to find Hazel standing before her. She lowered herself down to the floor.

"He left," Esme whispered.

Hazel's eyes turned murderous.

Chapter Thirty-Seven

"WHAT HAPPENED?" CADWYN asked breathlessly as she raced down the stairs.

Killian had an arm wrapped around Esme's lower back. Armel was on her other side. And Esme wondered if Hazel had actually gone to hunt down Tearlach until she heard her clipped response.

Cadwyn looked to each of the others like Hazel's explanation couldn't possibly have been correct. But when her green gaze landed on Esme, she exhaled a weary sigh.

"I—" Cadwyn furrowed her brow and shook her head, as if no words existed to convey her sympathies. So she took Esme's hands, pulled her gently away from Killian and Armel's support, then helped her to her room.

When Sully arrived not long after, Esme saw that all her guards had gathered outside the door. Cahir and Killian were the only ones dressed for duty, but they were all there, all with worried expressions, peering in through the open doors as Sully crossed to her.

He knelt before her, taking in her appearance quickly before meeting her eyes.

"I'll find him." His voice matched the anger in his eyes. "Drag him back here if I must," he muttered under his breath.

But Sully's ire wasn't the same as Hazel's. Sully was the only other person who knew about the Lifeblood Oath, and that it only protected her if the person she was bound with was near. How near? Neither of them knew.

"I broke it," she whispered, her breath catching.

A myriad of emotions played across Sully's face, and Esme wasn't sure if he was wondering whether he'd heard her correctly or if he was questioning the validity of her claim that the Lifeblood Oath could be broken. Perhaps it was only his worry over her safety multiplying.

After a moment, he settled on simply asking, "How?"

Esme cast a look around the room to make sure no one was listening. Hazel was arguing with Killian and Armel in the far corner, and Cadwyn seemed to be busying herself in the dressing room.

"I found her journal."

Sully's lips parted.

"All her spells...they were..." She pressed the heels of her hands against her eyes. "But I didn't think I'd actually...and then..."

Sully moved to sit beside her.

Esme tried to take a slow breath, hoping it might stem the flow of tears. But when Sully gathered her in his arms, she couldn't stop them. She buried her face against his chest and let them come.

After Marta delivered tea and several covered dishes, Cadwyn deftly shooed everyone except Hazel from the room.

"Need something stronger?" Hazel asked discreetly, cradling her own cup of tea.

Esme stared down at the cup that had somehow ended up in her hands. But before she could decide, there was a gentle knock at the door.

Cadwyn grumbled something under her breath about men being unable to listen as she went to see who it was, then stepped aside to reveal Cora. Cadwyn arched a questioning brow at Esme, who nodded that she be let in.

Cora carefully made her way over, choosing a seat across from Esme. She glanced between Cadwyn and Hazel, then leaned in toward Esme and vowed that Alpina would find Tearlach.

"No." Esme sat up.

Cadwyn plucked the teacup from her hand before it could slosh again at the same time Hazel handed her a linen napkin.

"I..." Esme mopped up the spill, then looked at Cora. "I don't want him...tied to this place. If he doesn't want to be here—" *If he doesn't want to be with me.* "If he doesn't want to be here, then..." Cora waited for her to continue, but it was too difficult to say the words, to make a statement that seemed so...final.

Esme exhaled and sunk back down onto the sofa. Without the teacup, she clasped her hands on her lap and stared down at them. "I told him to leave," she admitted softly. "To go home. He wasn't...happy here. And I thought—I thought it would be easier if..." She closed her eyes and took a shaky breath. "But now I don't know. Maybe I was hoping he'd choose to stay anyway. That if I told him he didn't need to stay on as my guard he might..."

"Stay for *you?*" Cora supplied.

Esme bit her lip and gave a trembling nod.

But he didn't.

"Tearlach has always been..." Cora began. "A man of his word."

Hazel huffed out a humorless laugh. "That's an understatement. Tearlach is the most stubborn man in all of Tremaene."

Cora agreed by inclining her head. "If he's no longer needed in"—she seemed to choose her words carefully—"an *official* capacity, it may take time for him to...realign. To accept that—"

"I don't want to be an obligation to him."

Hazel winced at the word. She'd made it clear that Esme was nothing more than an obligation when she'd first returned to Tremaene with Tearlach.

"He was—We were..." She needed to tell them. There was no other way to describe the way she felt, like Tearlach had been trapped there.

Cadwyn filled a fresh cup of tea and handed it to her with a nod, encouraging her to continue.

Esme took a deep swallow, then told the three of them about the Lifeblood Oath. And how she'd broken it.

The silence that followed felt as if it lasted an eternity.

"You didn't break the oath to send him away," Cadwyn stated with a sympathetic tilt of her head. "You needed to know."

"I suppose...yes." Tears gathered along her lashes and she brushed them away. "But I didn't tell him that. I didn't tell him how I really felt. Why didn't I just say the words? If only I'd—"

"No," Hazel told her firmly. "You're not doing that."

"But if I'd—"

"Let's say you *had* told him that you love him."

Esme sucked in a breath at Hazel's bluntness.

"And let's say he'd said it back. Do you really think it would have changed anything? That he'd suddenly follow his heart instead of his head? Instead of that rigid code of honor he wears like a damned shield?"

Esme's chest tightened. The need to crumple in on herself was nearly overwhelming.

"But he will come back."

She looked up and saw the conviction in Hazel's eyes.

"He'll come back when he realizes that there's more to life than upholding one's duty. And that this was never about some promise he made to the captain all those years ago, or the vow he made to you when you took the throne." Hazel took Esme's hand. "When he comes back, it'll be for *you*."

"You're just going to sit there while I sleep?" Esme questioned when both Cadwyn and Hazel appeared to settle in as she finally crawled into bed. She ignored her mind's unhelpful reminder that Tearlach had done precisely that on more than one occasion.

"Madoc invited us to play tomorrow night. I need to teach Cadwyn all my tricks."

"Is that right?" Esme stifled a yawn.

"Absolutely," Hazel assured as she went to speak with the guards stationed outside, then somehow returned with a deck of cards.

Esme might have laughed if she hadn't been so bone-tired. Instead, she burrowed under the covers and turned to face the windows.

The small crescent moons were still visible in the midday sky, and Esme wondered if he could see them too, wherever he was.

Tearlach? she reached out.

But there was nothing.

Chapter Thirty-Eight

ESME AVOIDED KILLIAN and Armel's all-too-knowing looks. Everyone seemed to think she was so fragile she might break at any moment. Which...she supposed was partly true. The two of them had taken it upon themselves to "keep her company" after she'd spent nearly a full day and night in bed.

At least her appetite had recovered somewhat. Though it would've been easier to eat her breakfast if she wasn't being watched as if she were an infant who'd just learned how to feed herself.

When Armel buttered another scone and Killian reached to fill her cup yet again, Esme pushed back her chair, snatched a plum, flung open the doors, marched across to her new office, and closed the door behind her before either could follow.

Taking her first full breath in what felt like days, she sunk down to the floor. But her reprieve only lasted a matter of minutes before her nursemaids were knocking at the door.

With a grumble, she rose, but was surprised to find Regan on the other side. Killian and Armel were predictably crowded behind him.

Quinlan and Harlow—her *official* guards that morning—mercifully allowed the poor page adequate space to breathe.

"Come in." She pulled Regan inside, shutting out the others.

He stumbled to a stop when she released him, looking stunned.

"Apologies." Esme stepped back.

"Not necessary, Your Majesty. I was only—" He thrust a folded note at her. "I was asked to deliver this."

For a moment, her heart stopped. Was it from Tearlach?

She wasn't sure how long she stared at Regan's outstretched hand until he began looking for the closest surface to set it on.

"I'll just leave this..."

"No." She grabbed the note. "Sorry. I..." The sight of her name written in elegant script had her nearly whimpering. It wasn't from Tearlach. Looking back up, she forced a smile. "Thank you, Regan."

He bowed his head, but didn't immediately turn to go. "Is there anything you need, Your Majesty?"

She had to hand it to him, he masked the pity in his expression much better than her guards.

"No. Thank you."

He bowed again and left her to read the note.

Esme,

I've heard you've been feeling unwell. I sincerely hope you make a swift recovery. The world is colorless without your cheerful demeanor.

Cheerful? She arched a brow, fairly certain no one had ever gifted her with that adjective.

I know full well that my dull wit won't cure what ails you—

in fact, I fear my mundane stories may have caused this malady.

Should you find it in yourself to forgive me, and desire a turn

about the lake or a stroll through the gardens, know that I am

forever at your beck and call.

Yours,

Jarlath

Unbidden, a smile bloomed. And for a moment, she felt like the shadow clinging to her evaporated. He had a way of lifting her mood. Even with a few handwritten words.

Things with Jarlath were easy. There wasn't anything unspoken between them. No tension. There was a contentedness he seemed to carry around with him. She suspected he put everyone he encountered at ease.

But the comradery she'd felt with Jarlath had been marred. He'd been unwittingly cast into the contention between her and Tearlach.

Esme set the note aside and stepped out into the private garden sanctuary Mairtín had created on the balcony. She let her eyes drift shut and angled her face up toward the cloudless sky.

For a short time, she managed to forget everything that had transpired. But when she opened her eyes with a long exhale, the slightly obstructed view between two of the potted junipers revealed the paddock, and the stables beyond. Which only reminded her of Tearlach.

Her grand idea that changing her surroundings would offer a bit of clarity turned out not to be.

There was a task, however, that might distract her long enough for her to forget. At least for a few hours.

Returning inside, Esme pulled the plum out of her pocket and set it on the desk, then took the top document from the stack of requests and settled in.

———————

A hand on Esme's shoulder startled her awake.

She twisted to find Sully peering down at her. He stooped to retrieve the papers that had fallen to the floor.

"My dear?" He looked her over when he rose, a deep crease of concern marring his forehead. "How are you faring?"

Esme blinked up at him as she tried to shake the strange sleep that hadn't felt like sleep at all from her mind.

"A bit tired, I suppose." She chuckled, but Sully leveled her with a stern look. "I feel terrible," she admitted, earning a nod from Sully. "I'd hoped these would serve as a diversion, but as you can see..." Taking the papers back, she sorted them into the correct order.

"Just like your father."

Esme looked up to find a wistful expression on Sully's face.

"Could always tell there was something bothering him when no one, not even your mother, could get him to set all of this aside for another day."

A smile forced its way onto Esme's face for the second time that day. It was nice to think her father was sometimes just as conflicted or confused as anyone else. She glanced over at the portrait of her parents. She'd only ever seen the self-assured king or the patient, adoring father.

But then, she suspected the image she'd built up in her mind was likely an idealized version of him.

"We all knew to delay delivering bad news until the storm had passed."

Bad news. Esme gave a heavy exhale. "Tell me."

"Roderick returned an hour ago."

"And," she prompted, though she already knew what Sully would report.

"Nothing to be found."

Esme pressed her lips together and bit back an expletive.

"Gather everyone," she told him.

———————

It wasn't a quarter hour later that her entire royal guard, as well as Cadwyn, were crowded into Esme's room.

She paced in front of the wall of windows, trying not to look at the concealed door like Tearlach might suddenly appear there, as Sully informed the others of Roderick's findings and how even the fertile lands surrounding the temples seemed to be receding more quickly than previously reported.

When he finished conveying the direness of the situation, Esme stopped her pacing and turned to face them. "We need ideas. Anything—no matter how preposterous it may seem. Don't hold back."

Unsure looks passed between them before Cahir spoke up. "What if Orianna took them, back when..." He trailed off, leaving them to fill in the rest.

Esme contemplated the likelihood, turning to stare out at the western grounds.

"Then wouldn't they still be—" Harlow began.

Esme spun back around. "Search the palace."

Chapter Thirty-Nine

ESME DIDN'T JOIN in the search, which Sully urged needed to be done as discreetly as possible. Rather, she went down to the kitchens just as the dinner preparations had begun and requested a few special additions to the menu, then found Mairtín and tasked him with arranging a trio of musicians to play through the evening. Finally, Esme put on a dress that was bound to draw attention, and once the dinner hour began, made a point of visiting with every person in the hall.

It wasn't likely her guards would find anything so quickly—if there even was anything to be found—but she was prepared to distract the staff for as long as was necessary.

And if they got lucky, and the missing pieces were located, she'd need to be ready. Which was why, once Esme returned to her room later that night, the chest with the priestesses' adornments sat waiting for her.

Simply the sight of it set her pulse racing, but a few deep breaths calmed her enough to move closer. She wiped her sweaty palms against her skirts, lifted the lid, and carefully removed each article, laying them out on the glass table.

When she reached the robe nestled at the bottom of the box, Esme took a step back. She waited for the unsettling, consuming sensation of the dark magic to lure her in, but the only things she felt were the pounding of her heart and the nervous tremors in her hands.

Without touching the hem, she lifted up the garment and pulled the box aside. The small silver beads clinked against the glass as the robe unfurled and pooled in the center of the table.

She shook out her hands, though it did little to dispel her rising panic.

The clock on the mantel ticked with each second, each minute, that passed as she did nothing but stand there, staring at the robe.

Esme wasn't a sensor like Hazel or Roderick. And yet she'd felt *something* when she'd touched the silver beading back at the temple. Could she detect the dark magic without touching it? If so, she might be able to help locate the missing items.

Then again, if she couldn't feel anything from a few paces away— hadn't even felt a twinge when she'd removed the robe from the chest— then what were the odds she could train her senses to feel the dark magic from any reasonable distance?

The longer she stared at the tiny, silver pieces, glinting in the flickering evening light, the less she wanted to try.

"I must," she resolved, then gripped the edge of the beading and ripped it from the silk with three hard yanks.

Coiling the long, tangled strand in her hand, she curled her fingers around it.

The pull was instantaneous.

Esme swayed on her feet as she closed her other hand over it, summoning her own magic in response. Thin, invisible vines interlaced, covering her palms, her fingers, her wrists like a second skin as she tried to contain the otherworldly power between her clasped hands.

Her heart thundered. But then a heavy warmth settled in her veins. She took a slow inhale as the dizziness subsided, trying to focus on the new sensations as they spread throughout her body.

It wasn't like it was trying to force its way through her the way the raw magic had when she'd traveled across the barren countryside. It wasn't trying to use her body as a conduit.

Her fingers twitched involuntarily, as if sparks of lightning were dancing along her skin.

It wasn't trying to move through her, she realized, because it was trying to become *a part* of her.

Her body and mind battled between tossing the strand aside and holding it tighter.

She concentrated on the warmth that felt deceptively good while reinforcing her own magic. Her vines slithered beneath her skin in a way that felt as though tiny lizards were crawling around inside her. Like birds fluttering around between her ribs.

It was unsettling, being so consumed by her magic. But she didn't stop. And soon enough, the strange warmth in her veins began to recede.

Once she was confident that only her magic dwelled inside of her—humming and buzzing loudly in her ears—she returned her attention to the tangle of silver in her hands. Pressing a finger against one of the wire-wrapped pieces, Esme tried to discern the sensation of the raw magic from the *other*.

It took several long minutes, but when the drone of her own magic faded into the recesses of her awareness, she felt it. A seed of darkness hiding within the raw magic. It thrummed like a heartbeat, like a living thing. Dormant, yet very much alive. Waiting until she let go. Until she let the protection of her own magic fall away.

Until she let it inside.

"Enough!" She cast the strand to the floor. The silver pieces pattered on the wooden slats, the sound echoing around the room.

Esme exhaled a long, shaky breath, but didn't release her magic. With a quick glance around the room, she spotted the metal tools by the hearth. The longest had a curved, pointed end, which she used to lift the strand of silver beads off the floor and place it carefully back in the chest.

The robe went in next. She tucked the fraying edges of the torn garment in before returning the other items to the box.

With the lid firmly latched, she shook out her hands and allowed her magic to retreat, shuddering at the feel of the vines receding.

Still, she felt prickly, inside and out.

Heaving the chest into her arms, Esme carried it into the bathing chamber. She wasn't about to let it out of her sight. Not after feeling its power. Its call.

She stepped out of her dress and down into the bath, then scrubbed every inch of her body. Her skin was red and angry by the time she dried off. One of the oils Cadwyn had blended for her was meant to help with sleep. She figured it couldn't hurt, and gently rubbed it over her irritated skin.

Once the chest was again situated in the center of the table in the main room, Esme pulled on her softest long-sleeved tunic and the loosest-fitting pants she could find, then climbed onto her bed, tucked her legs under her, and stared at the box.

She couldn't sense the dark magic from afar, so she'd have to rely on her guards to find the missing articles that Orianna had presumably taken. But perhaps the *connection* she had to the dark magic would help when it came time to destroy it.

Athdara had claimed that Esme would be shown the way, yet nothing had presented itself. Not in her waking hours or in her dreams.

Chapter Forty

WHEN ESME WOKE in a clearing ringed with tall trees and a dark sky above, she held her breath.

The owl swooped past soundlessly, and Esme exhaled her relief as she hurried to follow.

A not altogether familiar room in the palace materialized before her. Was it too much to hope that she'd be shown the location of the missing silver pieces?

The heavy tread of a boot stalked closer, but the man—she thought it was a man—paused just outside her field of vision. A stout crystal glass with amber liquid was cradled in his outstretched hand. The liquor swirled, and when the man lifted it to take a drink, he finally came into view.

Torin.

Esme stifled a groan at the sight of him. For a split second she worried that the missing fragments had been hidden somewhere in the suite he was occupying—or worse, that he had them in his possession—but she took a breath and decided that the purpose of the dream was most likely related to the ships he'd commissioned.

"What's taking so long?" he demanded of someone in the room whom Esme couldn't see. "It should've been done by now." Torin held up a hand to forestall the other person's response. "That unworthy, hedgeborn girl already laid waste to my plans once. I'll not allow it again."

Esme's lips parted at the insult, even if his impertinence was hardly a surprise.

Torin took another drink, then stared down at the glass. "An ill-timed death would be in order…"

Esme flinched at the ease of the remark as Torin sighed, like the idea of murder were nothing more than a meaningless contemplation.

"But the people love her too much; there's no saying what they might do. And any suspicion about her death would only complicate matters. Which is why"—he turned to whomever he was lecturing—"your role is crucial."

Esme couldn't quite make out his expression from her vantage point, but given his stance and the angle of his head, she could only assume the recipient of his ire was receiving a lethal glare.

"So explain how you haven't finished," he went on, "when your largest obstacle has up and left."

Tearlach? What did Tearlach have to do with Torin's plans regarding Periwen?

Torin moved to the sideboard to refill his glass, bringing Jarlath into view.

"No." Esme shook her head. "No," she told herself more firmly.

It wasn't…he wasn't…

Jarlath didn't want any part in his father's political games. He was simply appeasing him, letting his father think he would join in his schemes. The Jarlath she knew was kind and generous and…and honest. And would never willingly partake in something that would jeopardize Esme's position. He'd likely had to restrain himself when Torin had so casually mentioned killing her.

Perhaps he was just waiting until the right time to bring his father's subversions to her attention. Or maybe he had a plan to thwart Torin on his own in an effort to spare her from all the ugliness.

"How is it that I've built an entire armada that's ready to sail to the mortal realm, and the single task I've given you is yet unfinished?"

When Jarlath didn't respond to Torin's demanding tone, Esme breathed more easily.

"She's a foolish young girl. Seducing her should've taken no more than a matter of days."

Jarlath stretched his legs out in front of him, crossing one ankle over the other.

"Shouldn't take much longer," he finally replied. His voice was hard and menacing, without a trace of the gentle, soothing baritone she'd grown accustomed to. "As soon as she stumbles out of her own way, she'll realize that I'm the best option. The only option."

Esme's mouth dropped open as Torin regarded his son.

"The kingdom will be mine," Jarlath assured.

Torin grunted. "Don't forget who that crown belongs to. I'm allowing you to wear it, but I can just as easily take it away."

"I've no doubt." Jarlath waved off his father's threat like he'd heard a thousand of them.

Esme trembled, wrapping her arms around herself as goose bumps broke out across her skin.

———————

A violent shudder wracked Esme's body, jolting her awake. She scrambled to clutch the blankets to her chest.

Her breathing was ragged as she took in the darkened room, searching. Was she alone?

Biting her lip as a tear escaped the corner of her eye, she convinced herself that no one else was there. No one had charged into her room, needing to reassure themselves that it was only a dream that had threatened her.

"Tearlach?" Her voice quavered, her mind reeling with the realization that she'd been wrong about Jarlath.

So very wrong.

Chapter Forty-One

"WHERE'S JARLATH'S ROOM?" Esme demanded as she swung the door open, finding Killian and Hazel standing at attention.

Once Killian's startled expression cleared, he raised his eyebrows and considered her for far longer than her patience was prepared to tolerate.

It hadn't taken much time for the betrayal she'd felt upon waking from the dream to transform into something jagged and wieldy. So much so that she hadn't given it a second thought before she'd snuck into Tearlach's room, located a set of daggers amid the cache of weapons he'd left behind, then passed the remaining hours of the night using two stacked high-back chairs as target practice.

Esme hardened her stare; Killian's protectiveness was no match for her current mood.

She flicked a glance at Hazel, who hadn't said a word. Though, judging by the piercing look she offered, Hazel understood that Esme's desire to visit Tearlach's brother had nothing to do with anything remotely friendly.

At last, Killian acquiesced with a nod over his shoulder. "This way."

When they arrived outside Jarlath's suite, Esme looked around. "And Torin? Which one is he occupying?"

Killian gestured up ahead to the next door on the left.

Esme debated the merits of having a little *chat* with Torin first as she adjusted the ties on her belt. She hadn't donned her training clothes until after she'd pulled the last of the daggers from the furniture. But wearing armor when she spoke with the two men seemed...wise.

It also lent her an extra layer of courage, which had begun to wane.

"Wait here," she told them before forcing her way in, unannounced.

"What in the gods'—" Jarlath snapped before sucking in a breath and shifting his entire demeanor into a relaxed, easy posture. He tilted his head in an inviting way. "Your Majesty." He beamed. "I'm so glad to see you out and about."

Esme didn't take her eyes off him as she shut the door behind her back, wondering if she ever would've noticed the man beneath the mask. He was quite skilled, really. He might have strung her along for a long, long time.

"You're looking well."

Then again, with outright lies like that one, she'd have caught on eventually.

"I've just had tea brought up. Would you care to join me?" He gestured to the small seating area near the wall of windows where the tea service had been set. "Or perhaps a walk around the lake would better suit?"

"Is that your plan, then?" She finally spoke. Jarlath lifted one of his dark brows in what looked like confusion. But she was no longer fooled. "A stroll around the lake, through the gardens? Then I'll suddenly realize you're everything I've ever wanted? And the fact that you've no interest in your father's work or anything remotely political? Well, that only makes you more enticing as a prospect. Doesn't it?"

Jarlath took in a quick breath like she'd wounded him as a look of abject horror marred his features.

"Or maybe your aim is merely to get me alone again. Shielded by a curtain of willow fronds? Share another bottle of wine out on the balcony? Show me exactly how well matched we are?" She gave an exaggerated nod like she approved of his tactics. "Then again, if you'd just told off your father in front of me a few more times, it might have saved you some effort."

"Your Majesty...*Esme*..." He reached a hand toward her slowly, like she might otherwise spook. He tucked it behind his back when she glared at the offending appendage. "Are you...all right? You seem a bit out of sorts. Can I get you some water? Tea?"

"A walk around the lake?" she mocked, tilting her head and widening her eyes like the naive young woman he believed her to be.

"I always find that a little fresh air..."

She rolled her eyes. "Enough. It's time for you to go."

"I...I apologize if I've somehow made you uncomfortable." He bowed his head in shame. "I assure you, I never intended..."

"Uncomfortable? No. That's not it. I'm feeling more...vengeful at the moment."

He looked up at her then, but his mask was still firmly in place.

"You see, I've already eliminated one person who betrayed my family and stole a crown that wasn't rightfully theirs."

He straightened an inch.

"So you should know that I won't hesitate to stomp out *anyone* who has designs on my throne."

Wisely, Jarlath remained silent.

"Son, I've asked Olan to retrieve the—" Torin halted with a hand on the door that evidently joined their suites. "Your Majesty, I didn't..." He spared a scrutinizing glance at her unqueenly appearance. "See you there."

"Father, if you'll excuse us. Her Majesty and I were in the middle of—"

"Oh, how touching. You think you can shield him from all of this." Turning to Torin, she smiled widely. "Do stay," she insisted, gesturing at the tea Jarlath had offered. "You may as well enjoy the trappings of the palace. While you can."

Torin's nostrils flared. He shot his son an accusatory look. Then, with what must have been an immense amount of self-control, he straightened his spine, folded his arms over his chest, and regarded Esme with the kind of cool disdain she'd come to expect from him.

"Come now, my dear."

Esme ground her back teeth.

"Even you must admit this...*responsibility* you've taken on is far beyond what you anticipated. The complexity alone is staggering. More than any one person can reasonably be expected to navigate." His tone softened. "And with the land suffering as it is, how could I sit silently by while you took on the burden of the position all by yourself?" He furrowed his brow and adopted a look of fatherly concern. "The sacrifices you've already made, those yet to come...You needn't carry the weight of the entire kingdom on your shoulders. Not when an exemplary counterpart could alleviate the enormity of this incumbency. You deserve an ally, my dear. A confidant."

Esme felt herself sway, the temptation of what he promised enticing her far too much.

It *was* a lot for one person alone to manage. Especially for a person as inexperienced as she was.

She thought back on Cadwyn's act in the throne room—how she'd spared Esme from taking Orianna's life.

She didn't *have* to do it all alone. But trusting someone that much, like she had Tearlach...

Focus, she scolded herself, remembering what Torin had said in the dream, letting it set fire to the manipulative tale he'd spun.

Remember what they're capable of. Remember what Torin's already done.

He'd threatened her before. Would undoubtedly threaten her again. More than threaten, if he weren't so worried about appearances.

Esme arched a brow. "Your concern for my well-being is heartwarming, Torin."

A muscle twitched in his jaw at the lack of title—something he'd have to get used to.

"But I'd sooner pull out my own teeth than allow scheming, deceitful men like you and your son to *ever* sit beside me."

With a measured inhale, Torin regarded her, then began closing the distance between them. "The alternative is...less generous."

"Is this where you threaten me again?"

The expression that overtook his features was nothing short of bloodthirsty.

"You're smarter than you seem." He cocked his head to the side. "Because there just so happens to be a scenario that only requires one crown. One throne."

Esme lifted her chin, even as her boldness began to fracture under Torin's gaze as he continued to slowly advance on her.

When he was close enough that she could see her own reflection in his icy blue eyes, she yielded a step.

"Father," Jarlath warned an instant before Esme felt the grip of Torin's air magic wrap around her boots.

Chapter Forty-Two

HAZEL AND KILLIAN were through the door and between her and Torin before the panic of being trapped had fully set in. A half second later, the door to the adjoining room banged into the wall as Harlow and Armel burst through. Madoc and Quinlan blocked the main doorway, and Esme could see that at least two other guards were at the ready behind them.

Torin's hold slipped away, and Esme inhaled a breath as deep as she could. Despite how ragged it was, she held up a hand before Hazel could run Torin through with her raised sword. By the look in her eyes, she was more than willing to *thoroughly* defend her queen.

"Sit." Killian jerked his chin toward the chair beside Jarlath, who complied without hesitation.

When the rest of her guards lowered their weapons, Esme returned her attention to Torin.

"As of this morning, you are hereby removed from your position as Lord of Isloran." When he did nothing more than glare down at her, she felt a trickle of confidence return.

And a pulse of her magic. A reminder.

What was it about Torin that made her completely forget the power that dwelled inside her? He seemed to be aware of that vulnerability as well, or he wouldn't have tested his own magic against her.

When he'd followed her into the royal apartments and threatened her before, she'd needed Tearlach to intervene.

Not this time.

Yes, she was surrounded by her guards. But, too, there was no longer just cause for holding back her own magic if he did it again.

"And the ships—the ones you've commissioned for your...*expedition?*" She cocked her head, feeling bolder with each passing second. "As of this moment, they belong to Tremaene. And if you, or anyone associated with you or your family, set foot on any vessel, or so much as dip a toe in the sea, you'll discover just how unforgiving I can be."

Esme took a step back so she could address him and Jarlath both. "Be gone within the hour. I'll allow you to stay a *single night* in your family's home in Meallán."

Torin's lips formed a thin line and his nostrils flared.

"I'd advise against opening your mouth. You wouldn't want to forfeit your home in Isloran as well, or the meager portion of your family's fortune that I'll allow you to retain."

When Torin inhaled sharply, and his eyes took on the same malevolent gleam they'd had when his magic had wrapped around her ankles, Esme spun a thorny, invisible vine up his leg and torso, then twisted it around his throat.

"Not. Another. Word."

His face turned a mottled shade of purple as his magic fought against hers.

Esme raised an eyebrow and waited until Torin ceded with a jerky motion that was likely intended to be a nod.

"One hour," she repeated, then spared Jarlath one last glance. For his part, he seemed rather contrite—eyes downcast, hands folded in his lap. And he'd wisely kept his opinions on the matter to himself.

For a moment, she wondered what might've been—if Jarlath's path had diverged from Torin's demands. The way Tearlach's had.

Madoc and Quinlan parted to allow her through the open doorway—both giving her approving nods. Her lack of sleep must have been catching up with her, because the small gesture almost brought her to tears.

Out in the corridor, Esme found not only Sully, Roderick, and Cahir waiting for her, but Lord Lennox, Winifred, and Aindreas too. It appeared as though the presence of her entire royal guard had drawn a small crowd. She tried not to notice that nearly every door in the wing stood slightly ajar.

"Your Majesty, if I might recommend"—Esme braced herself, but Lord Lennox's smile disarmed her—"drafting a proclamation to be made public immediately."

"That…" She felt her shoulders sag. "Yes, that seems wise."

"I'd be happy to assist, Your Majesty," Winifred offered.

"Thank you," Esme murmured as her vision turned blurry. She blinked rapidly and rubbed her nose. *Sleep.* She needed sleep.

As she turned to leave, she saw Aindreas regarding her with the same look of admiration that Sully usually reserved for her. Sully's expression, however, was one of barely restrained rage. And the moment Hazel exited the room, he didn't hesitate to take her place, pausing for only a second to grip Esme's shoulder.

"I figured you'd want to personally see them out," Esme commented when Hazel moved to her side.

"Probably why Armel insisted I escort you back to your room instead," she grumbled. The gleam in her eyes hinted at all the ways she was imagining making Torin and Jarlath pay for what they'd done.

Esme looped their arms together. "Come on. Kitchens first. I'm starving."

Hazel hummed, leading them toward the stairwell. "I know the feeling. Annihilating an opponent—especially treacherous ones—always leaves me ravenous."

Chapter Forty-Three

ESME WALKED THE circumference of the throne room. The repairs had been completed prior to the ball, but she'd yet to step foot inside.

Harlow and Quinlan had respected her request to let her explore the rotunda alone. So, there she sat, in the center of the room, with the closed doors at her back, not wanting *at all* to recall the events of that night. But she forced herself nonetheless, closing her eyes and recreating the sight of Orianna standing before her.

Instead of meeting the woman's eyes, Esme looked past her, to where Orianna's throne had stood—gleaming and ostentatious.

The silver monstrosity had been encrusted with translucent and opaque crystals. And the white velvet cushion had been bordered with shimmery silver pieces, similar to those on the high-priestesses' robes. Yet the beads that had decorated Orianna's throne were more uniform in shape and size.

In her mind, Esme attempted to locate where the throne had landed after one of her storms had lifted it off the ground. The heavy sound of it crashing against the tiles still echoed in her ears.

But why would Orianna fuse the objects of power to something so stationary?

She wouldn't, Esme realized, dragging her gaze up to where the woman had stood before her.

Even in the safety of her mind—unmoving and locked in Esme's memory—the sight of Orianna made her blood run cold.

Suppressing a shiver, Esme looked higher, to the crown that sat atop her silvery-white hair.

The strands of tiny crystal beads that draped across her forehead had done a decent job of diverting attention from the silver spikes that ringed the crown.

The letter Esme had received from Jaime the morning after the ball suddenly made sense. Orianna had mentioned the power that the crown held. Esme had assumed she'd meant it as a symbol of the power she held as queen, not...

Clambering to her feet, Esme dashed to the doors and threw them open.

"Mairtín!" she called, seeing exactly the person she needed across the corridor.

He startled, as did the two palace guards standing sentry on either side of the main doors. But he recovered his composure almost instantly.

Esme hurried over, waving off his panicked look.

"Your Majesty, I can assure you that I conveyed your directives precisely. The missive you provided shall arrive at the Lady Isloran's home in—"

"Of course. Thank you, Mairtín." She'd given him an urgent request in the hour following her dismissal of Torin and Jarlath, wanting to assure Genvieve, the *former* Lady of Isloran, that she would be protected from any threats—mainly from her own husband. She hadn't wished to presume anything, leaving the decision up to Genvieve to either accept protection from the two guards who'd been sent to deliver the letter or take up residence at the palace for however long she required. Refusal of both was a possibility, but Esme hoped that if Genvieve no longer felt safe, she'd find the courage to leave.

Not for the first time, Esme longed to have Tearlach at her side, to talk things through with him. He'd know how to handle it. He'd know whether or not Esme had reason to worry.

"I appreciate your swiftness in relaying the message. But I wonder if you might assist me with something else now?"

"Always, Your Majesty," he assured her with a bow of his head.

"Do you happen to know where—" She made a quick sweep of the open area, then lowered her voice. "The...effects of the previous..." Esme gestured to her head in what she hoped would translate to *crown* or *queen.* "Were stored?"

His brows rose, taking her meaning. "I apologize, Your Majesty." He matched the quietness of her tone. "But I'm afraid I was never made aware of—"

"No, no. That's quite all right. I'll just..." She glanced back at the open doors of the throne room. Mairtín hadn't returned to his post until the days following Orianna's deposition.

If anyone had removed her effects or locked them away someplace, it would've been someone who'd been present that night.

Killian or Hazel, Sully, even Cadwyn could have—

No. *Tearlach.*

Esme could see the thunderous look on his face when he'd thrust his iron blade into Orianna's neck after Cadwyn's dagger had felled her.

If anyone had taken it upon themselves to secure the woman's stolen treasures, it would've been him.

When Esme opened the secret door to Tearlach's room, she wasn't in a fog of rage in search of something to throw like the last time.

The space felt different, even if nothing about it had changed. The sun had long since arced across the apex of the sky, but she could envision what the room would look like with morning light bathing the area between the bed and the small fireplace. *Cozy*, she imagined. Like her home back in Debarrow had been.

With an exhale, she closed her eyes and let the feeling—the memories—wash over her. Her small home had been so peaceful and secluded, away from everyone and everything.

Only...she hadn't been alone out there, not entirely. Is that why she'd always felt protected? Not because of the trees and animals who'd seemed to watch over her, or the comforting rain that so often cloaked her orchard and her cottage, but because *someone* had been looking after her? Making sure she was safe, even if she hadn't known he was there?

Perhaps something deep inside her had been aware of their connection even then, before Tearlach had been forced to confess it to her.

Allowing herself a rare moment to sink into that feeling, she stumbled back until her legs connected with the bed. She leaned against it and almost felt Tearlach there beside her.

It didn't matter that they weren't connected through the bond the Lifeblood Oath had forged. And it didn't matter that he'd left. Tearlach would haunt her memories and take up space in her heart. Always.

Esme opened her eyes and peered down at her palm. There was no scar from the cut. Not a visible one, anyway. Only a faint gray line where the ashes were sealed into her flesh.

Clutching the bedclothes, she scolded herself for letting him take up even more room than he already occupied in her mind. She'd gone in there for a reason, and ruminating about things that no longer were and could never be wasn't it.

With renewed focus, she looked around the empty room and considered what Tearlach might have done with Orianna's crown.

Burned it? Melted it into something he could surreptitiously bury without worry of it being identified if found?

Much as he might have wanted to erase all traces of the woman's existence, Esme knew he wouldn't have done that.

If she was being honest, she wouldn't have either, if the task had fallen to her.

Not because the crown or the throne or any of the other articles Orianna had crafted from stolen treasures might someday be useful or valuable. But because they'd forever serve as a reminder of what Tremaene had suffered through, what Esme and the others had fought against.

And how close they'd come to losing it all.

Destroying Orianna's effects and wiping her memory from Tremaene's history wouldn't change any of that, and would, in a way, diminish the sacrifices so many citizens—as well as Esme's parents—had made during the woman's treacherous reign.

So then...where had Tearlach locked away Orianna's belongings?

He'd have chosen a place where no one would see them, so some misguided person wouldn't be able to venerate the woman.

He wouldn't want them stolen either. Esme could still see flashes of gemstones and hear the jingle of bracelets Orianna had worn—no doubt worth a small fortune.

The dungeons? she wondered. Storing them in a location where palace staff would rarely, if ever, venture made sense. Though, for that very reason, the dungeons had likely been the first place her guards had searched.

The caves beneath the lake would've been an ideal location too. It was a place few knew about, but Tearlach hadn't been aware of the caves until Esme had discovered them.

"What about..." *The stables?* He'd frequented them often enough to keep an eye on anything he might have concealed out there.

And he'd visited them the night he left.

Much as Esme didn't want to relive that night either, she called up what the footman had relayed. He'd mentioned something about a pack that Tearlach had retrieved from the tack room or the loft, she thought.

Esme had assumed at the time that it was a pack similar to the ones he'd saddled Eimhir with the night they'd fled Debarrow. Likely, he had dozens hidden strategically throughout the palace and the various outbuildings. Perhaps even a few scattered around the city.

But if Orianna's effects had been hidden out there, might he have taken them as well?

If Tearlach wasn't coming back—Esme gritted her teeth at the thought—would he have trusted anyone else to keep them secure?

She couldn't help but scoff at the notion.

Then again...why wouldn't he? He obviously trusted her guards to keep *her* safe, what with him gone.

ERICA SEBREE

Chapter Forty-Four

AFTER CHANGING INTO nondescript clothing, Esme slipped back through Tearlach's room and lifted a cap from a peg near the door before sneaking out. The rounded brim came to a point at one end, and the material seemed well-worn, though she'd never seen Tearlach wear it. Judging by its placement on the wall, Esme wondered if the cap had been merely a decoration—something that'd always been a part of the room, even before Tearlach had claimed it as his own.

Esme tucked her hair up under the cap as she made her way down to the kitchens. With the chaos that seemed to erupt every afternoon at that hour, it allowed her to stroll through unseen. She swiped a harvesting basket on her way out, then crossed the open grounds quickly, before disappearing into the eastern gardens.

There, she gathered a small bundle of lemongrass and a few plums, waiting to make sure her guards hadn't caught on that she was no longer in her room.

But as she left the cover of the gardens and made her way over to the paddock fence, the thrill of her escape began to slip away, leaving in its place the all-too-familiar feeling of desperation.

She stoked the tiny, glowing ember of hope that Orianna's crown would be found, and quickly. Even as her thoughts attempted to smother that precarious hope, reminding her that even if she managed to track down the crown, and found that it contained the remaining fragments of the orbs, she still had no idea what needed to be done with them.

It wasn't until Edlyn's flank brushed against the fence that Esme noticed her horse. And was more surprised still when a hand reached out from beside her to offer Edlyn an apple.

She flinched, then noticed it was the same nobleman she'd conversed with out on the terrace during the ball.

Questions jumbled in her head at his sudden appearance. Instead, she asked, "Where did you get that?" gesturing to his empty palm as Edlyn made quick work of crunching the apple.

"I came across a rather out-of-place tree just yesterday," he explained, running his hand gently down Edlyn's cheek. "And I couldn't resist the intriguing fruit. Such a lovely color."

Esme looked between him and Edlyn, who was nosing at the man's hand.

"Not to worry; I tasted one myself first. Nothing amiss about them. They've a bright, crisp flavor." Finally, he spared Esme a glance. "Almost didn't recognize you."

She brushed a hand down the ill-fitting jacket. "How...did you?"

He leaned over and gently tugged at a wavy curl that had fallen loose from the cap. Esme hastily tucked it back under the brim, but the man only smiled.

"I won't tell," he promised. "Though I will venture to say that you seem more...comfortable in less formal attire."

If she wasn't already longing for her life back in Debarrow, she would've been at that simple observation. But she couldn't dwell on yet another thing she'd lost.

"I was told that all the guests had left days ago." She noted that he too was dressed in more casual clothing. His jacket looked soft and fitted in a way that came from years of wear, and his hair was unstyled, the golden tresses curling at the nape of his neck.

"I've an apartment at the south end." He produced another apple from his pocket, which caused Edlyn to stomp her hooves in excitement. "I came merely to enjoy the grounds once more before I return home."

For a split second, Esme considered abandoning her plan to search the stables and join him for the day. Her mission would surely end in disappointment anyway.

"I take it the ball was a success, then?"

It took her a moment to catch his meaning. "Oh, no. It wasn't... I didn't..."

"Forgive me, Your Majesty. It was improper of me to inquire. I'd just assumed that since the others had been sent home..." He trailed off. "If I might be so bold, I don't believe you require a male counterpart. It's quite evident—not just to me—that you're more than capable of leading the people of Tremaene."

Her eyes softened and her lips parted.

"Your Majesty." He stepped away from the fence and offered a bow. "I wish you well."

"I...Thank you," she replied as he took his leave, failing once again to ask for the man's name.

Edlyn nipped at Esme's jacket sleeve, demanding her attention.

"I don't have any apples. But I'll bring you some later. I promise."

Edlyn huffed, then turned away.

"Is that all I'm useful for, then?" Esme called after her with a smile.

With her basket in hand, she wandered over to the building, watching as a stablehand led a horse outside. Her fingers trailed along the blocks of stone that made up the lower part of the stable walls, thinking that there was something oddly familiar about creeping toward the side entrance.

Her mind provided a memory of Tearlach's workshop back in Debarrow. There'd been tables crowded with blades. She remembered the strange burning sensation she'd felt when her fingers had nearly grazed the metal—not knowing at the time that they were fashioned from iron. And she remembered Tearlach's watchful gaze as she'd pretended to study his handiwork. What she couldn't remember was how she'd found herself in his workshop in the first place. The way he'd glared at her made her wonder if she'd entered uninvited. Had she?

The quandary faded to the back of her mind as she peered around the corner. Another stablehand exited through the large double doors. Esme listened for a beat, and when no other footfalls were heard, she snuck inside and located the tack room.

Knowing one of the hands would be back shortly to muck the empty stalls, Esme made quick work of scanning the contents of the room. There were saddles, bridles, reins, bits, and harnesses. But every item had a place on a hook or a rod. There were no cupboards or closets, not even any shelves. Nowhere to hide anything.

Esme peeked her head around the doorframe, finding the aisle still vacant.

The light coming in from the large open window high on the north-facing wall illuminated mounds of straw piled up in the loft. After another glance down the aisle, Esme hurried up the ladder.

Motes of golden dust floated in the wide beam of light, luring her closer. Not wanting the floorboards to creak, Esme kept her steps light, tentative.

But when she neared the straw piles, she realized that Tearlach would never hide such valuables in something that would be stirred up, depleted, and replenished almost daily. Add to that how well lit that portion of the loft was...

She took in the rest of the upper level, shielding her eyes as she looked into the dark corners that even morning or midday light wouldn't reach. There were some crates shoved into the corner where the roof sloped down. One was filled with reins that had seen better days. Another held various harnesses—which, too, looked old and no longer useful.

Esme turned and eyed the dark corner on the opposite side. There appeared to be stacks of worn blankets that looked to be made of more holes than cloth. Why bother keeping them?

An owl was perched on a beam directly above, nearly tucked into the angle formed by the sloping roof. He shifted in his sleep and a single feather drifted down, alighting on a particular stack of blankets.

Esme didn't hesitate. She shuffled over as soundlessly as she could, then started tossing the blankets aside until a canvas sack was revealed.

Her heart sped up as she fumbled with the ties. But it only contained—

"Clothes?" she hissed.

Unfolding a linen shirt that was too close to her size to be a coincidence, Esme angrily stuffed it back into the sack.

As suspected, it was similar to the packs Tearlach had saddled Eimhir with back in Debarrow. But the one she'd opened—the only one that seemed to be in the loft—contained clothes only for her. Had Tearlach taken his own? Packed a separate one for himself, knowing there might come a time when he'd need to leave without her?

She refused to give that idea further consideration, and moved two of the tattered blankets to cover it up. But when she reached for a third, her fingers collided with something solid.

Esme stilled for a second, then whipped the blanket aside, uncovering a heavy wooden box.

A *locked* box.

Chapter Forty-Five

THE BOX WAS made of a dark, varnished wood. Not elder wood. Though after her trials with the silver beads the other day, Esme knew she needed to touch the object in question in order to feel the dark magic.

But why else would Tearlach use a lock? Surely it didn't contain items he'd need to take with him, or it wouldn't still be there.

Esme turned the heavy metal lock in her hand. She needed to know what was inside before attempting to bring the box back to the palace. How she'd accomplish that without looking suspicious, she wasn't sure.

The sound of boots on the stone floor below stilled her hand. When the stablehand began whistling, and Esme heard the telltale sound of a pitchfork scraping against the floor, she exhaled and leaned in to examine the lock more closely.

The crates of unusable reins and harnesses contained nothing that could double as a lockpick. She needed some sort of wire, ideally with a hooked end. A groan rumbled in her throat as she cursed herself for not wearing any hairpins.

Then again...perhaps she didn't need a *metal* hook.

Her magic coiled down her arms and around her wrists and fingers before she'd finished the thought.

Esme closed her eyes to better feel the vines. They prodded at the inner workings of the lock—lifting each of the pins in various combinations.

It felt as though hours passed while she funneled every ounce of her concentration into the lock. Her muscles started to cramp and sweat beaded along her forehead, and it wouldn't have surprised her if the harsh rays of sun that illuminated the opposite side of the loft were replaced by the soft glow of evening lamplight by the time the lock opened.

She stretched her neck and refocused, feeling and listening for any movement inside the mechanism.

Then, at last, there was a faint, metallic click.

Her breathing stopped at the sound.

Her vines receded. She sucked in a desperate breath as she wiped her palms on her pant legs. After a moment's hesitation, she removed the lock and lifted the lid.

Another worn blanket waited inside—its corners tucked around whatever contents were hidden beneath. Slowly, she tugged it loose.

And there, nestled in another blanket at the bottom of the box, was Orianna's crown.

Nothing more. None of her jewels or weapons. Tearlach must have known that there was something unique about the crown.

Esme couldn't look away. But staring was all she dared to do.

Yet even without touching it, she was able to confirm her suspicions. The spikes—and the uneven texture of the silver that connected them— had undoubtedly been fabricated from the orb fragments. And given how much silver had been utilized, she guessed that all the remaining fragments were there.

She collapsed onto her back and stared up at the rafters as relief washed over her.

———————

After asking Quinlan to find Hazel, Esme attempted to remove the crown from the harvesting basket. The protruding spikes of the crown made the task far more difficult than it should've been.

"How did I get it in here?" she muttered before finally managing to maneuver it past the handle, only for the tines of the crown to catch on the rough fabric of the sack she'd wrapped it in.

After removing the articles the priestesses had handed over from the elder-wood box, Esme placed the crown inside, using the cloth to avoid touching it directly. Then she stepped back to regard the immense, ornamental headdress, wondering how anyone could balance while wearing something so heavy.

"Enter," she called out when there was a rap at the door. At the sharp intake of breath, she turned to see a mix of shock and fury on Hazel's face.

"Where did you..." Hazel latched the door behind her back, like she didn't dare take her eyes off the ring of silver spikes that were protruding from the open box. She stalked closer, glaring at the reminder of not only what had happened that night in the throne room, but of her inability to stop it. To even fight back.

Having to witness Esme battle Orianna on her own, unable to move or speak, must have been its own kind of torture.

Esme wondered if Hazel had sensed the dark magic that night, or if Orianna's shield had acted as a glamour of sorts.

"Tearlach hid it out in the stables," she explained.

Hazel clenched her jaw. "And you think it contains all the remaining pieces?"

"I'm quite sure of it." Esme wasn't sure why Hazel even had to ask. It was obvious by the tension radiating off her that she sensed a great deal of the dark magic.

"I need you to melt away the silver."

Hazel blew out a breath and finally approached the table, considering the crown with a scrutinizing, detached look. "I don't want to damage the orb fragments," she admitted.

"What about Killian?" Esme suggested, well aware that Hazel's fire magic was the more precise out of the two of them.

Hazel bit her lip and narrowed her eyes at the crown. "No. Get Roderick."

———————

Roderick halted just inside the doors, eyes fixed on the elder-wood box Esme was holding. And the crown inside.

He blinked once, twice, then met her gaze. "What's the plan, then?"

"In here." Esme motioned for him to follow her into the bathing chamber.

Above the basin of the sunken tub, Hazel was fitting the thick wooden slab that had been part of Esme's sitting area table roughly a quarter hour earlier. Once she finished, several wool blankets were layered atop the wood. They weren't taking any chances—every drop of silver needed to be captured. Esme and Hazel had also agreed that even once it cooled, no one should handle the silver, for there was no telling whether the dark magic in the fragments could imbue the metal. Or anything else it touched, for that matter.

Hazel left the two of them for a moment, only to return with one of Esme's gowns. Without a second of hesitation, she ripped open the seam at the top of the bodice, then slid the metal strips from the garment.

Esme's choke of shock quickly turned into a laugh. "Do you need more?" she offered, her voice hopeful.

Hazel smirked, but shook her head.

The three of them worked together, bending and shaping the metal strips until they had the makings of a nursery room mobile. By some unspoken agreement, none of them used their magic to complete the task. It was as if they all feared the ramifications of using their own magic on an object that would then hold the crown.

Lastly, they used Esme's protective garments for the fine copper mesh that ran through them—hoping the openings would be narrow enough to catch even the smallest of the fragments—suspending the layers of fabric just beneath the place where the crown would hang. Roderick had assured them that copper required a higher intensity of fire to melt than silver.

When everything was in place, Esme climbed atop a chair, pulled on a pair of velvet gloves, and hung the crown and the beading from the ceremonial robe from the metal hooks they'd fashioned.

Roderick gestured for them to step back before lifting his broad hands to cradle the crown, without actually touching it.

Esme knew he could sense the dark magic like Hazel, but he didn't seem as affected by it. Then again, he wasn't one to reveal much.

After all the preparations they'd made, and precautions they'd taken, melting the silver seemed woefully anticlimactic.

Metallic drops burned through the fabric of the garments Tearlach had given her, leaving only the copper mesh. Esme had saved the small octagonal plate that bore a *T*, which had been sewn into the seam of the pants, near her hip. It was safely tucked into the pouch that held the ruby earrings.

As the last of the fragments clinked into the pile in the center of the copper mesh, Esme thought about their next steps. Hazel could help sort the fragments by element, she assumed.

But when she looked over at her, then at Roderick, she saw the weariness in their eyes. Their abilities had clearly taken a toll on them.

Instead, Esme wrapped the wool blankets around the cooled silver that had made a sort of abstract circlet in the center, then bundled it all into the sack she'd used to smuggle the crown inside. Hazel and Roderick untied the corners of the copper mesh, careful not to disturb the hundreds of crystal fragments caught in the center. They gathered the ends together as Esme placed the elder-wood box on the floor.

Roderick lowered it onto the wool blanket Esme had folded into the bottom of the box, then the three of them stood there, staring down at the mess of copper and crystals.

It was such a satisfying contrast.

Perhaps that was why Tearlach had kept the crown. He knew that one day Esme would want to destroy it.

Chapter Forty-Six

HAZEL HAD INSISTED on staying for dinner, despite how adverse she seemed to being in the same room as the dark magic. But when she finally left her alone, she made Esme promise that she wouldn't do anything other than sleep for the rest of the night.

"I swear," Esme replied far too quickly.

"Hmph." Hazel shook her head and made for the doors. "Just as stubborn as..." Her words were cut off as they clicked shut.

To her credit, Esme did sleep. But only because she'd laid across the foot of the bed after pulling off her boots and drifted off before she realized what was happening. When she woke later that night, the evening lights were still illuminating her room, and a fresh pot of tea and plate of small sandwiches had been left beside the box on the glass table.

Esme chuckled as she poured a cup, then pulled on the velvet gloves. After gathering a few of the fragments in a linen napkin, she settled cross-legged on one of the sofas.

Her plan was to only touch one fragment at a time, and only with the tips of her fingers. If the dark magic was more powerful without the silver casing, she feared she might not be strong enough to release her hold if she grasped even a single one in her palm.

She lined up the dozen or so fragments she'd gathered, spacing them far enough apart that she'd only sense the magic from one piece at a time.

"Shit," Esme cursed, realizing her mistake as she pulled off one of the gloves. She'd been too hasty in wanting the silver melted off to remember that the beading from the ceremonial robe had likely contained *only* fragments from the orb with the water magic. At least, that had been her theory, given that the women of the Triskele could only summon water.

With a groan, she dropped her head into her hands. She'd been too caught up in her anticipation—and desperation—after finding the crown to consider keeping the beads from the robe separate.

"Too late now," she sighed, then reached out to touch the first fragment.

Her muscles clenched. The pull of the dark magic was strong, even through such a small point of contact. It was a struggle to keep her hand where it was—a single finger poised above just one of the slivers.

Slow your breathing, Esme coached, closing her eyes to block out all other distractions.

But what was abrupt and forceful at first, turned sweet and alluring in a matter of minutes. The taste of it coated her tongue as the gentle vibration threatened to melt away every one of Esme's defenses.

She pushed past it, ignoring the warmth that spread through her and ticked up the pace of her heartbeat, all while relaxing her tense muscles.

With each exhale, she blocked it out, waiting to feel the trickle of raw magic beneath.

There.

She tensed a little, fighting to hold on to the faint, yet undeniable creeping sensation of earth magic. A magic she knew well.

Pulling her bare finger away, she used her gloved hand to place the fragment aside, then blinked at the pieces in front of her she'd yet to identify.

And the hundreds that were still in the box.

———————

When a knock came, Esme jolted awake, then groaned as she lifted her head from the arm of the sofa, straightening her neck from the uncomfortable angle.

There were three meager piles on the table in front of her: one for earth, one for water, and another for air. She hadn't been able to sense fire, or anything resembling her lightning. Why that still seemed odd, she wasn't sure—Lord Luxovious's memory of the summoning ritual had shown only three high-priestesses, each wearing one of the ceremonial robes. Fire simply wasn't required.

Only...she was almost certain she'd counted four orbs in the memory of their creation.

But that anomaly would have to wait.

"Just a moment," Esme called out.

When each pile was wrapped up in a strip of the wool blanket she'd cut up the night before, Esme tied colored ribbons to identify each. For the bundle with the earth magic fragments, she used a deep green color. Pale blue for water. And purple for air—which, in the early hours of the morning when she'd selected the ribbons, had somehow made perfect sense.

Noticing Cahir on duty when Marta brought in a breakfast tray, Esme gestured him in.

"I need Myles to find where the priestesses are staying," she told him once they were alone.

"I think...that is, Sully implied that we've already determined where the women are staying."

"Good!" Esme brightened. "Ask Myles and Hazel to go and escort them back here."

Cahir raised one of his blond eyebrows at the request. He didn't say anything, but Esme guessed that he too was questioning the likelihood that they'd willingly set foot inside the palace.

"We'll go to them," she decided. "Inform Sully. And...find Roderick as well." Out of all her guards, Roderick came off as the least threatening. His quiet, gentle nature seemed to make people look past his imposing size.

Cahir regarded her a moment longer before nodding his agreement and leaving to search out Myles.

"Have you..." Madoc moved into Cahir's vacated position near the door. "Has any progress been made?" Madoc had always been friendly with her, but that might've been the first time she'd heard cautious optimism in his voice.

"I believe so."

———————

They arrived at Sybil's Apothecary after the shop had closed for the night.

Esme looked up at the windows lining the second story as they waited.

A curtain fluttered in the candlelight a moment before the proprietress unlatched the front door. She was a tall, willowy woman with a black braid that nearly grazed the floor as she ushered Esme, Myles, Hazel, and Roderick inside.

She motioned them toward a curtained-off doorway, tucked into the far corner behind the long counter. "The stairs are at the back," she said, flipping the lock back into place. "And take this with you." The woman—who hadn't introduced herself, but Esme assumed was Sybil—handed a heavy wooden tray with a steaming pot of tea and several stacked cups to Roderick before disappearing into a smaller room at the opposite end of the shop.

At the top of the dark, narrow staircase, Esme expected to see a corridor with several rooms to choose from. Instead, the entire second story of the building was one large space, with comfortable-looking sofas, low tables, and large, tufted cushions piled atop thick, overlapping rugs.

The women of the Triskele were positioned—strategically, Esme guessed—throughout the room. But she wasn't about to waste time with power struggles or building up whatever depleted trust they had in her.

She bent down to unlace her boots, then swept her cloak off her shoulders and settled onto a cushion in the center of one of the many seating areas.

"I believe I've found all remaining pieces of the orbs," she told them.

"Where?" Moira stepped forward.

Esme had considered not telling them where the fragments had been hidden, given that they hadn't fully believed her explanation about the true origins of the Order. But ultimately, she'd decided that they deserved to know.

"Orianna's crown."

The women looked to one another, but Moira kept her gaze locked on Esme.

Roderick broke her line of sight by setting the tray of tea on the low table between them. Esme bit back a grin. She knew it'd be good to have him along.

When everyone was seated with cups of tea cradled in their hands, Ceridwen asked softly, "Did you bring them?"

Esme felt Hazel stiffen beside her—she'd been of the opinion that they not reveal anything, especially that they'd been found melded into Orianna's crown.

"No." Esme shook her head. "They're in a secure place until we're… ready for them."

Ceridwen and a few of the others nodded, seeming to be only curious. Esme couldn't blame them—she'd fractured their understanding of the world not all that long ago. Wanting a better grasp of their new reality was expected.

"You said you *believe* you've found all the remaining fragments," Moira reminded. Always the keen one.

Esme took a deep breath, then explained the different characteristics of the fragments and that they'd begun sorting them. She didn't want to reveal her connection to raw magic, or that she could feel the dark magic, for fear that they might draw similarities between her and Orianna.

"The fragments will need to be re-formed into the shapes of the original vessels," Hazel explained, "before any attempt can be made at releasing the magic."

"But how do you know you have all the pieces?" Keva asked with a slight tilt of her head that said she already knew the answer.

"I don't," Esme admitted as she blew out a breath. "I'm not sure anyone could fit them back together like puzzle pieces. Some of the shards are quite small."

"So you don't know if any of this will work," Keva accused.

"Not until we try."

"If we," Vevila began, darting a quick glance at Moira, "fuse them back together and *destroy* them without being certain that they contain every fragment from the originals..." Her eyes widened at the implication no one was willing to state.

They might accidentally release dark magic into the world.

Or perhaps nothing at all would happen.

Either way, Esme suspected they wouldn't get a second attempt at it.

Worse yet, if they altered the fragments in any way, *without* unlocking the channels, there'd be no way to summon raw magic. They'd have damaged their only means of access.

They *had* to get it right. There was simply no alternative.

"What is it you need from us?" Catriona asked.

Chapter Forty-Seven

WHAT ESME NEEDED from the priestesses was to know every detail about their summoning ritual. Because rituals were just spells, she reasoned. Lord Luxovious had fabricated every aspect of the Order, and the only thing that made logical sense was that he'd spelled the dark magic inside the orbs to summon the element it was entwined with.

The spell to break the Lifeblood Oath had contained similar components, only opposites. Or rather, the resulting state of the components—ash instead of fire. If she could surmise a similar reversal with the spell that summoned raw magic, it might break the dark magic's hold on the channels.

But the summoning spell contained only words from the Old Language and the requirement that the three high-priestesses at a given temple wear the adornments and perform the *ritual* as one.

Esme wondered if Lord Luxovious had designed it in such a way to ensure that none of the priestesses suspected that one, alone, could wield the immense power with which they believed the gods had blessed them.

Once everything had been explained, speculations and theories were voiced. Vevila questioned whether they could use the magic from one orb against the other two. And while Athdara had warned against *combining* the elements, Esme wasn't sure whether directing the magic of one against the others was the same.

When, in the early hours of the morning, they hadn't agreed upon a viable method to fuse the fragments back together, Esme, Hazel, Roderick, and Myles left. Though not before the women once again pledged their assistance.

Esme wasn't sure if they'd come to accept her explanation of how the Order had been created or if it was simply in their nature as would-be priestesses to serve Tremaene. No matter the risk.

———————

By some miracle, the council meeting had been pushed back until later in the day, which was fortunate because they would've been short one queen had it remained at the agreed-upon time. As it was, Esme found herself coming awake to the smells of stews and pies that signaled a midday meal.

When she finally made it downstairs, she found Myles waiting for her in the antechamber.

"Your Majesty." He stepped forward, his nervousness coming off him in waves.

Esme put a comforting hand on his arm, which seemed to remind him to take a breath.

He looked around, then lowered his voice. "I didn't want to ask last night, in front of the others. But I wondered if you need me to say anything about the redwoods, like we planned."

"Cahir didn't tell you?"

"Tell me what?"

"About what happened with Torin?"

"Of course not," he replied with dismay. "Cahir keeps everything related to his position in the strictest of confidence, I assure you. As do I."

"Very good of you both." Esme gave an approving nod, noting that he'd stopped fidgeting with the cuff of his sleeve. "As to the redwoods, while your suggestion was quite clever, it's no longer necessary."

He straightened to his full height, towering over her, as if he needed a different perspective to understand the information.

"Go on." Esme inclined her head toward the doors, indicating that he find his place before she entered.

He stared down at her for another second, like he wanted to ask more, but ultimately followed her directive.

Esme stood out of sight until the doors shut behind Myles, waited a breath, then gave a nod to the footmen.

Her councilors rose when she appeared in the doorway. It was strange having everyone's attention on her, and her alone. It always felt a bit unnerving, but more so that afternoon without Tearlach at her back.

As she made her way to the head of the table, she ran her thumb over the smooth, dark line on her palm.

"Good afternoon," she greeted. "Winifred, do we have any pending business from our last session?"

"Your Majesty, we can't very well begin until all members are present," Lady Audris declared.

Huh. She hadn't heard? Not even her attendants had informed her? Interesting.

"My apologies. Torin *is* absent. Thank you for bringing that to our attention, Audris. Always so astute." Esme gave her a smile that was more teeth than sincerity. "I'm afraid he won't be joining the proceedings today. Or in the future."

Ignoring the swift objections voiced by Audris and Pearce, Esme took a moment to glance at Myles. Seeing another person she'd chosen sitting amid her advisors only reaffirmed what she'd been considering for some time.

"Your concerns are noted." Esme held up a hand when Audris took in a breath that would undoubtedly voice her next complaint.

When the room fell silent, Esme informed them about what Torin and his son had been up to. And though she left out his plans to pillage the mortal realm, she made clear that Torin's actions constituted treason, and that any accomplices would be punished swiftly and similarly.

Rightly so, the objections that had been so loud before weren't renewed.

And with that matter handled, the meeting commenced with discussions and debates over topics that felt rather trivial.

Esme glanced at Torin's empty seat, thinking back on what he'd said when he'd tried to convince her of the benefits of having a counterpart, an ally.

Admittedly, she rather longed for that, at least some of the time. And if she couldn't have that sort of partnership with the one person she desired it with, then perhaps the alternative was to have multiple people who could fill different aspects of that role on her council. Rules be damned.

It took a surprisingly short amount of time for Mairtín to produce four chairs that matched the others in the council chamber, and only a few minutes longer for Hazel, Armel, Killian, and Cadwyn to claim their seats at the table.

What wasn't a surprise was how at home her new advisors seemed. And given the approving looks they'd offered when entering the chamber, they'd been expecting her to make such a move. Though, Cadwyn and Hazel's expressions had been more of a *took-you-long-enough* variety.

No objections were raised at their presence. In fact, the frozen looks on Pearce's and Audris's faces made Esme wonder if they were realizing that without Torin their small faction within the council was crumbling. Or maybe it occurred to them that Esme no longer cared how it might look to the public if she replaced *any* of them.

Pearce's expression hardened. "And how shall we refer to these *new additions*?"

Esme wondered what unsavory alternatives he'd kept to himself.

"I believe *Queen's Advisors* will do fine."

Chapter Forty-Eight

THE WOLF APPEARED *through a break in the fog, stalking closer. Esme closed her eyes, gripping the hem of her nightclothes. But it wasn't the wolf she feared.*

It was the first time she'd seen him since returning to the palace. Since taking the throne.

She hoped it would be the last.

She knew it wouldn't.

The wolf brushed past her.

Esme took a breath, preparing for the worst, then turned to follow.

When the fog cleared, she found herself looking down upon the main chamber of the Arlais Temple. The floor was made up of varying shades of stone in a nine-pointed star, with facets that radiated out toward the pillars circling the room. It was much like the floor of the Iola Temple in the mountains, where she'd first met with the unordained priestesses. The aesthetics of the Arlais Temple were more understated, so much so that Esme hadn't noticed the intricate tile pattern when she'd visited it only a short time ago.

A moment passed before she saw herself enter the space with the six women of the Triskele.

They gathered in the middle of the rotunda, where the version of Esme in the vision knelt down to place the three bundles of fragments equidistant from one another around the central point of the tiled star pattern.

Moira came forward next, clutching a pouch. Then, with hands that seemed far too steady for what they were about to embark upon, she loosened the ties and poured a boundary of unbroken ash in a circle around the three bundles, creating an inverse of the ring of blue flames Esme had seen in Lord Luxovious's memory.

When Moira stepped back, the seven of them joined hands, mimicking the formation of the summoning ritual.

"Seven?" Esme murmured. Not three. Would it matter? Would their combined powers be too strong? Not strong enough?

She knew the ritual wouldn't take, or the wolf wouldn't have shown her. Perhaps they needed additional participants.

As the chanting began, Esme strained to make out the words. Not only were they from a language she didn't speak, and muffled by the haze of the dream, but their combined voices seemed to layer atop one another.

No, that wasn't it.

She pulled herself closer, taking in each of the women's faces—eyes closed tight, lips moving together. They were all repeating the same words, she confirmed, but they didn't fade after they were spoken. The words were amplified as they reverberated through the space.

The noise grew louder, until all Esme could hear was a resounding peal so intense she could feel the vibration of it through the dream, in her own body.

Then it happened.

The spell summoned wisps of dark smoke, rising from the bundles that held the fragments—or perhaps the re-formed vessels, she couldn't be sure.

The smoke encircled everything within the ring of ash. But the boundary only contained the dark magic for a short time.

Tendrils of smoke whipped out, striking at each of them. Wrapping around them. Holding on.

Esme watched in horror as darkness surrounded each of the women. Surrounded her.

Then consumed them.

Only a matter of seconds, that was all it took. Then one by one, their bodies crumpled to the ground.

Until there was nothing left but seven piles of limp, lifeless clothing.

———————

Esme sucked in a breath. But as much as she wanted to escape the dream, she refused to open her eyes. She needed to remember everything, analyze every detail before the images faded.

Her exhale was rough and choppy. She shivered and felt tears streaking down her temples.

It didn't have to happen that way, she told herself.

It won't happen, she swore, forcing herself to think past the horrors she'd seen. Of the dark magic sucking them dry.

It hadn't corrupted them, not the way it had with Lord Luxovious. He'd...*used* the dark magic for his own ends. But in the vision, the magic had used *them.*

And killed them all.

Esme flattened her hands against the bedsheets and tried to focus her thoughts.

The three bundles, had they contained the fragments or the reshaped vessels?

The ash, what was it made of?

Seven women, not three. Had there been too many?

And what of the spell? Even if she could recall the chant, the echoes in the chamber and the veil of the dream had made it impossible to discern one word from the—

Another shiver ran through her body, and a chill settled against her throat.

The room had gone cold.

Slowly, Esme opened her eyes.

The specter of Lord Luxovious stood only inches from the end of her bed.

For several seconds, she simply stared at him. And he, back at her.

"You've accomplished a great deal. Your desire to deconstruct something you deem immoral is admirable. A fitting trait for a ruler."

Esme lifted her chin and narrowed her eyes.

"But you see, common magic, like one's own, must be guided. Measured. Or you risk an outpouring that will cause hardships, suffering...loss."

Esme's lips parted at his words. For the first time, she questioned whether his intentions hadn't been as selfish and power hungry as she'd always assumed. Was he right? Without something to restrict the flow, would raw magic flood the land?

She'd always assumed the elements balanced themselves naturally, the way they seemed to in Periwen. But if they didn't? If the rainy season lasted too long? If the winds caught an errant spark when the fields were dry?

She already knew the hardships that would follow.

"It will be much like your people are experiencing now. A deluge will not quench the soil, but drown it." He seemed to read her thoughts.

"The magic of this world requires control, or it will strangle everything upon this land. As you've seen, establishing such an elaborate structure is not easily done. Magic does not willingly bend. Are you prepared to do that? To give what will be required?"

Esme swallowed hard.

"You're young. You've many years left to serve. I, however..." He lifted his hand from beneath the folds of his dark cloak, and Esme saw the gray, gnarled fingers she'd seen in his memories. "I've been of this world for too long, sacrificed too much, yet I offer you what little I have left. You needn't bear the consequences of what's required to restore your world."

He tucked his hand away, concealing the sacrifice he'd made long ago.

Could she do the same? For Tremaene? For her people?

"When you decide to be the queen who will do anything to protect her people, you need only to call on me. Together, we can reshape this world."

Esme suppressed a shudder when the room went cold again. Her breath fogged in front of her face, obscuring the spot where Lord Luxovious had stood.

Together, we can reshape this world.

Chapter Forty-Nine

HAD LORD LUXOVIOUS not spoken those final words, he might've convinced her. Not to accept his help—she wasn't that stupid—but to rethink her approach about removing the obstructions to the channels. The *valves*, she was reluctantly inclined to call them.

Esme slipped from the bed and padded through the passageway to Tearlach's room. She didn't want to be...*Alone* wasn't the right word. She wasn't sure what she needed, but the weight of responsibility felt less like a stranglehold in the smaller confines of his room.

She drew the covers back, climbed into his bed, then stared out the window until dawn.

Her presence in the kitchens later that morning didn't cause as much of a stir as it once did. After a few nods to the other staff who were busy preparing for the midday meal, Esme claimed a work table beside Molly and helped knead rounds of turned-out dough.

The methodical movements had Esme's mind wandering to the many spells in her mother's journal. As her thoughts had been wholly occupied by Lord Luxovious's appearance the night before, devising alternative ways to merge the fragments, and how she might destroy the orbs with less... *grim* results, she welcomed any distraction her mind was willing to offer.

She visualized the pages where her mother had scribed countless spells, focusing not on the names—which Esme had little hope of translating—but on the myriad notations that indicated the care and practice Erena had taken to perfect each and every one of them. In secret. Hidden safely away so as not to risk harming others.

Use the caves beneath the lake to contain until mastered, she'd written.

When Esme had first seen the notation, she hadn't fully grasped just how quickly things could turn if a spell wasn't performed correctly.

And yet, her mother had utilized the caves to contain any untethered magic that might erupt from spells gone awry. Surely there'd been safer locations. Why had she chosen to practice spells with potentially volatile consequences so far underground, surrounded by pools of water? *Unless...*

Esme's hands stilled, her fingers sinking slowly into the dough as she stared ahead, unseeing.

The caves sat beneath rock and packed earth, and were surrounded by water—both inside and by the lake above.

After Erena had defeated Lord Luxovious at the end of the Dark War, she'd seen him imprisoned not only in sleep inside an iron box, but on an island. The sleep magic and the iron were to keep his physical form subdued, but the location might've been equally significant—buried deep underground, surrounded by water.

Perhaps entombing him on an island hadn't been because of its distance from Tremaene but about shielding the world from any lingering dark magic.

———————

Esme sunk into the hot water until even her chin was submerged. Her breath sent tiny ripples across the surface as she considered the smooth tiles that surrounded the bath and how she'd normally direct vines to crawl up them.

Instead, she summoned them beneath the water.

It felt different. The vines moved slower, yet coiled more easily. They didn't require a solid surface to climb. The tapered ends sought one another, intertwining in on themselves until they formed intricately woven spheres. And when directed toward the surface, Esme could feel her magic pressing against it like a barrier. There was a strange boundary created between the water and the air above, one her magic couldn't easily cross.

It wasn't at all like summoning roots or sprouting shoots from the ground. It felt almost like moving through the glamouring fog that stretched across the sea. As if her magic needed to operate differently within the two substances.

———————

It was early afternoon when Esme finally emerged from the bath, having tested the limits of her magic under the surface of the water until her fingers were wrinkly.

After barely tasting the food that'd been left for her, she spent the remainder of the day and into the night sorting fragments.

The pull of the dark magic grew stronger with each piece she added to the three piles. Even without Athdara's warning that she keep the elements separate, Esme knew that if they were merged into a single orb, it would be nearly impossible to resist.

If she attempted to destroy the orbs on her own, would she manage to succeed before the dark magic overtook her? Before it corrupted her? Killed her?

Lord Luxovious's words rang in her head. *Magic does not willingly bend.*

She had to assume that dark magic couldn't easily be destroyed. And if she couldn't destroy it, it would need to be contained the moment it was separated from the raw magic.

Esme feared that she might very well find herself trapped with it.

Chapter Fifty

"THE PRIESTESSES HAVE agreed to help," Hazel informed everyone who'd gathered in Esme's suite.

"Where?" Harlow asked, looking between Hazel and Esme.

"The Arlais Temple. It's the closest channel that's still active," Esme explained, then nodded for Hazel to continue.

"We believe our best chance at drawing the elemental magic out of the orbs is by reversing the Order's summoning spell. And because our queen has a"—Hazel gave Esme a lopsided grin—"connection to source magic, she'll use her power to funnel the raw magic from the orbs back into the channel the temple was built upon. If all goes to plan, only the dark magic will be left inside the orbs. Destroying those..." She took a breath, sharing looks with her fellow warriors. "Well, we've done it before." The others nodded solemnly.

Esme listened as they discussed various methods that'd been at least somewhat effective against the dark magic Lord Luxovious's underlings had wielded, while struggling to keep *his* memories of the war from emerging.

There were a few techniques that she suspected might work with her brand of magic. Even so, Esme couldn't stop picturing what the dark magic had done to her and the priestesses in her dream. Even with their combined efforts, she feared it wouldn't be enough.

Her guards posed additional strategies, but their voices became nothing more than a whirring sound. Esme looked around the room, humbled by their willingness to accept the risks. To stand against the very magic that had bathed their countryside in blood and ash.

And they'd do it again. For Tremaene.

Because they were warriors.

Every one of them knew how dangerous it would be. They'd seen battle. But the women too young to have been ordained as priestesses, they hadn't.

What if there's a cost in destroying the dark magic? she'd asked them that night, in the room above the apothecary.

Even then. We're with you, they'd said.

As unwavering as her guards, they'd sacrifice themselves to save Tremaene.

Sully rose from his seat. "Myles, alert the priestesses." Then he turned to the rest and issued a final directive. "We leave at dawn."

Tired as she was, Esme drew another bath. There was something about the water, about the expanding ability she had to move the fluid element around her body like a storm that made her feel more prepared. Like it might do more than contain the dark magic, but protect her from it too.

The water lulled her, swelling and settling with each of her breaths. When her heartbeat calmed enough that Esme believed she might actually be able to accomplish what she was about to attempt, she drained the bath and went to dress.

She pulled on her darkest tunic and matching pants. There was no point in wearing protective plates or her sword belt, though she wished she still had the garments Tearlach had made for her.

After tying back her still-wet hair, she searched the vanity drawers for the small emblem stamped with a *T*, then went to retrieve the pouches that contained the fragments.

Wanting to keep them separate, she stuffed two of the pouches in the deep pants pockets on either side of her hips. The third held the water magic fragments. She tied a strap around it, hung it from her neck, then tucked it under her shirt.

But when she reached the door to the passageway, she paused and closed her eyes. She couldn't just leave. Not without so much as a word.

It took longer than expected, writing the letter. Her gaze kept drifting to the shifting lights in the night sky, and she wondered what they might look like after.

Tearlach's room was dark, empty. Colder than it had felt before. Like even the memory of his presence was no longer there. Or maybe she'd just held on to the hope that he hadn't truly left.

But he had. Tearlach was gone.

And somehow that made stepping out into the corridor easier.

"Sneaking off to fix everything on your own?" Cadwyn's voice came from behind her.

Esme took a breath before turning to face her. She too was dressed in dark clothing, her red hair tucked under a headscarf.

"Like you did?" she challenged.

"I left camp to help you. Because you didn't need to do it all by yourself. Not then, and not now. Not...anymore." There was pain in Cadwyn's words. The guilt she felt for sending Esme off to Periwen alone was still there, like a wound that refused to heal.

A moment passed.

"You don't have to do this alone," she stated softly.

Esme didn't reply, just stared up at Cadwyn, eyes begging her to understand, to let her walk away.

"Then I'm going with you."

Chapter Fifty-One

CADWYN DIDN'T ASK where they were going as Esme led them out to the woods. It wasn't until they'd reached the rhododendrons that she spoke.

"I always wondered why your father wanted me to keep you away from this spot."

"My father?" He knew of the caves, what Erena had used them for?

Cadwyn nodded. "He said..." She seemed to consider her next words. "He said you could get turned around in there. Lost."

Trapped. The word hung between them, unspoken.

"I remember the day you were born." Cadwyn's eyes were wide and glassy, pleading.

"Cadwyn. Don't." Esme looked away, pressing her lips firmly together.

"And the day your mother asked me to watch over you."

Esme shook her head, her breaths becoming short, ragged.

"I swore I'd protect you."

"And you did. You did." Esme swallowed, looking over at where the entrance to the caves was hidden. "But you can't—" She shook her head again, then met Cadwyn's eyes. "You can't come with me. You know that."

"I know." Cadwyn's voice was barely a whisper.

"And you know that I love you."

"I know that too." Her voice broke.

Esme took a steadying breath. "Everything's going to be fine. Just… go back to the palace, have some tea. And tomorrow—" Another breath. "Tomorrow, it will all be better." She blinked back tears a moment before Cadwyn crushed her in an embrace so tight Esme felt like her ribs might crack.

After several minutes, Cadwyn pulled back and looked down at her. She gave an infinitesimal nod, kissed her on the forehead, then turned. She stood still for a second, then pulled her shoulders back and walked away.

Esme didn't move. Couldn't. She watched Cadwyn disappear into the shadows of the woods.

When the sounds of her footfalls faded into the distance, Esme looked around. Cadwyn was gone. No one had followed them. And yet, it felt as if someone was watching her. Watching *over* her.

Slowly, she turned in a circle, searching for any movement, listening for disturbances.

Perhaps it was only the trees, or the animals, aware of her presence. Whatever it was made her feel less alone. Protected, almost.

She moved toward the tangle of branches. They parted instantly for her. And the lantern, hanging on a hook just inside the entrance to the caves, sparked to life as she reached for it.

Her fingers stilled. She stared for a moment in awe at how easily she'd summoned it. Before she'd touched it. Before the thought had fully formed.

She blew out a breath, grabbed the handle of the lantern, then descended into the depths below.

Inside the vast space of the main chamber, the air was thick from the heated springs bubbling up into the largest pool. Esme stood in the center and turned, taking it all in. Wondering what would be left when she was finished.

Once all the hanging lanterns were lit, the warm, yellow glow made the space feel even warmer.

Esme peeled off her cloak and flung it aside.

Eying the massive pillars where the tunnel opened into the cavern, she pushed up her sleeves and shook out her hands. She moved toward them before thinking better of it.

Vines unfurled from the soles of her boots, slithering toward the pillars.

Winding around them. Tightening until the rock crumbled. Blocking her only way out.

Sealing her and all of the dark magic inside.

The rock beneath her feet trembled. Esme ducked her head and covered her neck a second before bits of rock pelted the backs of her hands.

"It's quite possible this was a spectacularly bad idea," she groaned.

Chapter Fifty-Two

ESME HELD HER breath until the reverberations ceased, then slowly raised her head.

A few of the lanterns had gone out, and were covered in debris, but nothing too disastrous appeared to have happened.

"And that was the easy part." She gave a mirthless laugh, then directed her vines to clear a small opening near the top of the closed-off tunnel for air.

When there were no more preparations to be done, Esme set the bundles equidistant from one another with the lantern in the center. There was something about seeing them arranged that way that reminded her of the triskele symbol. While the women of the Triskele had likely chosen the feminine mark because of their ability to sustain the land, the three spirals also represented the three elements priestesses were tasked with summoning.

Three elements. *Three.*

But there weren't only three elements, were there?

Esme shook her head and shoved her recurring unease aside, then reached first for the packet tied with the dark green ribbon.

She let out a slow breath and poured the earth magic fragments into her palm. When several seconds passed and she felt nothing of the dark magic, Esme closed her hands around the pieces and began funneling her own earth magic into them.

Though she started slowly, with only a trickle, her hands were shaking within moments, her own magic fighting against that which wasn't hers. She dropped the fragments back onto the unfolded swatch of wool and wiped her palms against her pants. Her hands were hot and tingling, made worse by the warm, humid air filling the room.

She tried again, forming a cocoon of vines around the fragments before picking them up. But no matter how much of her own magic she channeled into the knotted vines, the fragments resisted.

Unlike the last time she'd handled them, the dark magic didn't coax or tempt. It merely blocked her attempts, as if it knew what her goal was.

She tried using a similar method to encase the air fragments, producing a small cloud before carefully pulling the rain from it. When the fragments were encircled by only air magic, they looked as though they were hovering above her cupped hands in a gentle swirling wind.

As expected, every attempt she made to fuse the fragments back into their original shape failed.

Her shoulders dropped as she let her magic retreat. The fragments clinked together, returning to their small pile on the wool.

The same thing happened when she tried to fuse the pieces from the water magic orb.

By then, her entire body felt overheated and her skin prickled. Though not from the dark magic. The sensations felt different, almost like—

Her lightning.

That's what she was feeling. The fire of her magic had built up inside her.

She looked down at the three piles. Would fire have any effect on the other elements? Roderick's fire had simply melted the silver away. And he was far more skilled than she was.

Then again, maybe fire was...*necessary*. The summoning ritual used a ring of flames. What if Lord Luxovious hadn't added the fire element simply for show?

Was that it? Was that the answer to the question that had been plaguing her mind all along?

Maybe all four elements *were* required for the ritual, the spell.

Carefully, she brushed the earth magic fragments onto the stone floor and set the wool aside, then hovered her hands over the pile before aiming one small spark at it.

The fragments jolted. Some of the smaller slivers even seemed to melt, but they didn't quite liquify. They looked more like shavings of cold butter softening on a piece of hot bread.

And the result didn't last more than a second before the fragments returned to their solid state. Though they looked slightly deformed, less jagged.

She tried again with stronger bolts that ringed the outermost fragments in the pile. And while more of the pieces appeared to melt— some nearly melding together—they pulled apart as soon as Esme let go of her magic.

The attempts on the air and water fragments yielded much of the same.

What if...

No.

Keep the elements separate, Athdara had warned.

But Esme wasn't going to use all of her magic, only fire. That wasn't the same, was it?

Then again, Athdara had also claimed that Esme would be *shown the way* about how she was meant to release the magic, and what she'd been shown had resulted in her and all six priestesses dead. Without, she suspected, having released the raw magic from the fragments.

Try. Just try, she coaxed.

With a sliver from each of the piles, Esme set them beside one another—not quite touching. A small spark with three thin tendrils flared. The slivers melted for only a second before hardening again.

Leaning forward, Esme propped the tiny pieces against one another like kindling, then sent a single bolt straight down the center.

She held her breath as the sharp edges softened and drew together, melding into a small, glassy droplet on the stone floor.

With an unsteady hand, Esme reached out to touch it, finding it solid. Whole.

Chapter Fifty-Three

ESME SAT BACK on her heels with an exhale. It'd worked.

The small, opaque stone with a flattened bottom popped free from the stone floor. She held it in her hand. It was cool to the touch and felt like any ordinary pebble, polished smooth by river water.

After hesitating for a moment, she closed her fingers around it. Her shoulders sagged in relief as she sensed the dark magic's dormancy. Though she couldn't decide if that was actually a good thing. The raw magic, too, was quiet inside the glassy pebble. Perhaps because it was so minuscule an amount that she couldn't feel it?

Or she'd done something she couldn't undo.

"Too late now," Esme murmured.

The fragments hadn't repelled one another the way they had when she'd tried to merge the pieces from only one of the elements. And nothing else had worked, so what other choice did she have?

She blew out a breath and looked up at the ceiling imploringly, wishing once again that there were gods above who could offer guidance.

"Tell me what to do," she implored quietly.

When no answer came, she tipped the contents of the three bundles into a single pile, then stirred them around before sweeping them back together. Her lips pursed at the sight. She'd spent hours—*days*—sorting them.

The mound of fragments wasn't all that large. Though the original vessels had been rather small, she reminded herself. Still...given the sheer power they contained, Esme rose and put some distance between them and her body.

Sparing one last glance around the cavern, she whispered a final plea that combining them into a single object wouldn't be absolutely catastrophic—and that she might even survive the ordeal—then aimed her lightning at the pile of fragments.

When the heavy bolt struck the shards, they crackled and sparked. But even when the flash from the lightning died out, they continued to glow.

Esme yielded another step as the viscous substance merged into a shape that in no way resembled an orb. She grimaced when it seemed to settle into an uneven form, lumpy and pitted.

Smoke and light and darkness swirled within the knobby stone, and after watching it intently for another minute, Esme slowly approached it, still not sensing the dark magic.

She reached down to pick it up and pain shot through her skull.

Dropping the stone, Esme clutched her head. The pain pulsed through her once more, then subsided.

"Shit," she cursed, knowing she'd have to pick it up again.

It took several measured breaths before she was ready.

Shaking out her hands, she reached for it.

The breath was forced from her lungs. Her fingers spasmed like they wanted to let go, but she held on, covering it with her other hand. Her jaw clenched tight and her legs began to shake. She lowered quickly to the ground before her knees gave out.

Pressure built behind her eyes, and she struggled to keep them open.

Then the pain vanished.

And darkness surrounded her.

Though she could still feel the warmth of the stone floor beneath her, she knew she was no longer in the cavern. At least, not the one she'd trapped herself inside.

The darkness went on in all directions, seemingly forever.

No, that wasn't true, Esme realized as she tried to focus on the nearly invisible, shifting mass that surrounded her. The only light came from the stone clutched in her hand. She opened her palm and angled it so the light shone against the walls—if they could be called that. They seemed more fluid than solid, like the fog of glamour she'd crossed on her voyage back to Tremaene.

The air was thick, heavy, and smelled of—

"Magic," she breathed, holding as still as she could, like she might escape its notice if she didn't move.

But the seconds ticked by, and nothing happened. She didn't feel the overwhelming pressure from the raw magic trying to force its way through her the way it did when she crossed the barren land.

When the pounding of her heart finally slowed, she could hear the low, steady oscillation of the magic. Like waves against the shore. Like breathing.

Like blood. Thrumming through her veins.

Her eyes drifted shut as the feeling swept through her. Until the beat of her heart matched the rhythm of the magic surrounding her. Until her entire body was attuned to the vibration.

The steady drumming inside her ears grew louder. Her blood swelled, pulsing forcefully through her until it felt like her body could no longer contain it. Like her heart might beat out of her chest.

Too much, she gasped. *Too much.*

The stone clattered to the ground. And the cavern beneath the lake reappeared.

But the pounding in her ears wasn't replaced by the sound of water spilling from one pool to the next. It only intensified.

Then the relentless pressure she'd become all too familiar with started in earnest.

She reached for the stone, then pulled back.

What would happen to the dark magic if—or when—the raw magic forced its way through her?

It would gain control of far too much power.

That was why Athdara had warned her to keep the elements separate.

Needing a moment to think through her next step, Esme used one of the wool scraps to wrap the stone, like it might halt what was happening.

It didn't.

Her own magic strained within her, trying to resist the raw magic that bled in through the soles of her feet. She turned out the stone, then gathered all the swatches of wool and stood atop them.

A weak cry that was meant to be a laugh escaped her lips at how absurd the notion was. Because it did nothing to stave off the pressure building inside her.

Think, she urged frantically as water began to trickle down from the cracks forming along the walls.

"Water." Esme stumbled toward the nearest pool. It was one of the shallower ones, but she still had to hoist herself up to slide over the low wall on her belly. She swung her legs into the warm water and submerged herself up to her neck.

Her breath held. And when the pressure lessened, she sunk beneath the surface as every muscle in her body finally eased.

When she emerged, Esme pulled herself over to one of the seats carved into the ledge and pushed the hair off her forehead. Several minutes passed while she could do nothing more than strive to slow her breathing.

But her reprieve was short-lived.

Sheets of water covered most of the cave walls, shooting out in spots where the cracks had expanded. The drains that carried the water into the city beyond were nowhere near large enough to handle what was coming.

And it wouldn't be long until the magic found her again. She could already feel the pulse of it pressing against her temples.

The dark magic, however, remained suspiciously dormant.

The gentle swirl of the water in the pool started to churn, to rise. The larger pools were already overflowing, flooding the cavern floor.

Esme clambered back over the stone wall, made more difficult by the weight of her sodden clothes. One of her boots slid against the slick floor, sending a rush of water right toward the stone.

She dove for it. Her hip and shoulder collided with the floor as her fingers closed around the stone seconds before it could be swept away.

Her anguished cry echoed through the cavern as the pain returned— so much worse than before. Like the force had built up in the few moments she'd evaded it.

Every muscle in her body protested as she struggled to her feet, her vision flashing between the dark space where magic dwelled and the cave that was quickly filling with water.

Her stomach roiled. She swayed, then dropped back to her knees. The water was already mid-thigh, but she leaned over to brace her other hand on the ground.

Chunks of rocks fell from above, crashing into the water.

Esme squeezed her fingers tighter around the stone until they were white and numb.

Visions of Alastar flickered in her mind, of how he'd formed the original vessels. Only, she wasn't just undoing what he'd created. He'd funneled raw magic from the source into the orbs, but it had been Lord Luxovious who'd bound them with dark magic.

Her blood thundered in her ears as the water level rose.

Blood. Her magic mirrored the signature of raw magic. And her magic was in her blood.

Just as blood could bind two things, so too could it unbind.

If she allowed the magic in the orb to merge with her fully, would she be able to separate the raw magic from the dark? Or at least disrupt the connection between the two long enough for—

Something crashed into the wall of the pool nearest her, sending bits of rock and a deluge of water her way.

Now. Do it now.

Esme patted her hip before remembering that she hadn't seen her dagger since the night Tearlach had left.

Her eyes darted around frantically. A sharp edge of rock?

Another crash came from behind her. No time. She lifted her other hand to her mouth and bit down hard on the soft flesh at the base of her thumb.

The pain barely registered as blood ran down her wrist, spreading out in the water around her.

She moved the stone to her bloodied hand, and her entire body seized.

Esme gasped for breath.

The dark magic that had been lurking silently inside the stone roared to life.

No longer luring sweetly, temptingly. It demanded.

It took control of her body. Possessed every inch of her.

Even as the raw magic was finally free to rush through her, using her as the conduit it needed, the dark magic sought control.

Esme was trapped between them. Bound by both.

Or perhaps…she was the only thing keeping the two magics apart. But for how long?

Her body twitched, her muscles contracting from the dark magic's control at the same time the raw magic coursed through her veins.

Leaves and vines sprang forth from the cave walls, crowding the space more quickly than the rising water. Rain pelted her skin as wind whipped the churning waters into a whirlpool.

The cave coming down around her was no longer the greatest danger Esme faced. She was going to be consumed by the effects of her own magic. Drowned, battered, crushed by it.

She closed her eyes and focused every thought, every sense on the stone clutched in her hand.

In her mind, she saw bright sparkling light. Colors swirling through it. But at the center of it slithered a thin, violet, glowing strand.

The resemblance to the flames that had ringed Lord Luxovious's black cloak when he'd appeared to her almost broke her concentration.

She refocused on the rippling movement of the strand, swelling each time a tendril darted out like a whip to devour the surrounding light.

As the cave trembled beneath her feet, Esme slid a single, tapered vine toward the undulating purple strand, matching its fluid movements as it thieved the raw magic. And when its tendrils reached out for more, her vine slipped inside.

She grew more shoots from that single vine, taking up more and more space inside the purple light.

The moment its slithering faltered, she twisted her vines around it, trying to choke the power from it.

It fought back, lashing against her magic.

Then the raw magic began to react. Its colors shifted to muted shades as the mass of sparkling webbing pulled away, then contracted, constricting the tangled knot of dark magic in the center.

Inside her body, she could feel the battle. Her blood ran hot, then cold, like it was warring against poison that had infected her.

Esme's breath grew ragged, but she continued her own attack against the dark magic, sending jolts of lightning down along her vines.

The raw magic expanded once more, then coalesced to form a crackling sphere of light around the dark magic—and her own. It shone brighter, squeezing tighter and tighter until it became solid.

Esme couldn't see what was happening inside, couldn't feel her vines.

Then everything went still, silent.

And a flash of pure, white light blinded her.

The deafening sound that followed knocked her into the waters rushing past her legs.

She tried to regain her footing, choking and blinking against the glittering debris that clouded the air.

Through the crackling haze, she saw fire webbing up the cave walls, crumbling the rock.

She shot a look at the small opening she'd left when she'd blocked the entrance to the cave, then shoved through the rushing water, trying to reach it.

But it was too late.

Chapter Fifty-Four

ESME DODGED THE falling rocks, narrowly avoiding them. Then sucked in the largest breath she could just as the lake above came crashing down.

The swell of water shoved her forward, then yanked her back. She twisted, trying to see through the murky depths.

Another portion of the cave collapsed, pulling her farther from the surface and the faint glow she could barely see filtering through the debris.

Her lungs burned as she swam toward it. And for a second, she was back in the throne room, struggling against the onslaught of water Orianna had brought down upon her.

She banished the memory. If she was approaching her final moments, she didn't want her thoughts consumed by fear or the nightmares she'd lived through.

Her lungs tightened as she kicked her legs. The surface was too far. She'd never reach it.

Propelling herself up through the turbulent water, as mud and silt clung to her tattered clothes and rock abraded her skin, she conjured an image of Tearlach.

He was staring down at her with such unrestrained devotion. Then his arm came around her waist, and he tugged her close. Pulling her to safety the way he had in the darkness of the underground lake in the hidden pass beneath the mountains.

As her lungs seized, she let her arms drift down to curve around her midsection. She could almost feel his grip there, pulling her toward the surface.

The last of her breath escaped her lips as she held on to him.

The light above faded as her vision darkened.

The arm wrapped around her yanked harder, almost violently.

Her face broke through the surface and her lungs convulsed.

Esme sucked in a watery breath, then choked it back out.

She blinked the grit from her eyes as the phantom arm that had dragged her to the surface was replaced by Cadwyn's. She righted Esme as best she could, pounding her back until her breaths evened out.

Standing at the shore was Armel. The moment she looked at him, his horror-struck expression morphed into one of relief. Then exhaustion. It was *his* magic she'd felt, pulling her to safety.

He dropped to his knees and buried his head in his hands as Killian, Sully, and countless others rushed toward her.

Killian took her from Cadwyn, who was breathing rather hard herself, and carried her over the rocks and muck of the exposed lakebed.

Hazel reached out for her when they climbed up the shore, and cradled Esme in her arms as Cadwyn fussed over her.

Voices she couldn't make out hovered in her periphery.

She blinked slowly, trying to keep her eyes open.

Then the hands that were prodding at her were gone and she felt herself moving again.

She struggled, and managed to open her eyes once more.

The brilliant colors in the sky filled her vision. Not the colors of dawn or dusk. They rippled and sparkled.

The Loinnir Lights. Bright and vibrant and—

"It worked," Esme whispered as her eyes fell shut and her head rolled in toward Hazel's shoulder.

Chapter Fifty-Five

THERE WASN'T MUCH of it, the dark magic. But it was there. Lurking beneath the surface. Lying in wait until it could merge with her own. Until it became a part of her.

The slithering sensation was not unlike her vines.

Esme tried to summon for her own magic—just a drop—needing the reassurance that she still had control over it, but she couldn't reach it. Couldn't reach anything. Couldn't feel her hands as she tried to flex her fingers. Couldn't feel her legs, her toes.

Her desire to struggle toward waking was short-lived. And when the darkness cloaked her once again, she let it take her.

———————

Her cheek was pressed against something soft and cushiony. Over the sound of the rain pattering against the windowpanes, she could hear the deep, steady breaths of someone sitting near her.

Try as she might, her eyelids refused to cooperate, so she listened to the calming, rhythmic sound until the gentle touch of fingertips swept across her forehead.

"I can still feel you," a low, rough voice said. "With every breath, every beat of my heart."

Tearlach. Tearlach was there. In her room.

He'd come back.

Esme channeled the small amount of energy she had into her voice. But all she could manage was a barely audible hum before sleep pulled her back under.

————————

The room felt empty when she woke again.

For a moment, all she could do was listen to the sound of rainwater dripping from the eaves.

She wet her parched lips. "Tearlach?" she tried, though it came out as more of a croak.

There was no response.

Had she imagined it all?

It took several more focused breaths before she was able to open her eyes. Her body shuddered from the effort, but the sight through the open doors was strange and wonderful. Clouds. So many clouds. Big and fluffy. And below them, lush green treetops.

All Esme could do was stare. Though she was fairly certain that even if she wanted to see how far the effects had spread, she wouldn't be able to rise from the bed on her own. And she could already feel the heaviness of sleep descending on her again.

————————

"Tearlach?" she mumbled, feeling the bedclothes shift around her.

"No, dear, it's me." *Cadwyn.*

Esme's eyes slitted open to find her and Hazel at her bedside. "Where—" She took a breath, then started again. "Where did he go?"

They shared a pained look.

"Esme." Hazel reached for her arm. "Tearlach left. Don't you remember?"

"No, he...he came back. He was here."

"I'm afraid he...hasn't returned, love," Cadwyn explained gently.

"But he—" Esme's protest devolved into a fit of coughing.

Hazel helped her sit up, then Cadwyn brought a cup of water to her lips.

"More," she breathed after swallowing all of it.

Cadwyn chuckled. "Let's get you up."

Hazel moved to help support her under her arms, and the three of them somehow made it over to the sofa by the hearth, where pale, weak-looking tea and a myriad of bland-colored food awaited.

"How long have I..." Esme gestured to the bed as she stuffed into her mouth the thick piece of toast topped with a fried egg that had been handed to her.

"Four days," Cadwyn told her.

Esme groaned. "I need a bath. I feel so..." She squirmed a bit, trying to ignore the grittiness that seemed to coat every inch of her skin.

"Grimy?" Hazel supplied with a grin.

"After you eat." Cadwyn handed over a small bowl of cooked oats mixed with stewed apples.

It turned out that a bath wasn't an option since Esme couldn't stand on her own and a simple conversation had left her winded.

"I can do it myself," she protested as Cadwyn pulled the nightdress over her head.

"I'll not have you slipping and hitting your head," Hazel admonished, helping Esme step down to sit on the ledge of the empty bath. "Because I've no intention of taking your place. Now, lean your head back."

The letter, Esme remembered then.

Cadwyn grinned as she slowly poured warm water from a pitcher over Esme's hair. It felt so good, she hummed in contentment.

"Can you imagine," Cadwyn whispered conspiratorially, "if I brought in Leenan to fit her for gowns?"

Esme chuckled, recalling her experience with the brusque seamstress. "I don't think either would survive it."

Hazel looked up at the ceiling imploringly. "I don't know why I put up with the pair of you."

Their mingled laughter echoed off the tile walls.

After helping Esme into clean clothes and a freshly made bed, Cadwyn and Hazel left with the promise that they'd return later that evening. But even with her muscles feeling looser and her hair smelling a great deal better, she still felt...restless.

Too much had happened. Her mind churned, reliving every second in the cave, reimagining each scenario. She needed to sort out all that had transpired if she had any hope of processing it. So she rolled onto her side and pulled open the drawer of her bedside table.

But when she reached into the back and shifted the other books aside—her meager attempt at keeping her notebook somewhat hidden— her hand connected with a slender, cloth-covered object instead.

She pulled it out and scrunched her forehead. The worn canvas pouch wasn't familiar, but the shape inside was.

Esme hadn't seen her dagger since...*that night.* Her thumb rubbed against the *E* that had been carved into the smooth, wooden hilt.

The thing was, Esme *knew* she'd dropped the dagger in Tearlach's room before she'd fled. And hadn't come across it since. Not even when she'd gone into his room in search of weapons.

Had one of the maids found it and returned it to her? She didn't think so.

Esme turned it over in her hand, hoping to feel the warmth of Tearlach's grip.

She looked around the room, as if she might find him standing watch over her.

He wasn't there, of course. And suddenly, she felt even more exhausted than she had all day.

Curling back onto her side, she tucked the dagger under her pillow and kept her hand wrapped around it as she slipped into a dreamless sleep.

Chapter Fifty-Six

"THAT WAS QUITE impressive, what you did," a smooth voice said in the darkness.

Esme pulled herself up and stared back at Lord Luxovious.

"That's right. It's over," she told him with more confidence than she felt.

"My life's work, gone in a matter of minutes." He sighed heavily and looked off into the distance as if he were reminiscing about it.

"No one should have control of the world's magic."

"An oversimplification of a complex system, to be sure. Though I do wish you'd left the magic within its confines. It will take some time before I find a new use for it. So much of it can be...burdensome for just one person." He twisted his gnarled hand in front of the shadows of his face.

Was he implying that the dark magic had somehow...*returned* to him? But how?

"I destroyed it," Esme nearly shouted.

He tilted his head, considering her like she were a student who kept getting the answers wrong.

"Oh, child, you didn't *really* think you could destroy it, did you? Magic cannot be destroyed. It can only be transformed, reshaped."

"It...it freed you, then? The dark magic freed you from your sleep?"

"Oh no, certainly not." He seemed delighted by her confusion. "But mixed with a little something...extra, it will. It's a shame I won't have much use for you anymore. I've come to find you rather entertaining."

He didn't elaborate, like he was waiting for her to catch on.

It took only a second longer before she understood. It wasn't only the dark magic that had inexplicably returned to him, but her *blood.*

"It wasn't much, mind you, but it'll be enough. The great magic it's bound with will only enhance your power."

She thought back on the final moments in the cave, before its collapse. The orb had burst into a million glittering specks of dust, then drifted down into the water that Esme believed would suspend the remnants of the dark magic. But that wasn't all the water had contained.

She could see it, her blood spreading out like ink in the water, providing the perfect host for the unbound dark magic.

"Water is everywhere," Lord Luxovious added. "It connects everything."

A shiver went down her spine thinking of how the dark magic had returned to its creator across the sea. Bound with her blood.

Her blood was...*a part* of Lord Luxovious.

Suddenly the worry she'd felt at having a thread of the dark magic embedded in her seemed far less unsettling.

"You can keep that. For now," he responded to her thoughts. "Though I'll be wanting it back eventually. The memories too."

Her lips parted as she stared at him in horror.

"Until we meet again, young queen."

The violet flames ringing his dark cloak flared, engulfing him.

And Esme felt an answering slither under her skin as he vanished.

Epilogue

"MORNING, MALLORY," CARRICK greeted the older woman as she bustled in.

"Morning, dear."

"What's the word?" Being the proprietress of the tavern, Mallory always had a story to tell.

"Barram was at the tavern last night. He just returned from Rhoswen Harbor; you know? And he heard the most unbelievable tale."

Carrick grinned and leaned forward to rest his arms on the counter. "Tell me."

"Seems there's a man there who found a new land."

"New land?" Carrick chuckled. "Where?"

"Across the sea. Says the people there look a bit...different. All of them young with strange-looking ears. Pointy-like, he said. And their skin, it"—Mallory rubbed the tips of her fingers together next to her cheeks—"glistens. Shimmers."

"That's...certainly odd," Carrick admitted, though he was fairly sure that Barram had had the wool pulled over his eyes.

"Did he learn what this land is called?"

"Think he said Islaan...Something like that." She shrugged her shoulders.

Not a name he'd ever heard.

"Wait, no. That was the name of the province where the man snuck ashore. The land itself was called..." Mallory tapped her finger against her chin. "Tremaene! That's it." She snapped her fingers. "Pretty sounding, sure is."

Carrick felt the smile fall from his face. The image of a single gold coin with a *T* stamped on one side and a crown on the other rose in his mind.

He'd searched Tearlach's workshop all those months ago, after the metalsmith had taken off with Ffion. Even for a smithy, there'd been an awful lot of weapons. But it had been the gold coin he'd found under a stack of crates that had seemed most out of place.

"What else did the man tell Barram?" he asked. Mallory didn't seem to notice the edge Carrick's voice had taken on.

Her eyes went wide. "Said there was sorcery there. *Witchcraft.* Giant boats—bigger than you've even seen—moving fast across the water with wind in their sails. Only there was *no wind.* And at night, he said a man walked the streets without a torch or match and ignited all the lamps."

"Did he...converse with the man? With any of the inhabitants?"

"Too afraid." Mallory shook her head. "But Barram said the man overheard quite a bit. Seems they've got a new queen there. And not just any queen. They said she came back from the dead."

"What? How so?"

"Said she perished along with her kin nearly a decade ago."

"A decade?"

Mallory nodded. "But then, she reappears out of nowhere one day with her keeper and snatches back the crown that should've been hers."

Keeper? Could that have been Tearlach?

Mallory went on, saying something about strange, colorful clouds, but Carrick's mind had turned to the homestead at the far end of the village that'd sat empty since the night Ffion had fled Debarrow. To return...*home*, he realized.

Esme's Letter

How does one begin a letter like this? There's no good place, I suppose, so I'll simply start with my own beginning.

My parents showed me what a worthy leader should be. My mother stood up to untold power, knowing she might not survive it. Because that was the only way forward. And my father, he showed me how kindness can go so much further than heavy-handedness. If given the chance, I would have striven to become even a fraction of the leader I knew he was.

But there is one thing I can contribute to this kingdom. And so, I shall. Because I must. If I do not return, my wish is that Hazel will ascend the throne. She'll protest this, I'm sure. She might even claim that I'd gone mad in the end. But she possesses the strength, acumen, and resolve that Tremaene will need.

I also hope that Cadwyn, Armel, and Killian will stay on as royal advisors. Their combined wisdom, intuition, and stewardship is unparalleled, and I only wish that I might have had more time serving beside them.

I want the people of Tremaene to know, and to always remember, that they are stronger together—without shadows or secrets, without castes or divisions. Every citizen is equal in my eyes. And I hope, for as short a time as I wore the crown, they knew that.

And finally, I want Tearlach to know that I love him. I don't know why I couldn't say it before. I should have. I won't say that I've always loved him. At first, he frightened me—as was his intention. He accomplished that mission quite well, I'll admit. Though it didn't take long for my unease to turn to anger and irritation. Oh, how he infuriated me! But then, somewhere along the way, I found that he was exactly what I needed. What I wanted. Tearlach, you believed in me. You knew what I was capable of even when I didn't. Especially when I didn't. You were there. You were always there. And now...you're not. I let my anger overshadow what I truly wanted, and for that, I'm sorry. At least now you'll know what you meant to me. You have my heart, Tearlach. For as long as I have left.

It has been the greatest privilege of my life to serve Tremaene. Thank you for allowing me to do so.

Your queen,
Esme

DEAR READER

Thank you for reading *Wild Heart of the Magic*! Help new readers
find the Wild Heart fantasy series by leaving a review
on Amazon, Goodreads, or BookBub.

WILD HEART SERIES:

Wild Heart of the Storm (Book 1)

Wild Heart of the Crown (Book 2)

Wild Heart of the Magic (Book 3)

Wild Heart of the Darkness (Book 4) – Coming soon!

Wild Heart of the Dawn (Book 5)

ACKNOWLEDGMENTS

Thank you to the Cadwyns and Hazels and all the other fiercely loyal friends out there. Especially to Jen and Jim for being so wildly enthusiastic about every little detail in these stories. Thank you, Deborah, for sharing your love of the evil twin trope. To Chris, thank you for once again making sure my words are grammatically correct— even when that means changing the far more interesting variation of "amongst" to the ever so mundane "among." Thank you to Volodymyr with MiblArt for once again designing a hauntingly beautiful cover. And finally, my most sincere thanks to the small but mighty group of ARC readers who've found their way to this series. I'm incredibly grateful for every single review and post. *You're* the reason this series has reached so many readers. And your genuine excitement about the characters and the story...well, what can I say? It honestly makes me tear up. So, thank you. Truly.

ABOUT THE AUTHOR

Erica Sebree lives in Austin, Texas, where she works in public service as a graphic designer. She reads too much romance and drinks too much tea—usually at the same time. She makes frequent attempts at gardening, and will happily talk to any animal who crosses her path. She believes lists should be written in colorful ink, and dreams of one day having a farm sanctuary with many adorable cows. When she escapes into fantasy worlds, it's to places where magic is vital, animals are guardians, and a stubborn bodyguard's only weakness is the fierce, reluctant heroine he's sworn to protect.

Find her online:

instagram.com/ericasebreewrites

threads.net/@ericasebreewrites

tiktok.com/@ericasebreewrites

facebook.com/ericasebreewrites

goodreads.com/erica-sebree

bookbub.com/authors/erica-sebree

ericasebree.com

Newsletter:

bit.ly/WildHeartMail

ERICASEBREE.COM